For Grant
And our adventures

A Legacy of Ghosts

Vancouver, Oct 11 2019: Lydia, Old Haunts

I hadn't expected to see Vancouver again, let alone this misty view of English Bay. Perhaps the ghosts beckoned, but here I sit in the lounge of The Sylvia Hotel. The waves on the bay stir a wave of nostalgia for the days of my youth. So far away in time and distance and memory.

The memory interval compressed four days ago, when my great-niece Janey phoned. Would I talk to her friend Rennie? Rennie has a letter, she said, with instructions to find me, so I can tell her about Errol Flynn and her grandfather, Lachlan Flynn Jones. I met both men here sixty years ago in 1959.

The name, Lachlan, or Lachie as I knew him, woke a haunting memory of the tragedy that happened in this hotel, close to where I sit, in the same week I met Lachie and Mr. Flynn. My already sluggish blood froze. I caught my breath and willed my heart to resume beating, which at eighty-one is always a gamble.

When I drew enough air to speak, I told Janey my acquaintances with those men were brief. I didn't go on to say both acquaintances were trifling in comparison to the tragedy which had nothing to do with Mr. Flynn or Lachie at all. My heart might have stalled on hearing Lachlan's name, but my brain instantly signalled that a trip to Vancouver would be an opportunity, apart from explaining the erratic Lachie to his granddaughter, to tell Janey about my Uncle Michael. Before she sees my will.

I said I would fly to Vancouver, but I am pleased my older brother Mick, Janey's grandfather, came with me.

On this cloudy October morning, Mick and I flew in from Saskatchewan. The Regina airport is a short drive from where we reside on our family homestead with Mick's elder son and his wife, and the stragglers of their brood. So, I'm here for three reasons: to talk to Rennie, to escape the farm for a few days, and to tell Janey about her great, great uncle. My brother has his own agenda, not yet shared with me.

After putting away the few things I packed, because I have finally learned to travel light, I took the stairs, to make sure I could, but also because

R. Rigsby

I avoid elevators. From this window table, I can look at the bay and keep an eye on the entry for Janey and her friend.

Like me, Janey's real name is Lydia Jane Perrault. I've always been called 'Lydia,' or more usually, 'LYDIA!' by somebody wanting my attention, which, I admit, does drift. Janey is one of my large flock of nieces, nephews, greats, and great greats. They are my heirs, but not my descendants. I never married.

"Hello Auntie." I jump, planting the kiss that lands on my cheek extra deep.

"Janey!" I pull her down for a hug. Her ripe wheat hair envelops me in a cloud of herbal freshness. Of course, at nineteen, how could one be anything other than fresh? We hold hands across the polished wood and cover the obligatory recital of family updates.

"Your grandfather has taken himself to the aquarium where he will ogle fish for hours, a pastime that bores me cross-eyed," I say. "He will see you tomorrow after lunch with your father."

"Dad told me, but I get the feeling there's something else going on. Do you know what?"

I'm saved from answering when our beverages appear–a wine spritzer with lime for her, and a sparkling water for me. I would love a beer, but I have a story to tell. Janey's phone buzzes.

"Rennie is running late. Do you believe in Karma? Such a fluke that Rennie and I are friends."

I ignore her question. It's a perquisite of old age. I have thought much about predestination over the years, with good reason.

"How do you know Rennie, again? I'm sure you told me. A school friend?"

"Yes, high school. Rennie Flynn Jones. We graduated together. She's at university too. Except she knows why she's there." Janey looks out the window, her mouth a line of gloom on her usually sunny face.

I follow her gaze to the joggers trotting along the sidewalk. Why the doubt about her studies? Before I can ask, Janey turns to me, smile back in place.

"Tell me about Errol Flynn."

"I can't see how the little I know can help Rennie. I only met the man once. A perfect gentleman. That occasion is about two sentences in the story I want to tell you."

But all stories overlap, intertwine, and layer in ways that can't always be explained, and something of Mr. Flynn's and Lachie's story may help me with my ghosts.

Six decades ago, I anticipated a life that did not include changing diapers or baking bread. I would turn twenty-two on the fourteenth of that October of 1959. I looked forward to full adulthood, having landed a job far from Regina. At the end of my week here in The Sylvia, the twin deaths of security and predictability tempted me, but I chose to 'follow my dream,' which didn't become fashionable for another decade.

Where would I be now if I had given in to those temptations? How do we recognize those pivotal moments when one choice sets the course for the rest of our lives?

Like the choice made by my uncle. Memories of him come wrapped in a tissue of guilt, like other similarly clad memories. Is this another reason to tell Janey his story? And reveal my part in it? It will certainly explain my legacy.

"What do you want to tell me?" Janey brings me back to the present. "Did it happen in 1959 too? So long ago."

If Janey thinks 1959 was long ago, she's in for a trip to the dark ages and The Sylvia is the perfect venue. I'm prepared for flickering lights in the hallway, a lingering cologne, and whispers in the stairwell; hauntings that will beset me with the images, scents, and echoes of voices long dead.

"I will tell you about your great uncle, Michael Kerr. This story begins, if any story has a beginning, in 1927."

Regina, Oct 1927: Michael, A Shift on the Axis

The clock's pendulum swung, faltered, and stopped. Michael Kerr's pen stopped in mid signature. The clock had once hung in his grandparents' farmhouse, and he missed its steady tick as if it were his own heartbeat.

He finished signing his name and looked up. Just after five, an observation reinforced by a growl from his stomach. Time to lock up and go home. A long day, and a good one. Three new clients, including the Perraults, his grandparents' long-time neighbours. His practice had been open for less than eight months, but despite the lean times, people still bought or sold property and wrote wills. He capped his pen, closed a folder not yet dog-eared and creased, and locked all in the cabinet. He got up, stretching neck and back.

At the clock, he opened the glass cover, inserted the key, and wound seven times, as his grandfather had taught him. The clock ticked on. He plucked his overcoat off the coat tree and looked through the window. The streetlights had been lit, but their pale rings showed emptiness.

Outside he jiggled the key in the sticky lock on his office door. His office. He breathed chill air and pulled on knitted gloves. About to set off to join his mother and sister for dinner, he paused to watch a long low car pull up in front of The Prairie Arms Hotel farther down the block and across the street. He frowned. He was a part owner of that establishment, and a part owner of its auxiliary enterprise, as was the driver of that car.

Why had Paddy parked there? A change to the plan? Tonight was supposed to be the last run–they had all agreed. Their little operation had been small time, and not big enough to earn accolades from the temperance folks if the police shut them down. Yet, even with the blind eyes of friends in the constabulary, running whiskey to the states had always been risky. But they had found a better, and legal, way to make money.

Paddy got out and shut the door. Michael raised his hand in salute, but Paddy didn't look up and disappeared into the passage between the hotel and the building next door. Both shops in that building were dark: the hardware store, and the book and printshop. A movement by the stairs. Michael hadn't noticed the other man in the shadows. *Kesey.* He had only recently met the man and had only exchanged nods if Kesey worked the desk at the hotel.

R. Rigsby

A few seconds later Kesey ambled down the walk and went into the bookshop. Probably getting cartons, Michael thought. That was normal. But Paddy should have parked in back. The car door opened again, and a small figure slid out. Regan, Paddy's son, about five or six. He hadn't seen him since he was a baby. *What was Paddy thinking bringing him here?* Michael shuffled his feet, but from his years in the trenches, he sensed when Hell was about to explode.

The little fellow paused beside the car, then darted into the passage after his father.

Boom.

Regina, Oct 1927: Regan, Witness

His father had left his window down. Regan sniffed the cool air and hugged his stuffed elephant close to his chest.

"Regan, lad," his dad had said, "you stay here with Phintel." He had patted the elephant. "Lucky Phintel. When I come back, we'll go to Rudd's. I might have a penny for that gumball machine."

Regan thought of the gumballs. Red, blue, green, but couldn't help looking at the empty street where nothing moved. All the stores had closed. Everybody had gone home to supper. He wished for his mother's stew and a jam tart. But his father had sent her to bed.

He shivered in his light wool pullover. He should have worn his jacket, but his dad had said they would only be a few minutes and had left his own coat lying in the back seat.

"Stay here, Phintel." He opened the door, then trotted into the passage where his dad had gone. The dark closed in, and his feet slid on the brickwork. A light hung over a door about halfway along the building. He kept his eyes on that light until he reached the door and pushed it open to a landing. A flight of stairs led up to darkness, but another led down to a faint glow and loud voices.

"Come on Fitzroy. This is the last run, then we'll call it square."

"We've been square for a long time." His father's voice louder than Regan had ever heard before.

He stepped down the stairs, a flow of warm air on his face, his worn leather boots noiseless on the boards. At the bottom of the stairs a door showed a splinter of light.

"I'm done with this, like I told you before. Especially tonight. I've got the boy to think of, and Margaret...well, you know how it is."

A chair scraped.

"Oh, I know how it is. I damn well know how it is. This goddamn heap of a hotel has been a millstone around our necks and the only thing keeping it from dragging us down is–"

"No. I'm not going. We've been lucky, but you have legal beer upstairs. Business will get better. The states will catch up soon anyway."

"Look, you stubborn moron, we need this last run, like we said, and we're out of it."

Regan put his hand on the door. He wanted the man to stop yelling. He wanted his father to come out and take him to Rudd's for a gumball. He felt like he might wet his pants.

His father laughed. "Nope. I'm done now. See you around."

"You asshole."

Regan pushed the door to see a man punch his father who raised his fists and hit back. Another man pushed past him, shoving him aside. Regan skinned his hands on the rough floorboards.

"Come on you two, Paddy, Birch, knock it off!" The three men scuffled back and forth, then one of the men stepped back, tripping over Regan where he lay on his stomach. His father, laughing, stepped forward fists raised, then saw Regan and their eyes locked. His father didn't see the swing that caught him under the jaw. He teetered and fell, clipping his head on the edge of the table.

Regan pushed himself onto his knees, but a black mist filled his mind, surrounding a name. Birch.

Regina, Oct 1927: Michael, Setting the Course

Michael parked the car in the lane behind Abe Primnase's bookshop and shut off the engine. He clutched the steering wheel and dropped his forehead onto his knuckles. He should have gone home. What a mess. Paddy could be obstinate, yes. Once he made up his mind he wouldn't budge, and never backed down, especially from Birch's bluster.

It had been like that since they were kids. Bertram, *Birch*, McCandless, the big kid who liked to have his way, and Paddy Fitzroy the gangly kid who laughed at him. More than once he and Fred Bakker had stopped Birch from pounding Paddy, but Paddy always fought back and laughed while spitting out blood. Sometimes he had wished Birch would pound the snot out of Paddy. Pound that grating laugh right out of him.

Yet, when they signed up, the four of them hung together. Paddy had once dragged a bleeding Fred back to the trench, and Birch had shot a man about to skewer Michael with a bayonet. Birch. A nickname assigned in one of those fleeting moments of mirth. Birch's temper was legendary, but the name, Birch, had stuck. He must have liked it because he didn't knock a head off when called that. He probably liked it better than 'Bertram.'

But Paddy didn't deserve to die for his laughing obstinacy. When he went down, Michael hadn't thought the punch or clip to his head had been enough to do serious harm. He waited for Paddy to rise, to charge fists ready, and laugh. But Paddy hadn't moved. And now there would be consequences. His hard-won career would die before the year was out. Birch could lose the hotel.

Michael raised his head. No police car was parked in back or in front. If Mutch was on another call, he could be delayed. Michael jumped at a tapping on the window by his ear. In the pale glow from the loading dock light, he saw the hat shrouded face beside the car. His stomach lurched. *Paddy*. No. Kesey. He opened the door and got out.

"I'll take it from here, Mike." Kesey slid onto the seat in a vapour of alcoholic fumes. "McCandless is in the coal room. Trouble with the boiler."

Michael stood for a second. Why now, of all times, was Birch fiddling around with the boiler? The Arms had no guests and the beer parlour closed early on weekdays. He walked behind the hotel to the coal chute hatch and heaved it open. Birch looked up. On the dirt floor beyond the coal box, light from a kerosene lamp wavered in a circle. Within that circle lay Paddy's burlap-covered body. Birch stood in a shallow pit, holding a shovelful of dry earth.

"You took your sweet time. Did you take the kid to Moose Jaw?" Birch leaned on the shovel and wiped a sleeve across his face, leaving a streak of dirt.

"Jesus, Birch. Where's Mutch? You said you would call the constable. What are you doing?" Stupid question.

Birch stabbed the shovel into the ground, "What's wrong with the kid? He looked like a dead cat."

"He blacked out."

"How blacked out?"

"Like that guy in basic training. Just like that. I took Regan home and put him to bed. Couldn't wake Margaret. And listen Birch, it was an accident; let's get the constable. If we wait much longer it will really look bad."

Birch threw the shovel down. "It is bad. I can't even think how this will go down in the courts. You should know that. Just when we're almost finished. Trust Paddy to pick now to blow it."

"Margaret might have leaned on him."

"She knows those stills have kept us from starving. And kept her on whatever it is she's on. And paid for your fancy new diploma. In case you need a reminder."

"But it was an accident."

"Of course it was. But not a good time to have cops nosing around. Even Mutch." Birch picked up the shovel, jammed it into the earth and leaned his head on his arms. "You ready to say goodbye to your practice already? You don't even have the farm anymore."

"Kesey put the car in Primnase's garage. You're not going ahead, are you?"

"No choice. The Yank wants his fifty bottles and he'll come up here and bury me if I don't deliver. We need this last run. That broker is holding the shares and wants the cash tomorrow. Kesey can drive."

"Kesey! He's already half cut."

Michael closed his eyes. When he saw Regan, he should have walked away and not worried about what Regan might see in the basement. Should have gone home to his mother's pot roast. Then invited Lou for an after-supper stroll. They were engaged. At last, the banker's daughter had agreed to marry him. After a long siege of proving his worth with distinguished war service, a respectable degree, and a reputation for stability, the banker himself had urged his daughter to accept Michael's ring. Instead of prairie dirt under his nails, he looked forward to ink stains on his fingers and a comfortable living in a growing city. But all could vanish in a puff–the girl, the clients, and the esteem of peers.

Michael looked at Paddy. The burlap had slipped from his blank eyes.

"Paddy can't just disappear. What did you tell Kesey? And Primnase?"

Birch dug and dumped another shovelful. "I told Kesey that Paddy is fed up with his wife's problems and is leaving on tonight's freight. After the run, we'll sell the car and give the money to the wife and kid."

"Kesey might buy that, but Abe Primnase, not a chance. Fred neither."

"I told Primnase we don't need him to help tonight. His girl is feeling poorly, so I told him to read her some fairy tales. I'll tell him a fairy story myself later. If he makes any noise about getting Mutch, I'll remind him that his girl will be an orphan if he doesn't swallow that Paddy left town on his own. Fred can think what he likes."

"Margaret will never believe Paddy left her. He was a straight shooter from his first breath."

"If you have a better idea, I'm happy to hear it." Birch dumped another shovelful of earth.

Michael squeezed his eyes shut. Losing everything wouldn't bring Paddy back. And wouldn't help Margaret or Regan. "I'll help Kesey load the car." He closed the hatch.

R. Rigsby

Vancouver, Oct 11 2019: Lydia, The Past in the Present

Janey sits up and straightens her shoulders.

"Kesey. Is that name a coincidence? I saw Michael Kerr's name on that family tree Uncle Jasper made, but nobody ever talks about him. Nobody has said a word about him being a rumrunner. Wow. That's amazing."

Amazing, not shocking. But that's what happens to history. It's glorified in the present and it's easier, or makes for a better story, to gloss over the heartache and ugliness of the past. My mother never glossed over any of it. In 1959, my uncle told my father what happened, although I think Dad guessed long before then. Nobody fooled André Perrault. At least not for long.

"My parents knew. And my Auntie Lou and cousin Georgie. And your granddad."

"But it all happened so long ago. And that man's death was an accident." Janey taps her fingers on the table. She hasn't asked again about the coincidence.

"Janey, I'm so glad this thing with Rennie came up, even if she is missing in action. Apart from the chance to talk to you, I'm relieved to be away from the farm. So is your grandfather."

Janey grins. "Was Auntie Des very brutal?"

Desirée. Married to Mick's eldest son, Jasper, with whose family Mick and I found ourselves living this spring. Desirée said it would make more sense for Rennie to be the one flying somewhere. That's when I glanced at Mick and caught him shaking his head and mouthing, "Noooo." Together we persuaded the twin powers of Jasper and especially Desirée, who are not geriatric, that we old fossils could manage a trip to the west coast. We could have Thanksgiving with Kelsey and Gordon at their new house. Janey's brother Royce might even come home from Australia. I aimed a big smile at Jasper and Des, looking as capable as I could. Blink. Blink.

Janey waits for me to reply, eyes crinkling. Gordon, Mick's younger son, had the good sense to become a dentist, no, an *orthodontist*, here in Vancouver.

I shrug. "Once Des realized she would be cooking for two fewer people for several days, it was easier for her to agree."

"But it's temporary, isn't it? You living with them? Granddad was lonely after Gramma Noreen died, so I get why he moved in. But your house in Regina will be restored soon, right?"

I bought that house when I retired. It had been in the Croft family for decades. Janey stayed with me for a week when she was seventeen. We burrowed through albums of photos from my travels and a shoebox of ancient photos from my childhood. She said she loved my house with its vintage charm. That vintageness revealed itself in May, but the burst pipe damage was fixed, and my house has been ready for months. And as empty as ever. Call it the languor of old age, but I haven't had the drive to go 'home,' and I'm not sure I can explain it now.

Janey's phone beeps.

"Rennie has been called into work. I'm sorry, Auntie, but she needs the hours. But you can go on, can't you?"

Regina, Oct 1927: Michael, The Nightmare

Michael slept in fitful slices broken by soundless bombs and silent screams. He woke sweating, his blood pulsing in his skull. He hadn't had nightmares for years. And now a living nightmare. Paddy dead. He wished he'd never thought ill of Paddy, who so loved his wife and son. Regan.

Regan hadn't stirred on the drive home or when Michael carried him into the house, but apart from the deep sleep, he seemed alright. A seizure, Michael thought, like the guy from Weyburn who had signed up for service and was sent home before three weeks. He would borrow Abe Primnase's truck and check on the boy.

On the cold walk from his mother's house, he thought of telling Abe he needed a signature out of town. He knocked on Abe's door, his rehearsed speech ready.

"Morning, Abe. May I borrow your truck?" Abe's hair, which he wore longer than most men, stuck out and its grizzled texture matched that on his unshaved chin. Abe nodded and reached for the keys hooked on a nail behind the door.

"You know, Michael, I've been up with Lizzie all night. She came down with fever yesterday. She was burning and it got worse. I prayed all night it wasn't the influenza all over again. That I wouldn't lose her like I lost her mum. Thank God the fever broke and she's sleeping now."

The truck expired of its own accord in the yard behind the Fitzroy's house. Michael pulled the handbrake, wondering how often the truck died on Abe. Abe hadn't even asked why he needed the truck. Long shadows streaked the grass, but despite the early hour, smoke rose from the chimney. Margaret opened the back door.

"Ah, it's you, then. Did you bring Regan home last night? Paddy would have woken me. Where is he?"

"Abe asked Paddy to deliver an order." Michael didn't hesitate. "Because his girl was sick." He had no idea how that came so easily, then plunged on. "Paddy asked me to run Regan home. I didn't want to–er–wake you, so I put him to bed. I came by to make sure he was okay."

"That's kind of you Michael. Regan woke up yelling around midnight but couldn't tell me what it was about."

Michael's shoulders dropped. "Probably a kid's dream. Rudd's machine out of gumballs."

"I dosed him with my tonic and covered him up. He muttered about going to Rudd's, so maybe that was it. He's still sound asleep. Coffee?"

"Please." Michael followed Margaret into her kitchen.

"Are you glad to be back in Regina? Paddy said it took donkeys' years for you to become a lawyer. He was being funny. He's very proud of you."

Michael swallowed. "He's right about the years. I articled for a firm in Kingston after university. Nice town but couldn't wait to get back here." If he kept talking, he wouldn't choke. "Harvests improved this year?"

"For some, yes. Good enough on our farm that the Walters paid their lease with cash. And how is it that Paddy agreed to deliver that order? Abe Primnase's books or temperance pamphlets can't be that much in demand. Besides, I could use the car today. I'm going out to the farm this morning, but a walk will do me good. And Regan too."

Michael inhaled a sip of coffee but suppressed the cough. "Ah, well, I'm sure it was last minute, and you know old Primnase has his ways and insists on keeping his promises. I think the printing took longer than expected, because of Lizzie's fever."

"Yes, I see. Well I'll talk to Paddy about it when he gets home."

"Besides, that old rattle trap," Michael bent his head to the yard, "Is too unreliable for long trips. You'll see Paddy this evening at the latest. I should go, Margaret. Good coffee, thanks."

Michael shivered in front of his office door and stared at his face in the glass. He shivered again and fumbled the flat silver key.

No matter what rumours Birch let loose, Margaret would never believe Paddy had abandoned her and Regan. What was he thinking? He should have gone for the constable. He could go now. Instead of the 'Closed' sign in his window, he saw a 'To Let' sign and a reflection of Lou walking away. The police couldn't bring Paddy back either.

But the stills had to go. Tonight. He would see Birch this evening. He shoved open the door, casting a glance at The Prairie Arms, and then strode to the sanctuary of his desk and his appointment book.

Late that afternoon, Michael opened his door to breathe fresh air. Sometimes the radiator worked overtime, making his office stuffy. Or it was his head. He stared at The Arms across the street. After the war, when jobs were scarce, the hotel offered a chance. He sold the farm, moved his widowed mother and sister to a house in town, and he and Paddy each bought a share of the hotel from Birch. They were so sure that even with prohibition, they could make the place a friendly inn serving travellers or farmers treating their wives to a weekend in the city. For a while, it worked. They spruced up the lobby, opened the dining room, hired help, and offered specials. Travellers came– businessmen passing through, and some farmers stayed. But no wives. As if a shadow lay on its respectability. He didn't remember hearing anything bad about Birch's father. In fact, he heard nothing at all, and maybe that stated the problem. They hadn't known about the sideline in the basement, but when Birch invited them to join that enterprise, it too offered another chance. He had set his heart on becoming a lawyer.

He looked away from The Arms, westward to the lowering sun.

"We got a problem."

"What?" Michael jerked.

"Christ, you're a million miles away. How the hell did you survive the war? It's Kesey, he screwed up, I think he's dead."

"Come in. Now."

Michael locked the door and pulled the blind.

"I drove out after Kesey and followed him to the hill. I pointed him to the old trail close to the line of trees and waited while he went over the border. Next thing I hear shouting. Then the fireworks started. I stayed until daylight. A couple of uniforms with rifles waited by Paddy's car. The Feds must have got the Yank too."

From the bottom drawer of the wooden file cabinet, Michael pulled out a corked bottle and a glass. He splashed whiskey into the glass and the mug on his desk.

"That could have been Paddy."

"I doubt it. He could be pig-headed, but he was a good driver. He had a sixth sense about going south and keeping out of trouble. Not like that fool, Kesey."

"That sense might have told him not to go. Now he's dead, and Christ, Birch, your rotten temper has landed us in a shitload of trouble."

Birch held his drink between his knees and stared into the glass. "You know it was an accident. Paddy's bum leg gave out."

"It's not too late to call Mutch."

Birch shook his head. "No. We can still get out of this with our skins. If Kesey is dead, they might think he's Paddy. From the car. And they look alike. Except for the wooden leg." He drained his glass and whacked it on the desk. "So, if everybody thinks he's Paddy, who will ask about Kesey? Nobody. He disappears all the time."

"Make those two stills disappear, Birch. Mutch is a good guy, for a cop, but even Mutch has limits."

"I know. What about the kid?"

"He won't remember anything. I saw Margaret this morning. Regan was still dead asleep."

"If you say so. I told Fred and Abe that it looked like Paddy had run into trouble."

"What did Fred say? He's always said we should quit running. He told Paddy he shouldn't drive anymore."

"Fred was in an aisle, and his wife was painting the front counter, so I spoke quiet. He sat on a barrel and wouldn't look at me."

"And Abe?"

"Abe had to lean on the counter and hold his head. When he could speak, he said Paddy had made him promise that if anything went wrong, Abe had to make it look like Paddy ran his own show. He'll put a still in Paddy's barn and ditch the other. It'll give Mutch an excuse to ignore The Arms. Damn. I still have to pay that broker. Damn, damn." He slammed the door behind him.

Michael stared at the vibrating blind, but saw Margaret in her kitchen, smiling as she poured coffee that morning.

Regina, Oct 1927: Regan, The Awakening

Regan woke up, the quilts drawn up over his ears and Phintel beside him. They watched daylight push through the gap under the blind. Outside, the Croft's privy door squealed. His house had a proper toilet and running water.

He needed the toilet but heard voices–his mother's and that of a man. Not his father and not a man he knew. Regan got up and pulled the chamber pot out from under his bed. His mother would be annoyed, since it was for emergencies, but the toilet was on the far side of the kitchen.

He opened the bedroom door. His nostrils flared at the tang of wood smoke and coffee. The percolator bubbled behind the voices. His mother laughed. A mug, maybe the black one, his dad's favourite, slid on the wooden table. His mother, who seemed more awake than she had for days, clicked her tongue. She probably pushed wayward strands of brown hair behind her ear too. Or maybe the click was the spoon on the side of a pot. He smelled oatmeal mush.

Regan waited until he heard the truck sputter down the lane. Had he 'taken a little rest' as his mother sometimes called it? He had no memory of going to bed or what he had for supper. He looked down at Phintel's eyes glinting in the light. In those eyes he saw his dad wave and call him to get in the car. And telling him to stay with Phintel. A name came into his mind. He padded to the kitchen.

"Who was that man, Mummy?" Regan, with his too-long pajama pants pooling around his feet, clutched Phintel and looked at the black mug on the table. "Was that Birch?"

Margaret gathered her son in her arms. "No, my darling. That was a nice man. A kind man."

Regan let his mother lift him up onto a chair at the table. Usually, he would have climbed onto the chair himself. He was a big boy and didn't like help, but his head felt fuzzy and his legs wobbly. His mother placed a glass of milk and a steaming bowl in front of him. He barely touched the mush in his bowl and then found himself with Mrs. Croft while his mother walked to the farm. Mrs. Croft tucked him up in the big armchair in her kitchen.

When his mother took him home, he followed her while she swept, cooked, then swept again. He watched her stop often and look out the window,

R. Rigsby

but no long car came up the lane. With sundown, she fed him supper, and read to him.

"When is Daddy coming home?" Regan asked for the umpteenth time.

"Shhh, don't worry, he'll be home soon. Lie down now, here's Phintel."

Regan hugged Phintel, wishing his elephant could speak.

When he woke, the kitchen was cold. He found his mother asleep in the armchair by the front room window.

The next afternoon when he sat on the back steps, a policeman drove into their yard and met his mother coming from the woodshed. Her armload of wood tumbled around her feet when the policeman spoke. He half carried her into the kitchen and told Regan to go for Mrs. Croft.

His mother then spent the days weeping into her apron, if she was up, or in bed staring at the ceiling. Mr. and Mrs. Croft came every morning. Mr. Croft stoked the stoves and split wood. If his mother was up, Mrs. Croft left them, if not, he went and spent the day in her kitchen. Waiting. Waiting for his father. Waiting for somebody to tell him why he hadn't come home. He couldn't ask. It might have been his fault. He hadn't stayed with Phintel.

Regina, Oct 1927: Michael, Identity Crisis

Michael leaned on the bar in The Arms and ruminated on the sour thoughts in his head. The stills had been dumped. Primnase had seen to that. He placed one in the barn at the old Fitzroy place, with empty bottles and raw mash spread about to add flavour. Mutch's report must have had plenty of detail.

He looked up, surprised to see Fred dropping his coat on a hook. Fred enjoyed a beer or two, but rarely in the middle of the day. Unlike me, Michael thought. He had had beer for lunch every day for the last week.

Birch, too, lifted his brows on seeing Fred, but at Fred's nod, drew a draft without speaking, then turned to listen to a young man at the lobby door.

"Back in a bit, boys," Birch said, "My new man on the desk needs me."

"Who's his new man?"

"Oh, young guy, Jon Sorensen." Michael sipped his beer.

"Where's Kesey? Doesn't he work for McCandless?" Fred lowered his voice. "And I want to talk to you about Paddy. Not here, with McCandless around. I've tried to catch you at your office–"

"Afternoon gents."

Neither of them had noticed Constable Mutch. For a hefty man, he was light on his feet, and he had entered from the side door. Birch, reappearing, went behind the bar and slid a fresh-pulled beer to him.

"We got another call from the States," Mutch said, taking a deep slurp. "From the name stitched inside his coat, The Feds told us the guy they shot in that dustup down south was Paddy Fitzroy. But they can't release the body without next of kin identification."

Michael stared into his beer.

"Margaret?" Fred said. "There's no other family, and she isn't doing so well."

"She can't I.D. a frying pan in her kitchen." Mutch fixed his gaze on Birch. "Which is why I'm here. I need you, McCandless, as a friend of Paddy and a respected publican," he cleared his throat, "to accompany me to the morgue in Williston."

"I'll go too," Fred said, "if you don't mind, Constable Mutch?"

"Not at all. Probably even better with no next-of-kin."

"Now, hold on, Fred," Birch said, "you can't leave the missus on her own in the shop. I'm sure Mutch and I can convince the authorities we can identify Paddy."

"My wife can manage fine, Bertram. And Gerard's only eight, but he's already a big help."

Michael left his unfinished beer, nodded to Birch, and left. He went to his office and his desk. He held his head in his hands. He should go with Birch and Mutch to Williston. But he might not stop himself from telling everything to Mutch. Not that he wanted to hear it.

A week later, Michael thanked his mother for breakfast, pulled on parka and boots, and with his hands in pockets, he tramped to his office. His breath vaporised in the frigid air, a morning much like that when Fred was to go to Williston with Birch and Mutch. That morning, he woke to flames in his back shed. The fire brigade dealt with it in a hurry, but Fred had to stay while they investigated. He missed his ride to Williston. They put it down to paint rags stuffed in a linseed oil can. Careless of Fred and not like him at all.

Birch was shaken when he came back from the morgue. The body had caught one bullet in the face. Mutch hadn't shown any inclination to examine more closely. The clothes were a bloody mess, so Paddy's effects consisted of his coat, his billfold containing one dollar, and a penny that had been in a coat pocket.

Birch had slipped an extra bottle to Mutch, for his trouble. One of a dwindling supply, but nothing linked Paddy to The Arms. His death a tragic consequence of solo smuggling, not part of a ring. Ring? Michael stopped. Did Paddy wear a wedding ring? Margaret wore a gold band, but he was sure Paddy never had enough money to buy one for himself.

Regina, Nov 1927: Michael, The Longest Walk

On the morning of Paddy's funeral, Michael's sister, Jean, came into his office, just as he saw André Perrault to the door, who had booked an appointment for his father, Charles, to update his will. Michael thought he could have telephoned, but he was always happy to see André.

Jean and André gazed like idiots at each other before André tipped his hat and strutted as far as the lamppost outside. Michael rolled his eyes. That explained the visit. With a glance at André, Jean stepped inside to peek at the empty tray on top of the file cabinet. "Do you have more filing or typing for me?"

Michael would have scratched his head, since he usually let her know over dinner each evening if he needed help. But he had seen the sparks fly. Jean wasn't a flirt, so within the year, he bet, his mother would cry at Jean's wedding. Not with joy, although he was sure his gentle mother would feel a little joy, but because her upright Presbyterian daughter married a Catholic.

Michael shook his head and sat at his desk.

"How did you know André would be here?"

Jean merely gave him a *you're the dumbest brother ever look.*

"Does Mother know about you and André?"

"Not yet. I'm working on her. I've asked him to escort us to the funeral. She's always liked the Perraults."

Michael saw her to the door. With a toss of her red locks, Jean turned and joined André on the sidewalk. Michael reflected on his carefree childhood playing ball and Red Rover with André and his sisters before the war. Despite the age difference, he and André had been good friends. He hoped they could become even better friends. With a jolt, he remembered that he was now short a good friend. Whose funeral and wake would supposedly take place this afternoon.

The clock's mechanism clicked and wound. Michael put down his pen. The released spring prompted a whirring of gears before the clock chimed a hollow bong, followed by another. Time to go. No getting out of it.

Michael wondered how Margaret would cope at this sham of a funeral. She had stopped crying long enough for him to tell her that she would receive a monthly stipend from The Prairie Arms receipts. Paddy's investment would continue to support her and Regan.

"Does Birch agree?" she had said, and Michael assured her that was so.

Michael placed the deeds and wills of the current day's work into their folders then into the cabinet. He would love to file the events of the last two weeks as easily. Into a dark drawer never to surface again.

He shrugged into his parka, turned the sign to 'Closed,' and turned down the radiator. He locked the door and pulled on his knitted gloves. Down the street, he saw Fred outside his shop, erect and composed in his war surplus greatcoat.

Fred walked toward him. His son, Gerard, followed and greeted Michael with a good-natured grin. At a head-tilt from his father, he scampered back to where his mother locked their shop. Fred looked over his shoulder at Gerard, then at Michael.

"Mike, if you know more about what happened to Paddy, now is the time to tell me. For the sake of our friendship."

Michael wanted to put both fists in his eyes. Maybe to gouge them out.

"Fred, there's nothing more to tell. You were wise to stay out of the business, but we're all out of it now. And Paddy knew the risks."

"If you say so, Mike. I won't bring it up again."

Fred looked straight ahead, and they walked the longest block in the world to where Abe's truck shuddered outside his shop. Fred helped his wife and Lizzie into the cab, and Fred, Michael, and Gerard climbed in the back.

At the cemetery Michael watched Abe take a place beside Margaret, who held Regan's hand. Instead of being on the verge of hysteria, she stood calm and watchful. She was pale but walked unassisted. Paddy had never described her ailment, only saying she distrusted doctors, and made her own tonics. The recipe likely included laudanum from the bottle he had spotted on the shelf above the mugs.

Regina, Nov 1927: Regan, The Funeral

Regan gripped his mother's hand and shivered. She stood as still as the stone angel he saw above the heads of people on the other side of a hole in the half-frozen ground. The man from the bookshop held his mother's elbow on her other side, and his friend, Lizzie, stood beside him.

His mother hadn't cried all morning, even when Mrs. Croft came to help her dress, and then helped Regan too. He hoped she was finished crying now, and she would tell him when his dad was coming home.

Mr. Croft had driven them to this place–a cemetery he had called it and Regan had never heard the word. He had looked at the snow dusted field and the markers of all kinds, like the angel, but what they marked nobody had said. They had joined other people who spoke in hushed voices if at all, including two boys a little bigger than him.

The boys held their caps in their hands, and Regan removed his. He recognized one of the boys; had seen him in the shop next to the bookstore. The boy raised his hand and smiled, but at his mother's hand on his shoulder, joined the rest of the crowd in silence when a man in a dress spoke.

The man's words rose and fell in harmony with the November wind that pasted back Regan's hair and stung his eyes. Lizzie took his hand, but he shook it loose and jammed both hands in his pockets. Across the hole, a tall man stood beside a red-haired girl who held a white handkerchief.

Regan didn't know her, but she smiled at him. He looked at her handkerchief rather than the long wooden box suspended over the hole and the other faces surrounding it. He had looked at each of them, but his dad wasn't there. He had sometimes gone away, but he had been gone a long while this time. Could he be at home waiting for them? He closed his eyes waiting for the past to become the present.

The man thumped his book shut and his final words blew away in the wind. Six men, three aside, lowered the box.

R. Rigsby

Regina, Nov 1927: Michael, Kesey's Legacy

Michael shifted his boots on the frosted lawn then followed the crowd out of the cemetery. God, this was shameful. Margaret and Regan. Such a little chap. So lost and bewildered.

Mrs. Croft made sure everybody in her sitting room had tea and cake. Mr. Croft on the back porch offered the men something more fortifying, and Michael let him splash a little into his teacup. In the dining room, Jean perched on a chair with her arm around Regan who leaned his head on her shoulder and nodded to her soothing murmurs. Lizzie gazed up at them from a footstool. André stood behind Jean. Tall, square shouldered, with a strong profile, he held his teacup like an aristocrat from the court of the Sun King.

"André," Michael extended his hand and André balanced his saucer while taking Michael's hand in a decidedly farmer's grip.

"Ah, Michael," André said, "So sad. My folks knew the Fitzroys. Same church. Patrick, that's what we called him, taught me to pitch when I was a kid. Before the war."

Michael hoped his mother, who spoke to Mrs. Bakker, had embraced the obvious regarding Jean and André. His father, taken by influenza almost eight years ago, would have been delighted. He had said the Perraults were the most hardworking and successful farmers in the area. Given his father's lacklustre kinship with growing things, Michael thought he too had inherited the non-farmer trait. But his grandfather had homesteaded with diligence and André had inherited his own father's passion for the land. Charles Perrault was still a force in the community and his only son showed every likelihood of continuing that tradition. He was also an honest man who would love Michael's sister and future nieces and nephews. André deserved honesty and trust from him.

He glanced around. Birch had come to the Crofts with his wife and their children, Raymond and Marcella. Mrs. McCandless held Marcella on her lap. The dainty child's eyes were at half-mast and her thumb was in her mouth. Raymond and Gerard, bored with enforced solemnity, were in the back yard pitching rocks at the privy. Birch must have left, but Michael had overheard him commiserate on the sad loss of Paddy. With Birch, subterfuge was second nature. So much so that Michael found it easier to believe that it really was

R. Rigsby

Paddy's wake. He had to leave. The walk to his office would be a relief. On the way out, he spoke to Abe Primnase.

The print on the offer of sale blurred and the lines ran together. Michael couldn't attach faces to the names. People he had known for years. Instead, he saw Margaret at Mrs. Croft's, her face a porcelain mask. He would look out for her and the boy, for as long as they needed. Birch had agreed.

A beaky visage appeared in the glass of his office door. Michael set the page aside.

"Lock the door, Abe, and pull the blind."

"You wanted to see me, Michael?" Abe Primnase limped forward and folded into the chair in front of the desk, showing the shiny knees of his pants. He removed his hat and held it in his lap.

"It's all done, isn't it?"

"We've been through this. We can't go back to that business no matter how tough things get. Besides, apart from the still in the Fitzroy's barn, you dumped the other in Jessop's slough. Right?"

"Yeah, yeah, it's gone." Abe flipped his hand and slapped it on his hat. "Well, it was good while it lasted. But like you say, times are tough."

Michael opened a drawer and pulled out an envelope. He showed the bills inside. "This is for you. Don't put it in the bank, don't spend like a sailor on shore-leave, and don't tell anybody."

Abe stared at the envelope, then tucked it into his inside coat pocket. "McCandless know about this?"

Michael looked up, meeting Abe's eyes. "You'll see another envelope, much like that, every so often. Best not to inquire. Right?"

Abe nodded, again looking at the hat in his lap. "You're right, Michael. I miss Paddy. I wish I could do more for Margaret and Regan. I chop her wood and such, but I don't know how they'll get along."

"Don't worry. They're taken care of. Like you. And B–, McCandless feels Paddy's loss as much as we do."

Abe stared at Michael, but lifted his shoulders, got up, and left.

Michael remained in his chair. Usually, out of courtesy, he escorted his visitors to the door, but he didn't trust himself not to drag Abe back, to tell him what really happened to Paddy. He wasn't sure he could shake Abe's hand without telling him everything, the connection of skin on skin a conduit for confession. And confess to the source of the money. Abe hadn't yet missed Kesey.

They had lost the Yank's payment, but Birch had discovered a windfall in Kesey's room: a tin box stuffed with coins and bills. Kesey must have saved every spare nickel of his earnings from The Arms and his harvest money from the homesteads.

Michael opened his bottom drawer. He had insisted Birch pay Abe for the risks he'd taken. He'd insinuated that Abe might need incentive to keep quiet. Abe would never betray them, but it had made it easier to persuade Birch. Or not Birch.

He now wanted to be called Bertram. Or just McCandless. He said the nickname was part of the past, a past that Michael had to forget.

Birch, Bertram, used the rest of Kesey's cash to pay the broker and the share certificates went into the hotel safe. With the others. Rock solid shares according to Birch, already increasing in value in these crazy times when even schoolteachers put their savings into the stock market. At least teachers' investments didn't cost two good men. The rest of Kesey's legacy went into the burn barrel.

R. Rigsby

Regina, Nov 1927: Michael, Nobody is Anonymous

Michael stood up. He needed a change of scene. A brew at The Arms. Before he could pull on his parka, his office door opened, letting in a puff of tiny snowflakes and a tall young man.

"Mr. Kerr, can I ask you somet'ing?" A surprisingly deep voice and a slight sing-song accent not yet submerged under the vernacular. He whipped his worn cap off his head, releasing a thatch of fine blond hair. Jon Sorensen.

"What can I do for you, Jon?" Michael pointed to the client chair in front of his desk, but Jon, although taking a step forward, shook his head.

"It's about my friend Yig. Jig, er, Calvin, Kesey."

Michael turned and rehung his coat on the coat tree, then faced Jon who clutched his cap in both hands.

"Kesey? Sure, I know who you mean. Friend of yours, you say? Haven't seen him lately."

"Not for two weeks. He goes on benders, but he usually turns up, most often in his room at the hotel, sleeping it off." Then as if afraid he might forget them, he rushed the words, "We're going to Vancouver. To work for his brother. We were to leave last week. We bought train fare. We pooled our money. I promised to go with him."

Michael swallowed, envisioning Kesey's tin of cash. "Hmmm. How old are you, son? Don't your folks have a nice little farm? Do they know about this?"

"No, none of it. I'm twenty. Old enough to know I'm not a farmer. Jig and I have plans. Yeah, he's older than me, but when he's not drinking, he's good. He wants to quit, make something of himself."

"You work for Mr. McCandless now, don't you? Didn't you ask him?"

"He said he must have left town. That's why I got the job on the desk."

"I see. How do you know K–Mr. Kesey, again?"

"Oh, we worked the same threshing crew this fall. We have the same ideas. He said he should have gone west with his parents and brother five years ago. Said we'd have a better chance in Vancouver."

"Yes, but why do you think I can help?" Michael sat on the edge of his desk and resisted the urge to cross his arms.

"Because Mr. Fitzroy, the guy who's dead, told Jig that if he ever had a problem, he should ask you. Jig told me that, so here I am."

Michael gripped the edge of his desk. "Jon, perhaps Mr. Kesey has found work elsewhere." He chuckled his best avuncular chuckle, although a difference of thirteen years hardly qualified him for wise uncle status, "I'm a lawyer so I can't let you leave without advice. Go home and make your parents proud."

Michael closed the door on Jon, then turned and leaned against it, hands in pockets, eyes closed. Kesey, the anonymous drunk wasn't so anonymous after all. And some of that money belonged to Jon Sorensen.

Before he could regain the vertical, the door pressed against his back. He turned and opened it.

"André, my friend, what brings you to town in the middle of the week?" Michael stepped back but reached for his coat. "Do you have business we can't conduct across the way?" He bent his head toward The Arms.

André grinned. White teeth in a tanned face. "Non. Merely an inquiry on behalf of mon cher père."

Michael with André on his heels pushed open the door to The Prairie Arms beer parlour exchanging the scent of impending snow for that of stale lager and ashtrays. He dropped his overcoat on the hook at the door and took his usual stool at the bar where Bertram McCandless placed his favourite brew. André shook his head at McCandless.

Michael downed a long swig. "On the wagon today, André?"

"Well since I come to town, I will go and have tea with your mother. And your sister if she is to home." André placed both elbows on the bar, tenting his fingers together, and again showing his excellent dentition. "No need to smell of la bière, oui?" The mirror reflected the gleam in his dark eyes.

"Right. As if my sister doesn't know you're coming. I can smell scones from here. So, other than relentless pursuit of my virtuous sister, why are you here? What does cher papa need to know?"

"Ah, yes." André's accent switched to what could have passed for English learned at an upper crust private school. "When my unbelievably modern-thinking father sent me, his cherished and only son, to get an education in Toronto, he needed a hand on the farm. As you know, I have returned with a degree in agronomy which, of course, is not part of the present conversation."

"Of course, but you know I like hearing it." Michael gulped more beer and forced the jovial tone.

André resumed his normal speaking voice. "Calvin Kesey, known as Jig, has worked for Dad for a few years off and on, but he's disappeared. He's been known to do that before, but not this long–"

"Toronto." McCandless who had been washing glasses, wiped his hands on a brown towel.

Michael set down his empty glass. André sat up.

"Is that so? So strange he didn't tell Dad. Or pick up his belongings at the farm."

"I think it was a last-minute thing. So I overheard. He had a train ticket."

André caught Michael's eye in the mirror, but Michael met his gaze, then looked down at the fresh glass that appeared in front of him.

"I have to go," André said, "get the scones while they're still warm." He nodded to Michael. "Too bad about Kesey. When he shows up, he works hard. Dad likes him. Hope things go well for him in … Toronto."

Michael drained his glass and slammed it on the bar.

"Toronto, Birch?"

R. Rigsby

Vancouver, Fri Oct 11 2019: Lydia,_Pathways

Janey circles the edge of her glass with her finger. "Uncle Michael. If he had called the police, he wouldn't have just been in trouble, he would have lost everything."

"Yes. His conscience would have been clear, but bitterness and resentment might have bedevilled him as much as guilt. And he had no other trade."

"It's so sad. The times were hard, and social systems were poor."

"After the war, soldiers had trouble getting jobs, especially if maimed. Then in Saskatchewan, the wheat market collapsed. The prohibition years offered some people a chance." I look around the lounge. We have the place to ourselves, barring the single server. I, being caught up in my tale, had closed my eyes. When I opened them periodically to make sure my audience of one wasn't in a trance, Janey's face only expressed amusement or pensive sympathy, or like now, sad compassion.

"How do you know this story?"

"My uncle told me some, then my father and others filled in parts I didn't know. Mother told me what she knew when it was the only way to make me quit asking."

Janey's bubbling laugh has delighted me since she was a small child. "I get that. Just ask my mother. I'm still trying to get the whole story on Granny Marielle." Then she grinned, "But you can tell me. You two being friends for so long."

"You will hear some of it."

Young people rarely care about the pasts, scandalous or otherwise, of the older generation. I was an exception, and so is Janey. And I suppose Rennie.

Other than our shared interests, Janey and I don't resemble each other in any way. She's tall, blond, with grey-green eyes, and walks like an Amazon on duty. Me? When I was her age, I was short, well I'm still short, with mouse hair, hazel eyes, and freckles. Not that many freckles. Excuse me world, may I come through? Not that the world intimidated me, not at all; I found my own way of getting what I wanted out of it. Once I figured out what that was.

R. Rigsby

Janey's mother Kelsey, and her grandmother, Marielle, or Ellie as she prefers, were born knowing their missions in life.

"How is your mother these days? Still up to her neck in charity work?"

"She's organizing Thanksgiving Dinner for the people downtown. Mostly with The Finding Home Foundation. I hope she's taken our turkey out of the freezer."

I hope so too. Kelsey is a tough act for Janey to follow. Even though gifted with brains, humour, and a warm heart, Janey's still looking at a myriad of paths and doesn't seem sure of the one she has chosen. I at least knew which path I didn't want. And one of these days, I should write about the more memorable experiences from the paths I did follow, including the detours and dead ends. There were more than a few of those.

I don't think Janey raps the table intentionally, but it's a good way to get my attention.

"Oh, shall I go on?"

"Please, but, first, Kesey's money–it was used to pay for some shares, right?"

"Yes. In those years, many people invested in the stock market."

She's not asking for a history lesson, so I don't elaborate on how many of those speculators lost everything in the crash of 1929. And it's not yet time to tell her what became of those shares.

Janey nods and I wait for her second question.

"Was Regan's condition ever diagnosed?"

Regina, Mar 1934: Regan, Desertion

Regan duck walked backwards from his desk at the end of the row and slid out the rear door. He'd become quite good at sneaking away before the bell without alerting Twistle. Gerard and Raymond had told him how to do it. He usually waited for Liz, but she could find him outside. He ambled down the hall, pulling on his coat.

Through the glass in the front doors, he saw Gerard and Ray on the steps. They too had sneaked out early. Gerard was fifteen now, Ray too, and both boys were big for their ages. They leaned against the railing, with hands deep in pockets, but hatless in the March chill. Melting snow lay in patches and in dirty heaps where it had been shovelled off the stairs. The calendar spring would arrive with the equinox, but the prairie spring was weeks away.

Regan buttoned his coat and pulled his scarf around his neck. He left his woolen tuque stuffed in his pocket. Ray would take Marcella to her piano lesson. Gerard would work in his father's hardware store and Regan would help Liz in her father's shop. Or hang around with Gerard who never told him to get lost. Instead, he joked while he mopped winter mud, or in summer, swept prairie grit that blew into town on the never-ending winds. The dustbowl state of the farms and what people called a depression had closed stores and some families had moved away. He and his mother were okay.

Their farm had been leased for years, but Mrs. Walters only brought his mother eggs, butter, or a fresh-killed chicken. No cash. Yet, his mother paid their rent right on time every month, bought groceries, and kept them in good clothes. Not that she was always able to cook or shop. When she had one of her spells, he often cooked their supper. Something else he had become good at. He looked down at his new boots.

A few months ago, he woke to voices in the kitchen after one of his 'rests.' Mr. Primnase had been there the day before, but he remembered nothing after that. He smelled coffee and wandered in to see Mr. Kerr hand his mother an envelope. When Mr. Kerr left, his mother took the envelope to her room and then insisted he eat a bowl of porridge and a slice of ham. She said he didn't need to go to school. That afternoon they went to Rudd's, and he had his boots.

A sudden movement between the boys caught his attention. He would look silly if they saw him with his nose to the glass. Regan squared his shoulders, stood up as tall as his not yet thirteen years allowed and shouldered the door open.

"…and Dad closed the store last night." Regan heard Gerard say, then, "Oh, say, hullo Regan," and he grinned, "I didn't hear the bell." Ray laughed.

Regan laughed too. "Yeah," he said, "Early dismissal."

"Yup, us too. Even easier for you with old Twistle. He can't see to the back of the room. We had him for two years in a row."

The bell rang, and the leaders of the released swarm slammed open the doors and screeched down the steps. Regan moved closer to the big boys to allow the horde to pass. He saw Liz come through the door and angle her way towards them. She grasped her leather bookbag against her thin chest, her shoulders sharp despite the bulk of her winter coat. From under her beret, jammed on sideways, her hair stuck out in the usual clumps of wayward frizz. She looked prim and purposeful, until on meeting Regan's eyes, she smiled, and the sun came out.

Regan stepped aside to allow her a space between him and Gerard, safe from the ebbing stampede.

"Where's Marcella?" Ray said and stepped up one stair.

"Give her a minute," said Liz, "She hates being shoved in a crowd." Then, to Gerard, "Your Dad's closed the shop. When are you leaving?"

"Leaving?" said Regan, "Who's leaving? Why?"

"He is." Liz pointed her chin, which was eminently suitable for pointing, to Gerard. Gerard shook his head, but it wasn't in denial. "The store's gone broke," Liz continued, "Dad says you're going west. Vancouver, isn't it? Your granddad's?"

"Yeah, Dad will work in his shop. It's called Pinnace Appliances. Selling kitchen stoves. And fridges too. I'll go find Marcella."

"Can't he get a job here? So, you can stay?" Regan swung his arm as though to encompass a field of beckoning jobs, like ripe grain bending with the breeze. But Gerard disappeared inside without answering.

"There're no jobs here," Liz said. "A lot of people are leaving."

"You aren't, the bookshop is doing fine, isn't it?" Regan's eyes widened.

"Yes. We aren't going anywhere. Dad says so."

"There she is, at last." Ray lifted his arm in an unnecessary imperative.

Regan watched Gerard, who looked hypnotized, hold the door for Marcella, then accompany her down the stairs. Dark brown hair framed a heart-shaped face with blue eyes and a full-lipped mouth. She walked as if she were a queen bestowing the grace of her presence on the multitude. She glanced up and answered Gerard's smile with one appropriate to approving a vassal.

Regan narrowed his eyes. She never looked at him like that.

"Let's go, your ladyship," Ray said, "If we're late, it's me who'll catch it." He shoved her ahead of him and like a decapede, all five filed to the street, Marcella, Ray, Gerard, Liz, and Regan.

At the gate, Ray spoke over his shoulder to Gerard, "Dad said not to tell anybody yet, but he sold the hotel. We're going to Vancouver too. So, see you there!"

Regan stopped, and Liz, missing his steps, also stopped. The others carried on through the gate and up the street.

"Everybody's leaving," Regan said. "I'll never see them again."

"I'm not going anywhere," Liz said, "We'll both stay here together. We'll take over the bookshop from Dad. It'll be okay."

But it was too late. Regan's eyes rolled back, he sat down hard, and flopped over on his side.

R. Rigsby

Regina, June 1934: Michael, Prairie Arms Farewell

Michael walked into Primnase's Bookshop and inhaled the smell of musty books and printer ink. He ran his hand along a gritty shelf holding a few volumes of the Encyclopedia Britannica and a stack of old magazines. Nobody had appeared in answer to the doorbell's reluctant ding. Liz was in school, but Abe should be on deck. Swabbing, if not selling books. A broom stood in the corner over a forgotten pile of dirt. For God's sake, it wasn't like Abe didn't have time to tidy up.

"Abe!" he called, "Are you here?" In answer a toilet flushed, and Abe appeared in the doorway to what had once been the print shop. He hadn't printed a pamphlet or even a wedding invitation in years.

"Ah, Michael, so The Arms is sold, and the McCandless family is leaving Regina?"

"Bertram is already in Vancouver, looking at property. He did better than we expected on the sale. Michael reached in his jacket pocket for an envelope. "This is for you. Like the others, keep it to yourself."

"You know I need it Michael, for Lizzie, for her future, but I wish it weren't so." Abe pressed the envelope between his palms. "Too bad he didn't sell sooner. I could have helped Fred a little more. Then he mightn't have had to throw up his business and go live with his in-laws."

"Fred wouldn't have accepted. He didn't like you reducing his rent. He never wanted any part of the hotel, or the other thing."

"McCandless didn't want me in, did he? Fred told me. He didn't want Paddy either and only asked him when Fred said he wouldn't."

"McCandless thought Fred would join because we dragged each other through that war. Took everything I had to buy into The Arms when Fred wouldn't come in, but you already had the shop and owned your building. Bertram thought it would complicate things with too many shares. And The Arms was his dad's–he only sold us a piece of it each–it was his show to run."

"Well, if I hadn't this gimpy leg and could have enlisted with you guys…but it's all done now. I'll look after Paddy's family like we've been doing all along. Will you join McCandless?"

R. Rigsby

"I'm not going anywhere, Abe. I'll stay to look out for Margaret and Regan. And I'll wait; watch for a worthwhile investment." Michael walked to the door, Abe following.

Across the street in front of Miss Ariane's Dress Shop, André leaned against a lamp post, with what looked like a pocket novel held in one hand. He stopped reading and watched Michael and Abe shake hands. He was no doubt waiting for Jean, who was probably shopping for a new maternity dress, although nothing had been said. Number five. And he and Lou still waited on number one.

He would hear all about it at dinner, if anybody could hear anything above the racket of four children under seven, all of whom were deposited with his mother. His mother was thrilled when her first grandchild, the peerless Henri, was placed in her arms within ten months of Jean's marriage. She was equally delighted with David, Marguerite, and Jeanette. Whatever antipathy she felt about her daughter's marriage to a Catholic had long since evaporated.

Michael wished it were as easy for antipathy of any stripe to evaporate.

Regina, June 1937: Regan, Testament

Margaret moaned and her eyelids fluttered. Regan's head snapped up from the back of the chair. He rubbed his eyes, stretched the crick out of his neck and the tingle out of his leg. Across the room, the lace curtain on the open bedroom window lifted with a breath of dawn air, likely the last in another sweltering day.

Regan reached for the hand that trembled on top of the sheet; the skin showing every vein and sharp bone. He warmed the hand between his own, hoping today she would feel better, spiting Mrs. Croft's gentle suggestion that he must prepare himself. She had been in pain for years and never said so. She treated her agony in the only way she knew to protect her privacy or keep the thing inside her from becoming real.

It had become real enough when she fell outside Michael Kerr's office. Regan had left her in Miss Ariane's and was with Liz in the bookshop looking through a shipment of new titles.

Liz's father came in shouting, "Regan! Your mother fell! An ambulance is coming!" Regan rode with her to the hospital, a place she dreaded, but the doctors said there was little they could do. She insisted on coming home to her own bed.

Margaret opened her eyes and clasped Regan's fingers.

"Regan, lovey." Then stronger, "You've been here all night. When Mrs. Croft comes, you must go to bed."

"Oh, Mummy, Mrs. Perrault will come today. But I won't leave you." For the first time in days, her eyes shone. Her fair skin glowed and her smile widened. Regan's terror subsided.

"A little soup? It'll only take a moment to heat."

"No. I must talk to you. I don't have much longer. Don't look like that my darling, we know it is so." Margaret pushed herself upright and Regan plumped her pillows. "Listen, it's about your father. When he lost his leg in the war, he came home to your grandparents' farm. I didn't care about his leg. We married soon after."

"I remember him showing me his 'buddy, Woodside' and how he laughed."

Margaret shut her eyes tight, then opened them. "Your dad's leg never healed well. He said a one-legged farmer was even more useless than a one-legged husband. We leased the land and moved here. He worked for Abe Primnase." Margaret motioned for a sip of water, her steady breaths and strong grip reassuring.

Regan waited. He knew his dad worked for Mr. Primnase. Abe told Regan so in one of many conversations while he chopped wood or scraped ashes out of the stove. Regan had never forgotten one conversation.

In the spring after his father's funeral, while Lizzie and his mother baked cookies, Regan had helped Abe dig the garden. Or he dug, and I picked up worms, Regan thought. It was the worms that made him ask where his father had gone. Abe stopped digging, then took him to sit behind the shed. He took Regan by the shoulders. Regan could never tell anybody what he was about to hear.

He was such a little kid. He thought that knowing what had happened would make it possible for his dad to come back.

Abe had told him how some men made whiskey against the law. His dad delivered Abe's books and pamphlets, and sometimes those men hid whiskey in the boxes, and he took it to people who bought it. This was usually easy, but something happened and the police in the United States shot his dad. His dad was dead. His father was a good man, and a good friend, but times were hard, and men often did work they didn't like to keep food on the table. And not only food, but clothes and books and toys.

Like Phintel, Regan had thought. The day he showed Phintel to his mother, she hadn't smiled. She told his dad to take it back to Rudd's for flour and sugar. Regan had promised Abe he wouldn't tell anybody, ever. And he couldn't. His dad died because he had wanted Phintel.

He didn't think that now. Not entirely.

"Regan?" Margaret squeezed his fingers. "Your dad owned a share of The Prairie Arms. He put most of his soldier's pay into it after the war. And he bought that car."

Regan pictured The Arms, and something dark stirred at the back of his mind. The place gave him the creeps.

"When your father didn't come home, I knew something terrible had happened. Then Constable Mutch told me that the US authorities reported my husband accidentally shot in a 'border incident.' Mutch said he found a still in the barn at the homestead."

Margaret took a deep breath. "He had the cheek to tell me that your father's death was tragic but running booze across the border was risky. Pompous hypocrite. Your father…" A few careful breaths. "Your father did not have a still in the barn. He wasn't so stupid as to set up a still in his own barn. That was hogwash and I'd walked out there the day before. At that time, the Walters only leased the land and planted the garden; they didn't live in the house. I wanted to pull more of the fall onions. I went into the barn to get a sack and that's all that was in there–no feed, no hay, no tools–just those burlap bags hooked on the end wall. No still."

"When they told me your father was dead, I didn't think straight for a month. Michael Kerr said I would receive a monthly payment from the Prairie Arms receipts. Even after it sold, he's given it to me. That's kept us alive for ten years."

Margaret coughed. She lay back, her breathing ragged.

"Mummy, that's enough. Don't talk any more."

"I had you to think about, and no proof whatever that your father wasn't a bootlegger. He didn't make whiskey, but he did drive for Birch."

Regan sat up. Birch? Birch! The name rang in his mind.

"He always told me it was Primnase's books and pamphlets he delivered. Primnase never had that much to ship, but the money kept us from starving."

"Mummy, who is Birch?"

"I have something for you." She reached for the drawer in the side table, and Regan withdrew the painted box in which she kept her few baubles. "My mother's pearls, your grandmother Fitzroy's ruby ring, my gold earrings, my wedding ring and..."

Regan pulled out his father's pocket watch and looked at his mother. "Yes, your father's cufflinks and tie bar are in there too, but I don't have his wedding ring. It didn't come back from, the, you know. It's been on my mind lately. That's why I went to Michael Kerr's office. I thought he could ask for me." She lay back and breathed slowly.

"Can I get you something?"

"Yes." She pointed across the room. "In the top drawer."

Regan, expecting to fetch pills, got up and opened the dresser drawer.

"It's under the handkerchiefs." And it was. A revolver from the Great War. As an enlisted man, his dad had been issued a rifle. He raised his eyebrows.

"Fred Bakker found it and gave it to your dad. A gift for saving his life. Keep it, for ..." and she lay back holding her breath, then she coughed, and whispered, "It was Birch...made him deliver that load."

"I'll remember." He shut the drawer.

She took his hand again, then lay back and closed her eyes. "There's a trust for your education, Regan. Mr. Primnase and Mr. Kerr have been the kindest of friends. You must take their advice in all things." But the only name in Regan's mind was 'Birch.'

R. Rigsby

"Mother, Mummy," Regan kissed her hand. Margaret's eyes opened, and her smile returned.

"My sweet boy. I'm still here." But within the hour she wasn't.

Regina, July 1937: Regan, The Hunt Begins

Regan packed his few books and photographs and left the box at the back door. Then he emptied his bureau, including the item in his bottom drawer. He clicked the suitcase shut on the last of his belongings and lugged it to the bedroom door. Behind him, bare floorboards stretched to the bed, naked of sheets and quilts. His bedding, along with everything but the furniture, had been boxed and moved into the Primnase's garage. He had helped Abe pile the boxes on top of, and around, other boxes, some of which, including the old printing press, were covered by canvas tarps.

Happy Birthday, Regan, you are now officially an orphan at sixteen. But he'd really been an orphan since his father died, what with his mother's illness. She had her will prepared long before she collapsed in front of Mr. Kerr's office.

Regan, about to shut the door, paused. His mother had said she wanted to ask about his father's wedding ring. She wanted Mr. Kerr to ask...who? But the ring was likely buried with his father. It was a miracle he remembered most of his last hours with his mother. That morning, Mrs. Perrault came in to find him crying and still holding her hand.

"Regan dear, she's gone. Let go now," she had said. "Say goodbye and come with me to the kitchen." It was the kitchen that did it. So cold, like never before. Both Mum and Dad gone.

He had woken in his bed. A blackout. Or a bad dream. He had listened for the clink of the spoon on the mush pot and his mother humming to herself. He would never hear that again. Then Mrs. Croft tapped at his door and took him to her house where she plied him with fried eggs and johnny cake.

His mother's priest had come to see Regan that afternoon and told him of his mother's wishes for her service and interment. At the funeral, four men lowered his mother's plain pine coffin. She'd lost so much weight that four ten-year-olds could have managed it. His parents were now reunited, so the priest had said, when he patted his shoulder with a fat pasty hand. Liz and Abe stood with him at the graveside. Liz clutched his arm; she had needed his support more than he needed hers.

After the gloomy tea at Mrs. Croft's, Mr. Kerr had read him the will. The homestead was his, not that the Walters could pay much. Mr. Kerr assured him that the trust from his father's share of the Prairie Arms would continue to provide for his care and education.

Regan had clenched his jaw. He would rather have his mother back. And father.

In this house, he would never again see morning sun filtered by the frayed window blind, like visions returning in fragments. He'd hoped being alone here would prompt more memories, but if not, he had to go on with what he had. His last moments with his mother, and the shock that somebody called Birch had sent his father to his death, hovered in his mind.

He couldn't recall where he had heard the name before, and his mother never said who Birch was. She might not have known. He was probably a farmer with a still hidden in a ravine or a stand of trees. His dad probably met Birch and filled book cartons with booze. Mr. Primnase probably had to cooperate with this Birch too.

Regan looked up to see a stork silhouetted at the door. The stork removed his hat.

"Are you ready, lad?" Mr. Primnase stood slightly bent, his black coat hanging like bedraggled wings, and head bowed, as if, in honour of the dead, the house held an air of sanctity. Which would dispel the instant the couple with six kids moved in.

He didn't reply and picked up the suitcase. The kitchen smelled of Rawleigh's household cleaner, applied with Mrs. Croft's elbow grease. The floral linoleum glared as he walked across it. He should stop now. Drop everything, say he wasn't leaving, and snap some kindling for the stove.

Primnase plopped his hat on his head, picked up the box, and headed for his truck, shoulders rocking to his metronome limp. Regan followed and the truck rattled off. He looked straight ahead, refusing to look back, denying the water in his eyes the right to roll down his cheeks. He was sixteen for God's sake.

Primnase cleared his throat. "It's tough. I lost my folks young too."

He would move in with Liz and Abe, as his mother had wished. He hadn't much cared about where he would live, but Liz had offered her room. Which he refused; the storeroom off the kitchen suited him fine.

The truck wheezed to a halt in front of the book shop. The unit next door, once the Bakker's hardware store, had the same faded 'To Let' sign as when the Bakker's left for Vancouver. He missed Gerard. Would Mr. Bakker know Birch? Would Abe?

"Mr. Primnase, can I ask you something?"

Abe had stepped out but turned and looked at Regan. He pushed his hat back and mopped his brow with a handkerchief.

"Sure." His long face cracked in a smile. "If you're hungry, help yourself to the icebox. Liz baked a cake; it's in the tin on the sideboard. This is your home now."

"Oh, thankyou. But no, that's not it. It's about somebody called 'Birch.' Mum mentioned his name. Dad knew him."

Abe's smile dimmed. He closed his eyes, then his face pulled in on itself in frowning concentration. "Hmmm, yes, I mean no, that is, I've heard the name, but not for years." Abe shut the door and reached into the bed of the truck for Regan's box. Regan too, got out and picked up his suitcase.

"Do you know where he went? What was his real name?"

"Oh, I think he left here years ago. Nobody around here by that name. And your dad knew a lot of people."

Regan looked up at the red brick building. Knowing she would be there he saw Liz in her bedroom window. He ducked his head at her and followed Abe into the shop.

Who was Birch? Nobody ever mentioned that name. He would find him. Mummy said.

R. Rigsby

Regina, Oct 1937: Michael, The Rule of Three

At a tap on his door, Michael left his desk and greeted his visitor. Make that visitors: his client and a lad of about two.

"Mr. Pulaski, please come in, I have everything ready." He hunkered down to eye level with the youngster. "And who do we have here?"

"Richard, say hello to Mr. Kerr, there's a good boy. And take off your hat." Richard held out a small paw to Michael.

"Pleased to meet you, young sir," Michael winked at Mr. Pulaski.

A few minutes later, he tapped pages into order.

"Congratulations, Mr. Pulaski, the farm is yours. It's a good piece of land; the Perraults are your neighbours."

"Thankyou. Better than what I had in Manitoba. And congratulations to you too. A daughter, I hear."

Michael's heart filled his entire chest cavity, and he was sure his grin far surpassed that of any proud father. "Yes, in June. She has an incredible set of lungs."

"Ah yes, all of my daughters were so as well, but none like this one." He patted Richard's head. "Let's go, son, I'm sure Mr. Kerr has work to do."

Michael saw his guests to the door.

"Mr. Pulaski, tomorrow we will have a small gathering at the Perraults. To celebrate the christenings of my daughter and my two latest nieces. Please come. Bring Mrs. Pulaski and the children too of course. Around noon, I believe."

"Why thankyou kindly, Mr. Kerr, we will do that."

Michael parked in the Perrault yard, ran around to open the door for Lou, and relieved her of the cocoon in her arms: Georgie Kerr. A preposterous name for a girl, although it would have pleased his father.

"Uncle Mike, Auntie Lou," chorused a mob of nieces and nephews, "we have new neighbours, they brought cake," and a babble of other information.

"And how is your new baby sister?" Lou cut to the essential.

"She's fine." Henri, with seniority at age nine, commanded the conversation.

"She cries a lot," David said, Henri's second-in-command.

R. Rigsby

"She's a new baby," from Marguerite, the real commander, although she was barely seven. "Maman let me change her."

Inside the kitchen, Lou's sister burped four-month-old Marielle, and Jean came in holding her latest arrival. Lou unswaddled Georgie and the mothers lay all three baby girls side by side in a padded wicker basket. Michael smiled at his daughter. She would never have siblings, but she would always have cousins.

A hubbub of conversation from the sitting room and the aromas of coffee and fresh baking signalled that the celebration was well underway. A standing-room only crowd. The Pulaskis joining as if they had been neighbours for years. André and Mr. Pulaski engaged in the usual discourse on weather, crops, and stock. Lou's sister and Mrs. Pulaski discussed when to begin infants on solid food. Jean lifted her youngest son, Mick, from the hassock in front of the sideboard where he shoved cookies into his pockets. The Crofts had come too. Mrs. Croft bustled back and forth replenishing cakes and sandwiches. Why the Crofts, Michael wondered and then realized their son was married to one of André's sisters.

Michael sidled over to where his mother, with Jeanette on her knee, sat beside André's father, Charles, but refrained from joining the conversation on the liberal government's failure to help prairie farmers. He sipped his tea. He couldn't be happier. His life was complete, and the past was the past.

The kitchen door opened, and André welcomed Abe, Lizzie, and Regan inside. Marguerite, as official baby-viewing guide, took Lizzie's hand, and Jean showed her guests to the refreshments. The press of bodies and heat from the parlour's stove drove Michael out to the porch, where he leaned against the rail and admired the winter fields. Golden stubble and a dusting of snow over fields left fallow: a giant checkerboard of alternating gold and white. Beautiful. Everything was beautiful.

"Mr. Kerr," startled his reverie.

"Oh. Regan." He caught himself before asking Regan how he was doing. Margaret wasn't five months in her grave. "Good to see you. Settling in with Liz and Abe?"

"Yes, thanks, they're both very good to me." Regan shifted his feet, looked at the fields, and back at Michael. Regan's unease sent a prickle of warning to Michael's scalp. "Mr. Kerr, I've been meaning to ask you about my dad. My mother said he sometimes worked for a man called 'Birch.' Do you know who he is?"

Michael dumped the dregs of tea leaves over the railing and then set both cup and saucer on the rail. "Birch? There were a few guys in the war with funny nicknames. If he was from around here, he's long gone."

Regan poked at a crack in the wood. His shoulders slumped. "That's what Abe, Mr. Primnase, said too."

Liz opened the door but gave way to Marguerite. Brandishing her jump rope, she led the three Pulaski girls down the steps, all chattering about who should go first and how many jumps each could do per turn.

"Hello, Mr. Kerr," Liz said, "Regan, come in and have something to eat. You don't have your coat." Regan followed her inside.

Michael again looked at the fields above the heads of bobbing girls. Ah, Paddy. His ghost wouldn't lie quiet, would it? But at least he had Georgie. He wandered back to the kitchen to check on her.

David age eight, and Christine, age three, tussled over the basket of babies. David, with huge eyes and arms around Christine's waist, pulled her away. Christine held a wooden spoon with which she had been clearly intent on poking a baby. She scowled at Michael.

"Here now, Chrissie, you should give that to me." Michael gently took possession of the weapon. "Good boy, David, for minding the little ones. Off both of you go now." Michael sighed. Jean would know that Christine was jealous. No longer the baby girl of the family.

Michael looked down at a small figure who appeared beside him.

"Why hello, Richard. Meet my daughter Georgie. And her cousins, Marielle, and Lydia Jane."

R. Rigsby

Vancouver, Oct 11 2019: Lydia, Old Ghosts

Janey rests her chin on a hand, but the dreamy expression suddenly vanishes. "Oh, Auntie, look at the time. I've kept you talking for hours. I should be taking notes. Or recording this." Her face resumes its dreamy expression, then her eyes widen. I'm treated to one of her vivid smiles.

What's going on behind that smile? I don't ask. Like her grandfather, she will tell me when she's ready.

"Not to worry my lovely. But yes, I'm flagging. Your grandfather is probably asleep on the bench in front of the sharks. If he falls over, he'll give some poor sod a shock."

I'm glad Rennie didn't it make it this afternoon. Janey walks with me to the lobby where I kiss her goodbye and tell her I can find my own way upstairs. Five flights feel like a bit much right now, so I brave the elevator.

I tap on Mick's door in case he is back.

"If it's you, Lydia, come in. If not, my wallet is on the dresser. I'm too bagged to put up a fight." He sprawls on his bed, buttressed by two pillows, the television remote in his hand.

"Do you know how this works?" He thumbs buttons and thrusts the remote at the T.V.

"I know it's not a taser." He 'hmmphs.' I sink into the wing chair by the window, kick off my shoes, and prop my feet on the edge of his bed. "What happened at the Aquarium?"

"Nothing. I got tired. Took a cab back. Damn expensive ride for a twenty-minute walk. How's Janey? I saw you in the lounge, but I wanted to lie down. Did her friend show?"

"Rennie had to work. Janey is the same, you know lively, cheerful. She's almost three semesters in on an English degree but I'm not sure that's what she wants."

"She'll figure it out. After I left home, I flaked around Toronto for five years before I knew what I wanted to do. Had no idea how good a gig being a notary could be."

"Mick. I have a confession. Apart from an hour with Rennie, I came here to tell Janey about Uncle Michael. Because of my will."

Mick sighs and pushes himself up higher on the cushions. He tosses the remote on the bed. "Lydia, when you said we should stay here I guessed that was on your mind. And Janey will need to understand your wishes?"

"Yes."

"Then go with it. Tell her the whole story. When the time comes, she'll connect the dots."

I look through the window outlined with its tracery of red-leaved Boston ivy. It faces the building across the street. My room has the water view, but then I asked for that room. "Do you remember Grand-Père's stories about the ghost in The Prairie Arms?"

"He claimed it was his old hand Kesey."

"Mother would get so annoyed, but Dad would shake his head."

Mick too has also ridden a reversing train of thought into the past. "Dad said that the so-called ghost could have been anybody who didn't want to be seen in The Arms, and who scurried out the back door with a dishtowel over his head. Mother was never good with silly ghost talk. Especially when Henri kept it going about Jessop's haunted barn."

"Mother believed in Jesus, rain, and the price of wheat in Toronto. She did not believe in ghosts. When I came here in 1959, Kesey had been gone for over thirty years. Prophetic, considering, because here we are sixty years later yet and his fate ninety-two years ago still ripples forward."

"Doesn't it just." Mick suddenly sits up and swings his legs off the bed, stretches and rubs the back of his neck. "Enough about ghosts. I'm hungry."

We last ate on the plane. A rather good ham'n'cheese hoagie. But that was hours ago. Dear Des has commented more than once how much I eat for somebody no bigger than her twelve-year-old daughter.

Regina, June 1939: Regan, Evidence

"May as well do this now," Regan said. To which the empty alley behind the bookshop did not reply. He had all summer to read and somewhere in Abe's garage was another box of his books. Some were classics that he wanted to take with him to university. Dad, and a pang never failed to spear his guts when he thought of his father, loved to read. God knows he had lots of evenings when his wife couldn't function past four p.m. He stood in front of the garage and wiped his brow on his sleeve.

Unlike the wood-frame garage, the building he had called home for two years was brick, and each one radiated heat into his face. He squinted up at the building. The outside wooden staircase clung to the brickwork and led to a landing with doors to the second-floor suites. At ground level were back doors, intended for receiving goods. The door that had once opened to the Bakkers' hardware store hadn't received a delivery since the Bakkers called it quits five years ago.

He and Gerard wrote regularly. Gerard had completed a commerce degree and was now a junior manager in his family's business. His last letter enthused about Marcella, who still reigned in his heart. Regan quashed a vision of Marcella at seventeen and kicked a rock. Instead, he thought about Ray, who was absorbed in world events and the dire problems in Europe, so Gerard wrote. Ray never wrote, but Regan thought Liz kept in touch.

A year ago, he had written Gerard to ask his father about 'Birch.' Gerard replied. His father knew nobody who went by that name. A few other inquires were equally fruitless. Like Abe, people shrugged.

Last year, Abe had moved the cot and his armchair downstairs into the old print room. His bad leg had become arthritic, and it was too hard to run up and down the stairs. Regan had never seen Abe run anywhere, but he and Liz had assumed the cooking and household chores in proportion to Abe's increased alcohol intake.

Regan had moved from the storeroom to Abe's room with the window overlooking the back lane. From there he watched patrons of The Prairie Arms arriving or leaving from its side door. The hotel still made his stomach constrict in some unremembered way, but he watched it as if one evening, it would have to be evening, something happened that would explain his unease. He glanced at The Arms and quickly back at the garage doors in front of him.

He wished Liz were home, but her secretarial course kept her out all day. She had said she knew where to find his books, but, restless on a dull afternoon he had decided to just get it done. Abe hadn't opened the bookshop again, not that a line of customers waited at the front door. The street was as empty as the back lane, and Primnase was already semi-stupefied in his armchair.

The garage door scoured a furrow in the dirt, and the hinges complained as Regan pulled it open. Something feathered shot out straight at his head.

"Christ." He ducked and dragged the door open farther to light the jumble-sale of cartons, boxes, and broken furniture: some covered with old blankets or canvas or brown burlap bags, supposedly to keep out the dust. The missing pane in the one grimy window accounted for the resident bird.

"Should have brought the flashlight, owww!" He tripped on a small box but caught himself. "Shit. What a lot of rubbish in here." He walked to the nearest pile and pulled off the covering: an ancient quilt. He shook it, then coughed. "God, don't do that again Regan." He dropped the quilt and opened the boxes and trunks stacked in front of him.

One box contained kitchen utensils. In a trunk, linens, musty, and in another box, toys: faded wooden blocks, his train set, a stuffed blue elephant. Phintel. He picked up the elephant and shook it. Not too bad for dust. When he was little, he couldn't say 'elephant,' but he knew what he wanted when he saw it in Rudd's. His mother would have dragged him home yelling, but his dad had picked it off the shelf and handed it to him.

"Put it on the bill," his dad had told Mr. Rudd. It was the first time Regan had heard the term, but it stayed in his mind as something owed, something to be dealt with in the future, when the time was right.

He held Phintel. "You're missing an eye, old buddy, but you're coming with me to Toronto. Lucky you."

Regan froze. "Lucky Phintel." Dad had said that. Before he walked away. Down a passage between two large buildings... his armpits prickled, and his fingers gripped Phintel tighter. He knew which passage. And then, then, stairs, and his father's voice. And another voice, loud, angry. A name. Birch. His innards churned, like they did then. His bladder twinged.

He closed his eyes and tried to blank his mind, but that was it, nothing more in his head and eels writhing in his bowels.

He tucked the elephant under his arm and purposely went back to sifting the debris for the books. What else could Phintel show him? Why was his father there? With Birch? Never mind. Don't think. Let it come on its own. A large square of canvas covered a bulk of edges and points. Likely that old press, and yes, the box. "Hah!"

Regan lifted the canvas, but whatever had been holding the top edge gave way and the canvas, along with what Regan figured was two thousand years of dirt, bird shit, and dead bugs, fell forward in folds at his feet.

"Oh, Jesus." He coughed, put his arm across his face, and closed his eyes. When he opened them, he couldn't quite believe what they saw. The press was there, but so was something else. He backed away, then with rigid steps walked to the back door of the bookshop.

"You bugger. You miserable, conniving, drunken old bugger. You lied to me. You told me other men made the booze and made Dad run it. Not true, not true, you–piece of shit." Regan lifted Primnase halfway out of the armchair, knocking over the bottle and glass and pile of newspapers on the side table.

"Wha, wha, whacha, Reg'n stop lemme go!" Abe's slippered feet slithered on the newspapers, and equilibrium impaired, he slid forward clonking his bony knees on Regan's shins. Regan let go and trembled, fists at his side. The man on the floor, clutching a pen, reached for the pad of paper he'd held in his lap. Regan kicked it aside.

"That still in the garage. It's yours. You were the one hiding booze in boxes of books and pamphlets. You were the one! You were the fucking bootlegger. You made my dad go on that run! You *are* Birch! And you let my mother die blaming somebody else, even while you chopped her wood. I'm getting the constable–"

Regan took two steps back, one step forward and then watched the floor rush up to meet his face. *No, not nowww* flitted through is mind, but it was no use.

R. Rigsby

Regina, June 1939: Michael, Temptation

A car's handbrake screeched outside. More people had trucks and cars now, including Michael, but he'd been waiting for a particular vehicle: a cab from the train station. He glanced at the clock, assured by the swinging pendulum. Right on time.

It had been a tough decade, but lawyering was one occupation nearly depression-proof; although filing foreclosures didn't bring him any joy and he refused to deal with evictions. His practice had provided well for him and Lou, and Georgie's birth two years ago had fulfilled their dreams. She spent hours with her cousin, Lydia, at the Perrault farm. Lou's sister's girl, Marielle, often rounded out the general mayhem. As Jean said, when there were seven kids already, two more hardly made a difference.

Still thinking of the joys of family, Michael watched Bertram McCandless get out of the cab and straighten his tie. Always a broad solid man, McCandless had solidified more around the waistline, but his breadth of shoulder helped him carry it well. He wore a grey double-breasted suit over a white shirt. Cufflinks flashed as he took a valise and a black leather briefcase from the driver.

Michael rubbed his chin. Birch, Bertram, looked prosperous. He was prosperous. Why shouldn't he look it? They had done well when Bertram sold most of the shares before the crash. The man had a sixth sense for picking shares. All bought with whiskey money, then with Kesey's cash, slipped into the hand of that shady broker. Which might account for Birch's sixth sense. The shares they kept were good: increasing in value and paying dividends. Dividends that helped him discount his fees and pay for Regan's keep. What did McCandless want? They had been good friends once. He still owed him his life, but he had been relieved when McCandless left five years ago.

"If it weren't for Abe and Regan, I'd transfer my shares to Bertram and tell him to go hang," Michael said out loud but smiled when he opened the door. "You're looking well," he put out his hand, "Good times with the Pinnace people, I gather?" McCandless dropped his suitcase under the coat tree and took Michael's hand while looking around the office.

"Not much has changed here, Mike."

"Oh, I think the paint is different. Lighter green." Michael was about to lock the door, then caught sight of Abe Primnase staggering across the street.

"Primnase is coming here."

McCandless grunted. "We can talk later, but I'm going to Winnipeg tomorrow."

Michael opened the door and Primnase hobbled in. His bleared eyes focussed on Michael. Unshaven, he looked like he'd slept in his clothes. Smelled like it too.

"Abe, what's wrong man, did you fall down your stairs?"

"I wish I had. Or you'll wish I had. The kid found the still. Oh, Hi McCandless. Didn't know you were out here. Long time."

Abe looked and smelled of impairment, but his speech was coherent. Then the meaning of what Abe said penetrated.

"What still? You don't have a still. You got rid of that, what, twelve years ago. Didn't you? What the Hell are you talking about?"

"Christ." McCandless stood and pushed a chair toward Abe. Then he straightened his jacket sleeves and sat on the desk.

"Okay, Abe. You better have a good explanation for why that still isn't in the bottom of Jessop's slough."

"I don't. I took the small one and set it in the barn at the Fitzroy place, but on the way to the slough, I blew a tire. Was daylight by the time I changed it and I'd left Lizzie alone. I went home, backed the truck into the garage and piled the still in the corner. Covered it good. Thought I would take it away on another night. Then the weather got bad and stayed that way. By spring, it didn't seem to matter. None of the constables cared what any of us two-bitters did as long as a bottle or too made it onto their back steps."

"The kid found it. Regan? What happened?"

"He went nuts on me. Said I was the bootlegger who got his dad killed. Said I was Birch."

McCandless stiffened. "Nobody calls me that now."

"And I've never called you that. And I never told Regan either. He said he was going for the constable. Then he had one of his fits and fell flat on his face. I got Jon from The Arms to get him upstairs. He's sleeping it off."

Michael looked at McCandless who looked at his fingernails.

"Abe, why does Regan think you're Birch?" Michael said.

"I don't know. Margaret knew you, McCandless, were called Birch. She knew more about what we did than she let on, but it kept Paddy off the farm. Whatever she told Regan, he misunderstood." Abe, who had come in hatless, reached up as if to remove one, then let his hand fall to his lap. "He asked a few years back. I told him nobody called Birch was around any longer."

"He might not remember any of this when he wakes up." Michael reached for his bottom drawer. "He's probably out for the whole night. Let's decide what to do now."

A few minutes later, Bertram reclaimed a visitor chair and Michael leaned back in his own.

"Is he like that every day? He always enjoyed a tipple, but I never saw him drunk," Bertram said.

"He's gotten bad this year. Hardly ever opens the shop. Regan and Liz do their best."

"Will Regan really not remember?"

"He hasn't before, and he hasn't gone out like that for years. Last time was when his mother died. Abe put him to bed then too. Once he fell over in the schoolyard, and Abe saw him go out when he was younger. It's the same thing that happened that night. He doesn't know what he missed, so he doesn't know to ask."

"What if he remembers and asks?"

"Then Abe will tell him that if there was ever anybody called Birch he is long gone."

"What if Primnase is too drunk to remember that?" McCandless leaned forward. "Or Abe thinks telling Regan some version of the truth might help the kid. It sounds like Regan's not right in the head. Like an idea gets in, and it can't get it out. We both know people like that from the war: tedious, but not dangerous. Do you think Abe needs more reason to maintain his amnesia about the business?"

McCandless rubbed his fingers together, but Michael shook his head. He wished, not for the first time, that he could induce amnesia in himself, or like Regan, have a fit to erase his memory.

"Jesus. No. He'll do what we decided."

"He didn't do it twelve years ago, did he? He saved his own hide when Mutch was forced to find out where the booze came from. That other still could cause trouble if the kid makes it hard for Mutch to look the other way."

"Mutch retired."

"All the more reason to get rid of that still. Fred said that Regan had written Gerard to ask him if he knew a 'Birch.' Of course, he told Gerard..." McCandless sat back, "let me think...he told Gerard to tell Regan that 'he didn't know anybody who went by that name.' Which is true. Like you, he never calls me 'Birch.'"

"Regan is probably out for the night. Abe will talk to him. I'll check tomorrow morning as soon as I get back from Lumsden. Must get a signature."

"Okay, if you think you can get this straightened out, let's get back to why I'm here." McCandless reached down and slapped his briefcase on Michael's desk, popping the catches in one smooth movement.

Michael held his breath. Had Birch, Bertram, rehearsed this piece of choreography for hours or did he have a lot of experience heaving that black case onto desks? Desks whose apprehensive owners might dread the temptation the case was about to bring forth.

The temptation appeared as an offer typed on three pages of cream paper with a staple aligned at a perfect right angle in the left corner. Michael stared at the image of a sleek sailing ship on the top sheet.

McCandless smoothed the pages and tapped them with a knuckle.

"This is your ticket to get out of this town, if you want, but even if you don't want, and I really don't understand why you stay here at all, you can find a space in a decent building. But Pinnace could really use you in our new Toronto office."

Michael concentrated on keeping his face composed in polite interest.

"Toronto office?"

"Yes. To go with the plant expansion." McCandless leaned back and looked at the ceiling as if recalling a speech. "Despite the depression, Pinnace has done well, thanks to Fred Bakker's father-in-law and Fred too made some wise decisions. When I invested five years ago, they'd hit a rough patch. Fred wasn't keen on having me join, but his father-in-law had the reins."

Michael picked up the pages, scanning and flipping. He understood Fred's reluctance regarding Bertram, but there was no doubt the man could spot a sound investment.

"It's a good offer, Mike."

"So why ask me? Because Fred wanted you to? Or because not many people these days have liquid assets, and I might be interested. For old times' sake?"

McCandless, who had tilted back his chair thumped it to the floor and stood up. He tightened his fists at his side, opened then shut his mouth. Michael braced for the explosion, but to his surprise, Bertram burst out laughing.

"Fred did say that you might have 'considerations' as he put it. I respect that. But I still want you in. You don't need to decide now. Read it over. I'll stay at The Arms," he lifted a slat in the blinds and looked across the street, "for old times' sake."

Regina, June 1939: Regan, Flames

Regan woke in darkness. Not even a glow from the light over The Arms loading dock. Late then. And another spell. He lay back and closed his eyes to let images re-form. It was like weaving a dream out of vanishing strands of a curtain that lifted at the slightest puff of air, like that on the window in his mother's room. The image of his mother pushed aside all others.

She had rarely talked about his 'rests.' She had said it was like growing pains and would go away. Abe told him about the time his father drove him to the hospital. Regan had been denied a tart before dinner. In mid-howl, his eyes rolled back, and he crumpled on the floor. Abe said the doctors told his father he probably had a neurological disorder. They could test, but his mother had said no.

And here he was, eighteen and still dropping like a shot duck whenever, whenever what? Abe had urged him to see a doctor, and he would when he got to Toronto.

Regan blinked and lifted his head to listen. Scrapes, a clink, a rustle in the alley. A cat hunting among the ash cans. He dozed. When he opened his eyes, a rosy dawn flushed the brown wallpaper. Then the rosiness shimmered, he heard a crackle, and a tendril of smoke teased his nostrils. Regan shot out of bed and looked out the window. The garage was on fire.

Others had seen it. A firetruck clanged in the distance and shouting men ran toward the garage where orange flames tongued through the broken window. One man ran back toward The Arms, but Regan was pulling on pants and heading barefoot for the door. He banged Liz's door, yelled, then hurtled down the stairs and through the shop's back room, shouting for Abe, but his cot was empty. Must be in the toilet or already out there.

A man with a hose shot a stream of water through the splintered window while Sorensen and a few others pushed Abe's truck away from the blazing garage. The firetruck roared down the alley when Liz appeared at Regan's side. She pulled him out of the way. "Come on, we can't help, we can't save your books, or anything."

Books. Phintel. He remembered finding Phintel in the garage. Then what happened?

"Where's my dad?" Liz clinging to his arm, squeezed, and looked around.

"Liz, he's probably passed out. Most likely in his chair."

"He wasn't there when I came out."

A few hours later, Regan and Liz waited by the smoking remains of the garage and the charred lower flight of the outside stairs. Jon, ash-smeared and dripping stood with them. A few other voyeurs stood about watching and waiting. Two firemen prodded through the steaming fragments with shovels, then one put out his arm stopping the other. They looked at what they had uncovered, looked at Regan and Liz, and one of them shouted at the chief to call the constable. And the coroner.

"Nooooo." Liz staggered against Regan.

Regan and Liz sat, chairs side by side, at the kitchen table. Liz had stopped sobbing but snuffled into her handkerchief. Regan had one arm around her and the other cradled Phintel.

When he had taken Liz inside and passed Abe's empty chair, Phintel's one eye gleamed at him from the floor. The edges of the black fog rose in his head, but Liz had stumbled and with one arm around her waist, he had picked up the toy and brought all of them upstairs.

He looked down at Phintel. And then he remembered. He lifted his arm from Liz's shoulders. He rubbed his eyes. He saw the dilapidated press exposed when the canvas slipped, but beside it, dented and broken, was a still. He remembered the shock of revelation; that it was Abe's still. He remembered yelling at Abe, shaking him, he was Birch.

And he again remembered that night so many years ago when he hugged Phintel and watched his father disappear down a passage between two buildings. This building. And The Arms next door.

He had followed his father to a door and stairs. He remembered a man shouting and his father's laughter, then, nothing, except somebody saying 'Birch.' But Phintel had helped him get this far and Abe must be, had been, the Birch in the basement and who made his father run a load of whiskey across the border. Hidden among boxes of temperance pamphlets.

Had Primnase threatened his father? Regan couldn't think of any time Abe had threatened anybody. But now he was gone. Something made his dad take the job when, from what his mother said, he didn't want to go. His mother. She greeted Abe, fed him cookies and coffee, and thanked him every time he came to help. She hadn't known Primnase was Birch.

Regan got up, leaving Phintel on the chair. At the sink he poured a glass of water, drank what he could, rinsed and spat, and watched it swirl down the drain. Abe had helped him through the last few years, and before that. He thought of how often Abe brought books, brought Liz to play while he strung a new clothesline or cleared the pipes, and one day out of the blue, he had delivered a brand-new washing machine.

And now everything good he ever felt for Abe swirled away like spit down the drain. He braced his hands on the side of the sink, and again fought down the dark fog.

"Liz, Regan!" echoed up the stairs, followed by thumping footsteps and Mr. Kerr panted into the kitchen. "Dear God, Sorensen told me. I was in Lumsden. Have they told you anything?"

At their shaking heads, Mr. Kerr pounded downstairs to talk to whoever was in charge, he said, as if it would help. Still, it was good of him to come and help them when the inescapable became official.

R. Rigsby

Regina, June 1939: Michael, Revelations

Michael stopped at the foot of the stairs to gather thoughts which heaved in and out of his head in sync with his panting breath. He couldn't have. It had to be an accident.

Outside, a fireman who still shovelled through the stinking rubble advised him the coroner had removed the human remains. The fire chief and the constables too had left. They should have the preliminary report shortly.

Michael paused. He should get back to Regan and Liz, but instead he detoured through the Prairie Arms side door and into the beer parlour where Jon mopped the floor. His hair hung damply in strands, fresh from his bath after the filth of firefighting.

"Jon, is Bertram McCandless here?"

"No. Last night he said he would leave early to catch the train to Winnipeg."

"Did you see him go?"

"No. The fire, you know. Out there all morning. The women who clean and cook start at eight. He was gone by then." Jon had stopped sweeping and watched Michael. If he wondered at the interrogation, he didn't ask. Michael thought it best to deflect his curiosity.

"Ah, yes, too bad I've missed him." He patted the Lumsden papers in his inside pocket. "Who called in the fire?"

"I did. I sleep here when not at the farm. Something woke me, but I always have one ear out for guests. Or vagrants rattling the back doors. I heard glass break and when I looked out, I saw smoke coming out the garage window. I ran downstairs and phoned. Then I went out to hook up my hose and do what I could. It wasn't enough."

Jon clutched his mop handle with both hands and he and Michael stared at each other. Abe's death had suddenly become real.

Later that long day, Michael escorted the coroner's assistant and a constable up the stairs to see Regan and Liz.

An accident they said. Most likely, although they were still investigating. It looked as though Mr. Primnase, perhaps under the influence, had gone into the garage with a lantern which had somehow ignited the sacking and canvas, and the extremely flammable printer's ink. He might have tried to contain the blaze but was overcome with smoke. The investigators had discovered, and here the constable cleared his throat, the remains of a still.

Liz put her face in her hands and leaned against Regan who put his head on the table. Michael ran a hand through his hair and rubbed his eyes as if they too felt the sting of hot smoke.

Vancouver, Oct 12 2019: Lydia, Beach View

The birds in the vines outside my windows chirp me awake. I laze under the comfort of the duvet. Last night, instead of turning down the bed, I drifted, like a phantom myself, to the window. I pulled the chair around, leaned my forearms on the ledge, and summoned my ghosts. I hoped they were paying attention to this story, although we all know the ending. While I pondered those years between my birth and the war, I watched pewter wavelets lap the beach until my eyelids drooped.

They aren't drooping now, and I call room service for toast and an extra-large carafe of coffee. If Rennie doesn't show today, there's still more to tell Janey. A tap at my door. Oh, boy, that was fast, but it's Janey. Mick hovers behind her smirking. He knows how much I love early starts.

"Grandad and I are going for a morning walk. Come too?"

"Morning? More like crack of dawn; it's barely light. What time did you get up?"

"I stayed at Rennie's–a few blocks away. She's got another shift." I hear the elevator open and a cart jangles toward us, pushed by a big smile, which is all I see above the carafe and silver dome.

"Come in, have some toast. Let me gulp a cup, then we'll go." Mick relieves the tiny lady of the tray, and she leaves with an even bigger smile.

We march along the bayside path. I wipe my watering eyes and blow my nose. I march to keep warm, but Janey, with the resilience of youth, faces the wind and breathes deeply. She takes our hands and laughs. She's always cheerful but now she's positively buoyant.

A food truck is parked next to a semi-glassed gazebo housing two picnic tables. Mick beelines to the truck. He joins us in our gazebo refuge with hot chocolates and steaming wraps. He and Janey look at the beach while they eat, but I swing around on my bench to look at the intersection of Denman and Davie. I used to work in an office on the third floor of a long-gone building on Davie Street. For Joe Mason. I often ate my lunch on a bench near here during mild weather, and sometimes it was a good place to come and think. Even in bad weather. Joe always knew where to find me and was always happy to hear my thoughts. Often it was useful.

I turn around to face the beach, and Janey finishes her hot chocolate.

R. Rigsby

"A teacher once told us about the 'dirty thirties,' she says. It was baking hot, and the wind never stopped. Dust in everything. Her great grandparents up and left their farm and never went back."

While I was entertaining myself with visions of good times long past, she has been mulling over the hardships of the '30s and how the struggles of those times influenced peoples' choices. This narrative has got her thinking.

"Do you remember that Granddad?"

"No, I was too young, but Henri remembered. Seed blew away before sprouting or the crop died off in the drought. Our grandfather and Dad switched to a mixed farm–ran a few head of cattle on fields they let go fallow. They were lucky. You've seen the slough–it's deep and spring-fed so lots of water for the stock and garden. God. That garden. Henri said he watered it before he was seven, and we started about the same age. Watered it every day all summer long."

Janey leans back against the wall of the gazebo, smiles at me, and waits.

It's a good thing I rehearsed the story last night. I catch them up on those parts and the rest comes easily. It's getting so I can't remember what I had for breakfast, but I remember this story as if I had written it. No, that's not true, I always remember what I had for breakfast.

Regina, July 1939: Michael, Denial

The service concluded and Michael rose with the congregation, glad to escape the stifling heat of many bodies packed in a small space. He offered his own prayer of thanks that there would be no cavalcade to the cemetery. Abe's remains had been cremated and Liz planned to inter his ashes in her mother's grave in private. Truly, ashes to ashes.

Michael watched Regan and Liz follow Reverend Cole downstairs to where a luncheon awaited in the church basement. He nodded at other mourners filing past, like the villagers of Hamelin Town enthrall to the tune of the Pied Piper. Or like starvelings on the scent of coffee and ham sandwiches. One figure split away and went out the church door rather than down the stairs.

"Lou, you go ahead." He handed Georgie to Lou. She nodded and followed her sister and brother-in-law who held Marielle. Michael followed McCandless into the wedge of shade on the porch.

"Jesus, Bertram, where have you been all week? We have to talk."

"In Winnipeg," McCandless lit a cigarette. "Two more shops will bring in Pinnace appliances."

"Come on. Primnase was supposed to dump the still, not burn the garage down and himself in it. Did you try to help him?"

"No. I left at daybreak in a cab. He might have been drunk and knocked over the lantern. Who even uses lanterns these days?"

"How do you know about a lantern? Abe knew better than to take a lantern in there. Again, were you with him?"

"Are you insane? I can't believe you're asking me this." McCandless leaned in close.

Michael stood his ground. "Abe Primnase was a good man. He made our business a lot easier when he offered to move bottles in his deliveries."

McCandless dropped his cigarette and ground it to bits. "You think I don't know that? And I am sorry he's gone. Mike, it's a shame, but you of all people know that now no secrets will slip. Forget the past. You sign that contract, and you'll have a strong investment in Pinnace, which, I tell you will boom." McCandless lit another cigarette and stepped away.

"Aren't you coming down? Give your regards to Regan?"

R. Rigsby

"No. I've been seen at Abe's funeral, that's all that's needed. The less I see of Regan, or he of me, the better. I'll come by your office in an hour or so. And I had nothing to do with this."

Regina, July 1939: Regan, All Good Men

Regan saw Mr. Kerr join the receiving line of sombre expressions. They shuffled forward to where he and Liz accepted the condolences and trite words of comfort with stoic smiles. He couldn't believe how equally trite words of thanks rolled off his tongue. Incredible how many people attended. If they only knew. Yet the image of the cruel whiskey runner who sent his father to die was out of focus with the gentle bookshop owner everybody had come to mourn.

Regan adjusted his tie. It had been Abe's, but he had never seen him wear it. Not a favourite then. Abe had taught him how to knot a tie, how to polish his shoes, and had helped him choose the suit he wore. For Toronto, not this memorial.

Mechanically he shook hands. He looked at his watch. Was Abe's death his fault? When the firemen had found the body, he hoped it was a mistake. Not Abe, a tramp. Had Abe intended to set the fire? What on earth was he doing? Yeah, stills were illegal, but that one hadn't been used in a long time. Why not load the thing, then dump it in a gully out on the prairie?

Did the still in the garage prove Primnase was Birch? Would the police have believed his accusation that Primnase was a rumrunner who killed his father? Especially in his enraged state. And with only a beat up old still as evidence. Was there yet equipment hidden in The Arms' basement? And who was the guy he saw running away from the fire?

"Regan." An older man of medium height extended his hand and with the other squeezed his shoulder. Fred Bakker, and behind him, taller, Gerard.

"Mr. Bakker, Gerard. So good of you to come all the way out here." Regan looked straight into Gerard's eyes. They were now the same height.

"I hadn't seen Abe since we left five years ago, but I should have," Fred said. "He was never the same after your dad died. I understand he had a tough time in the last year or so."

"Dad," Gerard said, and Fred looked at the line of people waiting.

Regan turned to Liz beside him. She had been listening to Mrs. Croft who had walked on but still clung to her hand, "Liz. Gerard and Mr. Bakker are here." Liz's frozen smile thawed and lit her face.

Later, with people holding sandwiches and teacups, Regan joined the Bakkers. What remained of Fred Bakker's brown hair was grey, but he stood straight and slim in a dark suit.

Gerard smiled and popped the last of a cupcake in his mouth. In the next few minutes, Regan learned that Pinnace Appliances, with the help of an investor, had acquired a small manufacturing plant in Toronto five years earlier, which they had now outgrown. They had weathered the depression and within the next two years, would lead all contenders in household conveniences. Regan thought of the washing machine Primnase had delivered when he was a kid. His mother had burned her washboard.

"Gerard," Fred leaned toward Regan, "is off to Toronto this fall to join Research and Development in our new office. Liz says you're going to university in Toronto, so Gerard can show you around. We're always looking for good men."

Regan nodded at Gerard's warm smile. He hadn't much choice in abandoning him five years ago. And neither had Ray. Or Marcella.

"Marcella? And Ray," Regan said to Gerard as Fred moved off to speak to Michael Kerr, "Liz says they're with their mother at an island resort and no boat for another week?"

"Yes, Liz keeps tabs on all of us." Gerard laughed. Then he sobered. "Sorry, and sorry about Mr. Primnase. Like a father to you. As for Ray, he's fine, Marcella too. We haven't announced it yet, but we're engaged."

Regan set down his teacup and leaned against the table behind him.

Gerard looked around the room and frowned. "Mr. McCandless isn't here."

"I'm not sure I would recognize him." Regan looked for any middle-aged male he didn't know. In fact, he couldn't remember ever seeing Ray's dad. But then the family left Regina over three years before Abe took him in. Mr. McCandless once owned The Prairie Arms. Regan shivered. So ironic that Primnase took him to live beside the one place in town that gave him the willies.

"Marcella's only seventeen," Gerard continued, "But before I leave, we will ask permission to marry next spring. Ray knows. He's all for it, but he's still spouting gloom and doom about the situation in Europe."

"Does Liz know? About the engagement, that is, not Ray's fretting over Hitler." If Liz knew, she hadn't shared it with him which made Regan wonder what else she knew. Like Gerard making the jump to Toronto.

"Oh, I'm sure," Gerard stifled another laugh, "She and Liz write each other often."

People had started leaving, saying goodbye to Regan and Liz. Regan felt some of them were on the verge of thanking them for a swell party. The room pulsed with relief and lifted spirits. For some.

R. Rigsby

Regina, July 1939: Michael, In for A Penny

Michael joined Lou who held Georgie and Marielle each by the hand. Lydia, grasping a cupcake, stood beside Georgie. Marielle was doing her best to pull away, a determined look on her red-cheeked face. Georgie's eyes shone with the verge of tears. Michael pushed thoughts of McCandless and his deal to another part of his mind and picked up Georgie who leaned into his shoulder and put a finger in her mouth. He patted her back and kissed her curly blond head.

Holding Georgie with one arm, he relieved Lou of Marielle's hand. "Ellie, where do you think you're off to? On a mission? And Lydia, by the looks of your face, you've had cake."

"A lot of cake," Lou said. She nodded to her sister coming across the room and straightened her gloves. "Michael, we're going home. Georgie and Marielle need naps. You stay and visit. Take Lydia to Jean; she's over there." Lou took Georgie out of his arms, and her sister reclaimed Ellie's hand.

Michael picked up Lydia and smiled as he watched Marielle and Georgie leave with their mothers. Jean called the little girls the three mutineers; there was no end to the mischief they concocted. Joining Jean and André, he handed the youngest mutineer to her father who tucked her into the crook of his arm. Lydia surveyed the crowd with solemn eyes.

"Where's the rest of the brood?" Michael brushed crumbs from his lapels.

"At Mother's," Jean said, "Henri and David in charge. Marguerite to watch Christine, and Jeanette to mind Mick. She," nodding at Lydia, "threw a conniption and we decided it was easier to bring her. She napped through the service. So did this one," she elbowed André who grinned and shrugged, then his black eyes lost sparkle.

"So sad, eh, Michael. I was fond of Abe. I can't see him being so careless, but then he'd been battling a few devils lately. I heard about the, er, circumstances–"

"Regan," Michael said, "Do you remember my youngest niece, Lydia Jane? A young lady who knows what she wants and how to get it."

Regan looked into the little face with its bright hazel eyes and cap of light brown hair. "Is she big for her age? I don't see many kids," he smiled.

R. Rigsby

"She's smaller at this age than any of the others." Jean said. "Takes after André's mother, who was petite."

Lydia held out her cupcake to Regan.

"Why thankyou," he laughed, and took a pretend bite. "Mmmm, delicious." He smiled at Jean and André, who then put Lydia down on her own sturdy legs. "Thankyou for coming."

Jean grasped Regan's hand with both of her own. "Regan, we hope to see you again before you leave for Toronto. Please come to dinner."

"I would like that. Ah, I see Mrs. Croft is leaving. Excuse me." Regan patted the top of Lydia's head and again smiled into the serious hazel eyes.

"That poor boy." Jean said, "Michael, he's no longer a child, but we must keep in touch with him. I couldn't spend as much time with Margaret as I would have liked." She looked at the limpet clinging to her leg.

Michael stared at his sister, wondering how a housewife, with a talent for farm management, had found time to nurse the ill. Especially as a mother of six children with one on the way. He had no idea that Jean even knew Margaret that well. What did Margaret tell her?

"Some of Margaret's ramblings made no sense toward the end, but she adored Regan. She was so grateful for all you did for them."

Michael excused himself. Across the room, Fred Bakker had caught his eye. He had spoken to Fred and exchanged the usual pleasantries, but Fred had asked for a minute when the crowd thinned. Fred got right to the point.

"Mike, you need to know the facts about Pinnace. It's a strong company, but I won't tell you everything is rosy. We may have been over-optimistic about the new plant."

Michael hoped his surprise didn't show. "It's not going under is it?"

"I'm certain not. We're coming out of this depression. Business has picked up steadily. But we may have to pull out of the plant deal. It'll cost, but we can absorb that."

"But you need a bigger plant?"

"Yes."

Liz Primnase tapped his arm. "Mr. Kerr. If you have time, I would like to hear Dad's will."

"Of course, Liz. I'll go to my office now. Come when you're ready. If you're up for it."

"No point in waiting. It won't get better."

An hour later, Michael wrote his signature on the bottom of a creamy page. McCandless placed it in his briefcase.

"You won't regret this, Mike. Pinnace will manufacture the best home appliances in the country before the end of year." He stood up and brushed invisible lint from his pants. He looked at Michael, but the door opened, and Liz Primnase stalked in.

Michael half rose from his chair. God, she was so like Abe.

"Oh, I'm sorry," she said, "I didn't realize . . ."

"Not to worry, my dear, I'm leaving," McCandless's chortle sounded almost genuine. McCandless, with a flourish, offered Liz the better visitor chair and picked up his briefcase.

"I'll have the rest of the documents sent through as soon possible, Mike. Are you sure you won't reconsider the other part of the deal?"

Michael, at the door, offered his hand.

"No, Birch, I'm not going anywhere."

R. Rigsby

Regina, July 1939: Regan, Birch Exposed

At Regan's tap, Liz opened her bedroom door. She wore a frock, one could only call it a frock, which must have been her mother's. A mother gone sixteen years. Mothball scented, it was dark blue with a dropped waist and a pleated skirt. A square collar outlined in white piping drooped over her shoulders.

"Don't look like that," she smiled, one of the few times in weeks. "It was in Dad's bureau."

"Oh. No, I mean yes, the dress is old, I guess, but it's a nice colour on you. What bureau?"

"This one." It had been in Regan's bedroom before Abe moved downstairs. The top drawers stood open and piles of clothing, family photos, and books besieged the ransacked dresser.

"Oh, you've started sorting your dad's things." A cardboard box of papers and the battered footlocker from beside Abe's cot waited on the floor. "You shouldn't have carried that up yourself!"

"It's not heavy. It's Dad's day-to-day clothes and that wooden chest. This," she pointed at the box, "is full of papers from his desk. And there's still more in the bureau."

"I'll get tea and toast."

Later, Regan sat cross-legged on the floor with the wooden chest in his lap amid piles for keeping, donation, or burning. Liz sat with her long legs tucked underneath her dress and sipped her tea. Regan gazed at the debris of a life not necessarily well-lived. But Abe had given him a home, was good to his mother, and maybe was a better friend to his father than he knew. They could have argued, but his dad decided to do the run. He thought of Phintel and the bill at Rudd's.

"What are you thinking? You're okay, aren't you?"

"Sure. wondering what to do with all of this. Should set a match to it." Regan looked at the heaps, then at Liz's face, "Oh, God, Liz, I'm sorry, I didn't mean that. Here." He slid the box aside and handed his handkerchief to Liz whose face had blotched before the first tear flooded her already red rimmed eyes. "Let's finish later."

"No." Liz blew her nose. She handed him a folder from the box of papers and took one herself. They riffled through pages and folios, finding ancient receipts, bills stamped paid, orders for printing pamphlets, invitations, and lost dog notices.

Regan opened another folder expecting to add it to the mountain destined for the incinerator, but a name caught his eye: Frederick Birchmann Bakker.

"Liz. Look. Here. Birchmann. Fred Bakker's middle name."

Liz riffled the other pages in the folder. "Yes, lease agreements. What of it?"

"He's Birch! The man who killed my father."

"Regan! Stop talking, don't think."

"I thought your Dad was once called Birch, I thought he killed my father, but I, I, didn't let him explain–"

"*My* father! Never mind that for now. Put your head down. Relax, big breaths, there now, that's better." She stroked the back of his neck.

Liz parked Regan at the kitchen table while she scrambled eggs. She placed the toaster in front of him and Regan focussed on it, opening the doors to flip the bread. Just look at the toast, Regan. Just look at the toast.

"Better?" she asked after they ate, to which Regan nodded, grateful he hadn't lost the entire day asleep. "Tell me why you think somebody called Birch killed your dad. And why you think he was my father." Her mouth set in a hard line and her pale eyes frosted over. "Dad hated setting traps for the mice and threw spiders out the door. He would never have harmed your father."

Regan breathed in slowly, and told Liz what his mother had said, and what he remembered. "When I found the still, I knew I had found Birch. I shouted at your dad. Then I blacked out."

"So that's what happened. When I came home, he was upset, but I thought it was because he was worried about you." Liz paused and studied the pattern on the teapot. "That old still wasn't his. I found it when I was ten. Dad was storing it for somebody and kept forgetting to get rid of it. He said. I know he wasn't Birch." Her eyes glittered.

Regan crossed his arms and dropped his head. "He must have been trying to move it. Why didn't he wait and explain to me in the morning? When I wasn't so full of rage. I'm always better after a 'rest' as my mother said. I'm, I'm sorry. You must hate me. Abe wouldn't have tried to move the still if I hadn't gone crazy."

Liz's long fingers pleated an already pleated fold in her dress. "Regan. You know how he's been. Not always thinking straight." She took Regan's hand. "And I could never hate you. What else do you remember."

He told her about waiting with Phintel. He was cold. He went into the passage. The dark stairs, his dad's voice, and a giant yelling. And waking up in his bed. And months later, how Abe had told him his dad was dead.

"Did he mention Birch?"

"No, and I'd forgotten it. I didn't remember again until my mother said the name. I asked Abe once if he knew Birch, but he didn't."

"But Regan, the American police killed your father, not Birch."

"But Birch made him go." Regan looked at the crumbs on his plate and instead saw Fred Bakker in the store. Fred Bakker always asked about his mother. Had he worried about the gun?

Liz rubbed a sparse eyebrow. "Regan, I don't think Mr. Bakker is that Birch."

"Who else then? With a name like that?"

Liz looked over her shoulder at the half-opened window and shimmering heat rising from the rooftops across the street. She looked at Regan and pursed her lips. "Birch is an unusual nickname, but you shouldn't assume it's Mr. Bakker."

"Why else would your dad have the still? Fred made him store it."

"But you were in The Arms basement."

"Yes, but he might have forced Marcella's dad, Mr. McCandless to cooperate too." Liz nodded but plucked at a loose thread. "Fred left and put his whiskey money into his father-in-law's business. And Gerard, too, he, he," Regan's voice caught.

"Regan, who took you home that night?"

"I don't know. I never thought of it." He closed his eyes. "Probably Birch. Fred Bakker."

"So, you remember an argument, and then you woke up in your bed?"

Regan sighed. He was just a little kid. "Maybe your dad took me home."

Liz shook her head. "I was sick all that night and Dad stayed with me. The next day Dad wrapped me in a quilt and brought me downstairs to his chair in back. A man came in. He said your father was dead. Dad went to pieces right there in the shop."

"Probably Fred Bakker. He's Birch. It's his fault."

Liz's mouth retained its stubborn line, "Why couldn't your dad have taken you home before he left? And although you remember loud voices, two men talking below an echoey stairwell might sound like an argument to a child, don't you think?"

"We should finish." Regan placed his plate and cup in the sink. Liz tapped her fingers on the edge of the table, then got up.

An hour later, they had sorted the last of the papers.

"What's in that?" Liz said. Regan pulled the wooden chest onto his lap. He released the catch, and the lid sprang open from the pressure of a fat envelope inside. Liz picked it up.

"Look, Regan." She showed the bills inside. "This wasn't in Dad's will. It must be yours."

"No. Abe opened a bank account for me this spring. Michael Kerr has my trust, but they decided I should look after my own allowance. That's yours, wherever it came from." Regan thought of the blackened remains of the still. And the other blackened remains. "Fred Bakker paid your dad for his silence and used his pamphlet deliveries for cover. His death was Fred's fault too."

Liz fingered the cash. "Regan, there's something you should know."

But Regan had stood and placed the box on the dresser. "You can sell this dump and move."

Liz saw a folded piece of paper in the pack of cash, but looked at Regan, eyes wide. "You mean move with you? To Toronto?"

Regan jerked as if poked with sharp stick, "Well, no, no, I didn't mean that."

Liz's hand froze.

"What is it I should know?" Regan said.

"Nothing. Nothing important."

Regina, Aug 1939: Regan, The Cellar

Regan closed the larger of the two suitcases on his bed. Tomorrow, the train to Toronto. After his degree, a decent job and financial independence. He'd asked Mr. Kerr about selling the farm, but he advised him to keep it. Good land close to town would increase in value, and for now, his trust would pay his tuition and a modest monthly allowance.

What would have happened to him and his mother without Mr. Kerr? Phintel didn't really blink, did he? With his one good eye? Regan laughed at Phintel who sat in the smaller case beside a photograph. It was the only picture Regan had of his parents and him. He was about four, and they had just moved to the house in town. Big smiles. His Dad had a job that didn't hurt his leg, his mother was strong and well, and he was a happy little kid with two parents.

"Phin, old buddy, the happy times there died with Dad." And the happiness here died with Abe. Fred's fault. But if Abe hadn't died, he wouldn't have found Birch. He would destroy Birch–he'd promised his mother. He closed his eyes and saw Fred and Gerard at Abe's funeral. Both smiling at him, both sorry for him. Or had Fred smiled about something else? Did Gerard know about his father's former career? What would Marcella think of the Bakkers when she found out?

Regan lifted Phintel who rested on the item swathed in his mother's pink gingham apron. Regan unwrapped the revolver and spun the barrel. Always clean and oiled. Ironic that his father's death would be avenged with a gun Fred Bakker had given him. He sighed and replaced Phintel on his steely bed.

He wanted to go to Vancouver and deal with Fred Bakker right away, but then what? He wasn't a fool. It wouldn't take much to work out that he wasn't in Toronto, and Liz knew about Birch. Birch would have to wait for the right plan. He had time for that.

And time now. No Liz for another hour. Not that he expected conversation. She was never a chatterbox, but she had been positively mute for weeks, and each evening after supper, had gone to her room. She was still angry with him about Abe, but tonight they would talk.

Yanking his shirt out of his pants, he shook the tails. "Bloody hot day, right Phintel?" He then turned, went through the kitchen, picked up a flashlight from a drawer, and keys from the hook downstairs. He passed the burnt-out garage and unlocked the back door to the Bakker's old shop. Its basement had a low ceiling over bare dirt and homed a few empty wooden boxes. If there had been a distillery here, nothing remained of its production. Regan sighed and climbed the stairs, relocking the door. The bookshop basement contained the boiler for the whole building, and he had been down there many times to shovel coal and stoke the furnace. That left one alternative.

The Arms' side door was propped open to let in air. Regan crossed in a few quick steps. As he remembered: stairs. A short flight up and a longer flight down. Murmurs of conversation and a fug of beery tobacco smoke hung in the stairwell. Below, black quiet. He switched on the flashlight.

The stairs creaked with each step to the door below. He turned the knob and pulled. Locked? Then remembering, pushed, and stepped into the cool of an enormous cavern. He expected a stink of mildew, or soured whiskey mash, or dead mice, but instead scents of wood polish and soap, and a whiff of beer. The flashlight beamed around what wasn't a cavern at all, but a largish room with shaded windows above a radiator. Plank floorboards underfoot. Something drifted across his face. He swatted at it imagining bats or giant spiders, but it was a string. He pulled, and a single bulb lit the dusky room.

Against one wall a few tables, and chairs in cantilevered stacks. Castoffs from previous décor choices or extras. A deep shelving unit on the wall by the door held crates of crockery, glasses, and utensils. All gleaming. Bars of soap tumbled in a box and a basket of fresh linens waited distribution to the rooms upstairs. A broom and dustpan hung from hooks. Jon Sorensen and his obsessive tidiness. At the funeral, he had told Regan he hoped to buy the hotel one day. Regan sniffed and located a broken beer keg on the far side of the shelves. Probably awaiting its return to the brewery.

"If a still was ever in here, it's long gone now." He hadn't spoken loudly, but the room's acoustics bounced the sound around his ears. "Whoa, that does echo." He stepped to the far side of the room, lifted one of the blinds and saw feet walking by. His memory clicked: from his father's car, he saw these windows with their sills level with the sidewalk. He whirled holding the flashlight like a weapon, his heartrate surging. But the room was just one of homely purpose and innocent of ill deeds.

Boots clomped up the front stairs. He twitched. A few patrons arriving for after-work refreshment. Chairs scudded across the floor overhead and voices bellowed for service. It would be awkward explaining to Jon, if he came down for more glasses, why he was there. Regan pulled the cord and quietly shut the door. He leaned against it and closed his eyes. His pulse beat in his neck. What else happened that evening?

An argument. His father's laughter? Smells? Nothing. There was nothing in this storeroom either. No equipment, not even bottles or corks, and no ghosts.

"Damn." That was a waste of time.

Regan pushed away from the door shaking his head. Fred Birchmann Bakker had done it. And the man had the nerve to shake his hand and all but embrace him at the funeral. Gerard too. Gerard had to know. He and his dad were close. The Gerard who had let him sit in the hardware store, who smiled over cake at the funeral, was a fraud.

Outside, the sun on his shoulders eased his outer chill. Nothing could ease his internal gloom. The storeroom, cool in summer, would be frigid in October, but he hadn't felt cold that evening. He remembered a breath of warmth on his face. The radiator under the windows.

Regan walked to the back of the building and lifted the coal-chute hatch. He shone his flashlight into the depths. On a dirt floor deeper than the level of the storeroom, the chute ended in a wooden bin half full of coal. He bent over the hatch and saw a brick floor on the back half of the dim grotto where the boiler and its sprawl of pipes sat like a fat octopus. Beyond it a flight of stairs, likely to the kitchen.

"And so what, Regan?" It wouldn't make sense to have a still in the boiler room. Not safe, and anybody might come down to stoke the furnace or get a bucket of coal for the stoves. "Nothing concerning my dad down there." He let the hatch thump shut.

R. Rigsby

Regina, Aug 1939: Michael, The Letter

Michael locked his office and pocketed the key. Time for lunch. Or at least dessert. Despite the lack of anniversaries or birthdays in this last week of August, he felt like celebrating.

Yesterday, he had seen Regan off on the train. He hoped the elation that lightened his step wasn't relief. Of course not, he was happy for Regan–a young man embarking on a new life beginning with an education in a fine university. He might even become interested in law.

Michael had arrived at the station before Regan and, hands in pockets, strode up and down, ignoring the sun baking the platform planks. He hadn't seen Regan since Abe's funeral, but then there was no need. Regan handled his own banking and allowance with gratifying responsibility. Michael hoped that indicated a growing maturity and focus on the present and future, rather than the past. It had been over two years since Regan had asked about Birch.

Regan's step on the platform and the whistle of the eastbound train brought Michael's perambulations to the present. He was surprised that Liz hadn't accompanied Regan to say goodbye, but her absence made it less awkward to hand Regan the envelope of cash. Regan asked if it was from of his father's share of the Prairie Arms investments. He had said yes, the investments had been carefully managed.

Michael told Regan he would do splendidly in the coming years and shook his hand. The conductor called for final boarding. Regan had looked at Michael and at the train, the engine steaming, passengers chattering as they climbed the cars' short stairs.

Michael remembered the catch in Regan's throat when he thanked him. He angled across the street to The Arms. Liz was washing the bookshop windows. Good girl. They hadn't talked since reading Abe's will in which everything went to Liz. She had said she might go to Toronto. She and Regan could become engaged. They were young, certainly, but he couldn't imagine either of them with anybody else. He altered course.

"Liz, that looks good. Are you doing okay?"

R. Rigsby

Liz stepped down from a box, dropped her sponge in a bucket, and wiped her hands on her apron. She smiled, but it had a new twist he hadn't seen before.

"Yes, Mr. Kerr, thankyou."

"Getting this place cleaned up to let out? Or sell? Or are you reopening the shop?"

Liz shook her head "It was never closed. Dad just didn't bother most days."

"It's been a hard year. You did your best, and I can't imagine what it was like. Good for you for taking that secretarial course. Liz, if you need a hand, or if the shop has debts, let me help."

"Thankyou, but there's no debt. Dad paid everything right up to the last tax notice." Michael almost stepped back, cursing himself for being an idiot.

"Yes, Abe was careful that way. And he had loyal customers even through these bad years. You'll do fine, you're a smart girl."

Liz's mouth quirked. "I was planning to see you, and if you're not on your way to a meeting," she inclined her head toward The Arms' front stairs, "could you step inside?"

Without waiting for an answer, she opened the door. Michael hesitated, and a tingle of trepidation crawled along his backbone. He followed Liz into the shop.

"I have something for you. I'll be right back."

Michael placed both hands on the counter as if to push it across the floor. This had better not be what he thought it was. *Oh, Abe.*

Liz returned, eyes like winter ponds, and handed him a sheet of paper. Michael stared at the creased page with Abe's unmistakable perfect script.

"Dad left this in an envelope of cash. A lot of cash. I'll keep that, but the letter is for you. I read it."

Dear Michael,

Thank you for helping me write my will, although you laughed and said it unlikely to be read in your office. You said that by then you too, if still among the quick, would be waiting for God and praying for a place in that meagre slice of heaven reserved for lawyers. I don't think there's much chance of heaven for either of us, but in any case, I'll stand before the Great Judge before you. I'll put in a word on your behalf.

I'm not well. I wish I could help it, but when the shadows reach out, I push them back the only way I can. I see Paddy Fitzroy in those shadows. I blame McCandless, because I know I did not hear the truth on why Paddy drove that last run when he told me he was finished. Paddy needed the money as much as any of us, but he had promised Margaret. I wish I knew why Paddy went, but Lizzie was sick that night and I never got to ask him.

Before Margaret died, I was at her place chopping wood. She brought out cider, and we talked about Paddy and the good days before the war. Then she said she still didn't understand why Paddy drove that night, because she was sick, and the Crofts had gone to Estevan. There was nobody to mind Regan. Then Margaret said that you had brought Regan home. It was the first I'd heard that Regan had been with Paddy. That surprised me as much as learning you were there. You didn't go anywhere near The Arms after hours. You only kept track of the money. McCandless and I distilled and bottled. Paddy, or sometimes Kesey, drove.

I think of Kesey too. He'd told me he was going to Vancouver, so I was surprised he went to Toronto. I said so to McCandless. I expected him to blow up and call me a fool as he often did, but instead he said Kesey changed his mind. Fred asked me about Kesey after he disappeared because Kesey used to do small work for him–like picking up shipments at the station. Fred said that on that night, he had come down the alley intending to catch up on bookkeeping in his shop. He saw Paddy's car leave the garage, and he swore Kesey drove it. But I think Fred was mistaken because Kesey and Paddy looked alike.

And that's all I thought until the other day I was in the alley at the incinerator. Jon Sorensen came out with rubbish to throw in. Jon's not good with small talk. Before I could mention the weather, he asked me what I knew about Jig Kesey and why he left town. I inquired why he asked after twelve years, and he said that old Charles Perrault had been in The Arms with André. Jon said Charles' clutch is slipping, but he said that if Kesey went to Toronto, why would he leave his rucksack and a train ticket to Vancouver in his bunk on the farm? He might have gone on, but André said they had to go.

So lately I've been thinking that Paddy didn't do the run and it was Kesey, like Fred saw, but then where did Paddy go? He wouldn't abandon his family. It's on my mind a lot. I told Regan when he was a little chap that his dad did the best he could for his family, and that is true whatever happened.

When we cleared out the equipment, I was afraid. The books and printing had barely kept food on my table before I joined the business. Lizzie's Mam had one good dress to her name when she passed, and I couldn't bear to part with it. She was buried in her second best–a constant reminder that I don't want Lizzie to settle for second best. Those envelopes from McCandless always arrived when Lizzie had grown another six inches. But I managed to save something from each one for her. For her future. I know I can rely on you to look out for my girl like you have for Paddy's lad. Like you do for everybody. No wonder you haven't moved to a fancy office worthy of your talents and

The letter ended there. Michael looked at Liz, sure that she too pictured Abe in his chair, his legs crossed, writing this last missive.

Michael rubbed his brow. "Liz, that money is your father's share of the invested profits and compensation for the risk. I'm sure Mr. McCandless will keep it up–"

"I've already written to him. I told him I don't want anything to ruin Dad's good name and I don't want any more money. Instead, I've asked him for shares in Pinnace. I'm sure he'll agree, don't you think?"

Regina, Aug 1939: Michael, Reprieve

Liz went back to her window washing. Michael folded the letter and breathed out slowly. All it said was that a man had driven to the border, and another had left town. Liz now knew they had all run booze out of The Arms, and that McCandless paid Abe. He'd told Birch from the beginning that Abe knew nothing of Paddy's death to betray, and he would never reveal what he knew about the business. But Birch was Birch.

He placed the letter in his inner pocket. Abe didn't finish and explain why he wrote it. Had he seen his own doom in those shadows? Through the window, Michael saw Liz pick up the sponge. She wrung it out, squeezing, squeezing.

"What are your plans for the shop?" Michael joined her outside and thought a return to the original conversation was in order. As if the intervening ten minutes hadn't happened.

"I'll keep the shop open for a while, but I want to turn this place into my own secretarial school. That cash and the insurance money for the garage will help."

"What happened to going to Toronto? I assumed you and…since Regan's left, I thought you would too?"

"No. And Regan won't come back."

"Liz. I'm sorry. I shouldn't make assumptions. But you and Regan have been close since you were children."

"Yes, well, not as close as I thought. Maybe his condition affects his thinking. On the day we cleaned up Dad's things, we found the leases for Bakker's store. Regan almost blacked out. I was baffled but made him eat and rest. Then it all came out. Regan's mother told him his father had been killed by a rumrunner called Birch. Because of the still, he was convinced my father was Birch. He fought with Dad. I told him that believing my dad, of all people, was Birch was ridiculous. Then we found the leases and now he thinks Mr. Bakker is Birch."

"Fred!" What? Why?"

"Because Mr. Bakker's middle name is Birchmann. When Regan went on about his mother saying Birch killed his father, I tried to reason with him. The US police killed him, not Birch. How did he get that name?"

"Oh. Look, Liz, it was a long time ago, in the war. A silly thing about trees, but the Birch name stuck. At least with Paddy and me."

"Then I read this letter. You, McCandless, Paddy, Kesey, and my dad were in it together and responsible for Mr. Fitzroy's death. When I came home from class the afternoon before Dad died, he was upset but wouldn't tell me anything else. After the, the, fire, I wondered what possessed him to try and move the still that night, alone."

Another shiver went up Michael's spine and he looked at Liz standing there, so alone and vulnerable, but at the same time not. She had always been a self-sufficient girl.

Liz's mouth had resumed its new twist, a bitterness which Michael thought would be permanent. Betrayed by her father, and now by Regan. And by him. He should have told Abe to wait on moving the still and he should have helped. McCandless too. Or he was helping, until the lantern tipped.

"Mr. Bakker wasn't part of it," Liz went on, "yet he's the man Regan blames. He doesn't even know about you."

Michael sucked air. "The times, Lizzie, the times. I hated it, but after the war we didn't come back to the rewards we were promised. Your dad never went to war, because of that old accident, but he suffered too. And when your mother got sick, he was desperate. We all were. There were few jobs, little business, and poor crops." When Bir, Mr. McCandless inherited the hotel, and his father's sideline, it kept us alive."

"Regan saw the money. He thinks Fred Bakker paid Dad to keep quiet. I never showed him the letter, and I won't tell him that Mr. McCandless is Birch. I heard you call him that on the day I went to hear Dad's will."

Michael put his hand out as if to pat her arm, but Liz stepped back.

"We argued again the night before he left," she said. "He doesn't want us to be together. I told him to forget about Birch, to let it go. I told him to go to Toronto and make himself a life. Nothing will bring back his father."

"Do you think he will? Let it go?"

Liz shrugged and suddenly looked like the parentless girl she was.

"Knowing Regan, I doubt it."

Instead of going to The Arms, Michael returned to his office. He uncapped his fountain pen and opened his appointment book. Liz had her life in order, no need to worry over her. And Regan? In Toronto, a change of scene, a course of studies, and a new life to help him find perspective. Regan would realize that nothing could be gained by confronting Fred. Michael placed his finger on his next appointment and smiled as a whirring of gears heralded his clock's imminent chime. Regan just needed more time. He would be fine.

Vancouver, Oct 12 2019: Lydia, Déjà vu

I shift my behind on the bench. Mick is probably stiff too. He helped with the litany of miscommunication and misunderstanding; he had heard about me throwing a fit when Mother and Dad wanted to go to a funeral. Christine probably pinched me. I have a hazy recollection of a man eating my hand.

Janey sits with her back to the wall and her legs stretched out. She looks as comfortable as if sunning on the beach in July. It's most definitely not July. "Did anybody have any idea that a war would start?"

Mick fields this one. "Dad said he worried all summer. He read every paper and listened to the radio at Granny Kerr's. Sometimes Mother and Dad left us with her and went to the movie house which played newsreels. Henri was only eleven in 1939, but even so, they worried about conscription if the war lasted a long time. Everybody worries for their sons, and now daughters, when there are wars."

Janey nods. "Rennie's cousin went to Afghanistan." Her phone buzzes.

"I'll go back to Rennie's and bring her to you after lunch. If you're okay with that?"

"Nothing that a bowl of soup won't fix," I say.

"Dad says he's taking you out?" Janey looks at her grandfather.

"Correct. You run along and we'll go back to the hotel. If this old bird can walk that far." He's extricating himself from the bench and holding out a hand to me. I get to my feet without tipping over.

"I'll race you. Old bird my foot."

From my favourite table, I watch Mick waiting on the sidewalk. I had a bowl of delicious vegetable beef soup and a croissant. Being a tad early for something alcoholic, I ordered a pot of tea and a slice of cake. Chocolate Ganache Torte according to the menu, but when I think of cake, I see a large wedge of my mother's eight-inch chiffon with another inch of butter cream icing. This tiny piece would suit a dolly at a child's tea party. But it's good, and I can order another. I have the means.

When Gordon comes, depositing girls and scooping Mick, they are going off to have a father/son lunch and a stroll. Mick hasn't yet seen fit to liberate the bee in his bonnet. He may let it buzz when Gordon takes us, including Rennie, home for dinner tomorrow.

Gordon drives up and Mick opens Janey's door. She has her hair wound up in a knot on top of her head, but I prefer it flowing loose. Rennie gets out of the back seat. I inhale crumbs. Lachlan. Strawberry blond hair cut boyishly short, but so becoming; it shows off her cheekbones and full mouth. There's nothing boyish about her figure, although she is petite and slight. She wears glasses. I have time to quell the unsettling illusion before the girls appear in front of me.

"Rennie, so good to meet you at last."

"Miss Perrault, I'm sorry I kept you waiting all day yesterday." She clutches her backpack to her chest as if it contains a lost masterpiece.

"Quite alright, my dear. Janey and I had more time to catch up." Except we haven't. I need to ask about her studies.

"Auntie," says Janey, smiling. She caught me wool-gathering. "Could you tell Rennie why you were here when you met Rennie's grandfather?"

Rennie nods. "Please. I've shut off my phone and I'm all yours." She opens her mouth but closes it without saying anything.

"Well then, why don't you both order something and we'll start."

"It's a ghost story, isn't it," says Rennie, "With secrets! I'm dying to hear it."

I laugh. After all, I have more tea and another slice of cake on the way. Then I look at her. What does she know about ghosts in The Sylvia?

"Hmm, when I first saw this place, I didn't know about ghosts, but I was sure it had secrets."

From where I sit, I can see the vines and tendrils reaching to mask the windows. Most leaves are autumn pink, but some have already shifted to red like a warning that the year is coming to an end. It occurs to me that by October 14, 1959, many things had come to an end, but nine days before, I only thought of beginnings, especially my first real job–a secretary for Mr. Gerard Bakker.

Regina, Mon Oct 5 1959: Lydia, Life Begins

My life began on the day I stared into a cold cup of coffee at The Cecil Café in Regina. Where I no longer waitressed. I gave up that career when I enrolled in the secretarial school upstairs. Mother and Dad had said that I could take the training, and get a job, but I couldn't use the money they had set aside for my wedding. They didn't say what would happen if I didn't snag a husband in the next few years, but sometimes I know when to keep my mouth shut.

I loved the course. I took shorthand faster than, Miss Primnase at least, could talk, typed fifty words per minute, and knew how to find out almost anything about anything.

Miss Primnase more than once said, "You girls must find whatever information your employer requires and quickly. You must know how to use newspapers, directories, and encyclopaedias, and which material to request at a library."

This wasn't news to me, because libraries were places where I spent a lot of time for free, and I had used Henderson's Directory to find businesses in town that likely employed secretaries. Or even filing clerks.

I touched the engraved certificate propped against the saltshaker: my fine new diploma from Miss Primnase's Secretarial School. I had a secretarial diploma, but so far, no secretarial job. After a morning of tramping about downtown applying for work, I was relieved to sit and check the want ads yet again. It was October, with my twenty-second birthday a little over a week away. My stomach growled. I didn't have enough change for soup and wasn't about to break my last ten-dollar bill. It would slide through my fingers like a broken egg. If Mr. Ho weren't out buying vegetables, he would dish out some soup for free. Wait for Mr. Ho? Or go home to Uncle Michael's where I could make a sandwich?

"Oh, good show you *are* here!" Miss Primnase banged open the door.

Well, where else would I be when not thirty minutes before I had borrowed her Leader-Post and pointed down here? She had been talking to a man, so I suppose she could be excused for not understanding my newspaper semaphore.

"I have a job for you, Lydia."

A job? My fixation on food vanished.

R. Rigsby

"You must leave immediately," she added.

"I can leave right now." I gathered my purse and coat and handed Miss Primnase her newspaper.

"No, no, you will get on the evening train with a client, who is travelling to Vancouver."

Vancouver? I had never been west of Saskatchewan. Nor east. Vancouver was a real city. Regina called itself a city, and as a kid I thought it was huge. Then when I moved in with my Aunt Lou and Uncle Michael, my impression of huge lasted three days.

I gulped out, "Sure, of course," and hoped that the flutter in my stomach was anticipation and not terror. I followed her out the door, thinking hard. She hadn't specified in which capacity I would be employed, but after this morning's disappointing hunt, and not one ad circled in the paper, I wasn't about to ask who, what, or even how much. I had a job and, better yet, I was leaving town on a train. If the job meant washing my boss's socks, I didn't care. But I thought I should demonstrate some degree of curiosity.

"This client of yours requires a secretary?"

"Mr. Gerard Bakker, an old friend as well as a client, needs a stenographer typist."

I thought, Bakker, Bakker, I know that name from somewhere. From filing for Uncle Michael? But Miss P went on.

"His secretary, er, missed the train. He wired me from Sudbury late on Friday night. He has interrupted his trip from Toronto but must continue to Vancouver this evening."

In Miss P's car I caught a glimpse of the station. My prospective new boss got on a train in Toronto, but his secretary didn't, and he needed a replacement. I was sure Miss Primnase had other girls on her list, but none who could leave Regina with two seconds' notice. She knew I needed a job.

She drove me home to pack, only telling me that Mr. Bakker was on his way to a convention where he was to give an important speech. Auntie Lou was out, thankfully. It didn't take me long to stuff the few shoes and clothes I owned into my mother's old carpet bag and fill my brown canvas holdall. I grabbed Georgie's umbrella. She was at work, so I guess I stole the umbrella. On the way out, I saw a letter for me on the hall table. I stuffed it in my purse.

Regina, Mon Oct 5 1959: Michael, Premonition

Michael switched off the hotplate, lifted the percolator and watched coffee stream into his mug. Thick black coffee in a thick white mug. His favourite. A few chips, but a survivor of his busy office for over thirty-two years. Like him. The first twelve years were rough, but his practice had had smooth sailing in the last two decades, and in a few years, he would plot a course toward retirement. But not yet. It had been a busy morning; he had earned a beer as a reward.

He looked at the unfiled stack of paper on top of the cabinet. Georgie hated filing and loved her job at the bank. Liz helped before the school took all her time. Now she placed students with him for practical experience. With any number of fingers and eyes in his files, he had removed a few sensitive documents. Except he had forgotten about that letter.

It had slipped out in the spring but was now deep in a locked desk drawer. He'd thought about burning it, but on rereading, reconsidered. In the meantime, the stack grew. He could ask Lydia again.

Lydia. So bright, so bursting with passion to see the world, to do anything but marry a farmer. That would be death to her. André and Jean didn't understand. Henri and the other girls were dependable and dutiful. But having lost David forever, and because Mick, after that last blow-up with André, wouldn't return for a good long time, if ever, they dreaded Lydia's independent streak. He sympathized with Jean's fear of losing another child to a world beyond that which she and André knew best. But that's what young people did these days.

Marielle had gone to Toronto at the first opportunity. And Lydia would jump at any opportunity. The three mutineers. Or two mutineers. One had been remediated. Georgie would likely stay in Regina. She had a young admirer.

Sipping his coffee, Michael wandered over to the window as he often did, but The Prairie Arms waited, as squat and ugly as ever. Its basement windows still eyed pedestrians at street level as if the hotel had been punched into the ground by the weight of time and history. And as ever, he couldn't not go there. Should he have left when McCandless offered? Would the ghosts who rose in his mind every time he looked across the street have stayed behind?

He saw Liz go into the Cecil, her coat flying out behind her, then he leaned against the doorjamb and looked around his office. Not much had changed since he opened in that spring of 1927. Apart from fresh paint. Usually green. Still a one-man show with one desk, one good swivel chair, and a few chairs for clients. He'd swapped out the original desk and chair but kept the coat tree. He liked that coat tree. And the clock. He swallowed the last of his coffee and almost reconsidered the beer when his telephone rang.

"Michael Kerr speaking."

"Michael? Yes, sorry, I didn't expect you to answer your own phone. It's Gerard Bakker."

"Well, this is a surprise, Gerard. How are things in Toronto?"

"Ah, good, but I'm here in Regina. On my way to Vancouver, annual conference, you know. And I have a problem, somewhat embarrassing. Would you have a copy of the latest confidential report from Research & Development?"

Michael sat down. He'd had shares in Pinnace for over twenty years; was on the board for Pete's sake; but rarely attended meetings. He signed proxies to the chairman confidant that he had a firm hand on the tiller, so to speak, proved by the increasing number of zeros on the dividend cheques. Years ago, he'd told the board that he only cared to see year-end financials.

"I'm sorry, I haven't received R&D reports for years."

Gerard sighed. "I had hoped that this time because it's a major release…but never mind. I'll get a copy. But I have another question for you. Or two questions. They're personal. Do you have a few minutes?"

"Well as it happens, I'm finished my early appointments. How far away are you?"

"At Liz's school. I'm going to The Cecil. Can I buy you lunch?"

"Sure thing. Fifteen minutes." Michael sat on the edge of his desk. After the Bakker family moved away in, what, April '34, he and Fred had kept in touch. When the war started, Fred wrote of his anxiety for Gerard when he and Raymond left early in 1940.

Ray didn't come back, but Gerard did, in time to say goodbye to Fred before he died. Michael had gone to Vancouver for the funeral. He'd seen Birch. Bertram. He was the only one left who knew him as 'Birch.' Stood beside him at Fred's graveside that November, while an icy reminder of another grave, another November, blew down the neck of his coat.

He stood up and again looked across the street at The Arms and its neighbour building. They appeared as they always did, but deep in his guts, he knew something had changed. Or had been set in motion.

Regina, Mon Oct 5 1959: Lydia, Between the Lines

On the way back to the school, Miss Primnase handed me a set of hieroglyphics on a scrap of paper.

"Mr. Bakker came to my office this morning." She glanced at me and of course, caught that look on my face. "He has business here today, so left this with me. You must make some calls before we meet him. You may use my office while I teach my three o'clock class."

I looked at the note, turning it over in case I had it the wrong way around. No prizes for penmanship. At the top I made out that I should call Sylvia Hodel. No number, but below it I saw the words 'book a dll roon.' *Aha. I must book a double room at The Sylvia Hotel.* I made out the next scrawl, barely, but the one on the bottom looked like a doodle and was partially scratched through.

"What happened to Mr. Bakker's secretary?"

Miss P grimaced. I didn't think it a strange question. "Nothing you need to worry about, Lydia. Let's just say I had to find him another girl. I don't know why…" She bit her lip.

Why that edge in Miss Primnase's voice? There was more to this than a secretary missing a train. Another girl? Obviously from her school. A year or two ahead of me? We might have met when I worked at the café and before I scraped together the money for my tuition. I liked to think of it as 'scraped together,' but I squirmed thinking how I obtained the rest of the money.

"Oh, is she from here? Would I know her?"

"Yes." Miss P's shoulders dropped. "You may as well know. Marielle Tremblay. But until I understand what has happened, keep it to yourself. I don't want to alarm her parents. Her father was transferred to Halifax. Have you heard from her?"

"No, but…," I bit my tongue. Ellie missing a train? If she was in trouble, she would call me. She always said I was the best at coming up with good explanations for our bad decisions. When we were seventeen, Georgie smuggled a beer into the Broadway to share with Ellie and me. "I'm sure she's fine," I said. Although I couldn't think of a single good reason for her being so irresponsible. She had worked in Toronto for about a year, for a company called Pennant, no, not that. She got the job because her new boss's secretary left to get married. Her new boss. Mr. Bakker. No wonder the name sounded familiar.

She wrote that he was kind, but I wanted to read about the fabulous restaurants and shopping, the museums, and the beauty of the lake. When I was young, I used to sit on the edge of our slough and squint my eyes until the water looked like the ocean. Or at least I imagined it that way. It's a big slough though.

Miss Primase had parked behind the school. She glanced at my squinty eyes, then narrowed her own. "Now don't worry about any of that. Trot yourself up to my office and work on that list. You have an hour before we leave." She got out and left me to catch up.

I shut the car door and looked up at the weathered brick. The Prairie Arms next door might one day qualify for heritage status, but there was little to admire in the square building that had been in the Primnase family for years, according to Uncle Michael. When Miss P started her school, she converted part of the bottom floor to live in and ran the school above. Her business grew and she took over the other half of the upper story so that now, in addition to her own office, the school consisted of a meeting cum lunchroom cum library, a lavatory and cloakroom, and three classrooms, in which Miss P employed two other instructors.

Where Miss P now parked her car, a garage had once stood. Uncle Michael had told me about the sad death of Miss Primnase's father after I found the letter.

In the spring, I had rounded out Miss P's program with practical experience in Uncle Michael's office. He had asked me to file several weeks worth of folders and papers. He'd never had a secretary, but Georgie and Ellie too, like other students, had each had a practicum. He had made no allowances because he was our uncle or father. Georgie still helped sometimes, but now she had a job at the bank, and Miss P had sent Ellie to Toronto.

Uncle Michael had set up a folding table and a guest chair for me. While I worked, he sat at his desk, sipped from his mug, and made notes with his favourite fountain pen. He had turned sixty-five in April, but, like my mother, he looked young for his age. Mostly silver in his dark hair, but he still had hair.

I hummed to myself as I ordered folders and sorted papers. Uncle Michael periodically went to the kitchen for coffee, or to the file cabinet where he riffled through drawers. He then opened the bottom drawer, took out a bottle and sloshed some in his mug.

"Here's a name I haven't come across before." I was really talking to myself, as I smoothed the creased letter which had slipped out of a folder.

Uncle Michael came over. I looked up to catch a fleeting expression of grief, quickly masked by his usual good-natured calm.

"Oh, that. Way before your time Lydia."

I didn't say that most of what I filed was way before my time.

"Good old Primnase. I still miss that man." He plucked the letter out of my hand. "I'll hang onto this." He tossed it onto his desk.

Another Primnase family couldn't live in this town, but I wasn't curious until I had caught that look on his face. "Oh, what happened to him?" Uncle Michael then told me about the burning garage and the death of Mr. Primnase. So sad, but it had happened so long ago. But why that look on my uncle's face?

Most of Uncle Michael's stories, which he shared with a reminder that I had his confidence, were ancient history. However, listening to him talk, which seemed to happen best after he'd opened the bottom drawer, helped to while away the time during the dullest of jobs. I heard about old friends, old events, funny war stories–the first war that is, he was too old for the second– schoolyard bullies, funerals, and weddings. Mostly I nodded my head but sometimes my ears perked up. I liked to hear about when my parents met although the big foofaraw over the difference in their religions seemed silly.

"Abe. Primnase. He wash a good guy." I might have missed some sloshings into the mug. "And Abe, he didn't deserve that. He would never tell what Fred told him about Keshy." An hour or so later, Uncle Michael clacked a key onto my desk and said he was going to The Arms. "You can lock up when you're done, Lydia, and push the key through the mail shlot. I have another."

I worked for a while longer but kept looking at his desk. When I unslung my purse from the coat tree, an invisible hand pushed me over there, and I read the letter.

R. Rigsby

Regina, Mon Oct 5 1959: Michael, Questions

Michael faced Gerard over a table in The Cecil's quietest booth. Gerard looked up at the ceiling, then at the red papered walls and gold fringed drapes.

"Sure changed from when Dad's shop was here. Except for the ceiling. They just painted over the pipes."

"How is it you don't have your reports? Aren't they extra-confidential?" Michael said. They had already covered the small-talk over bowls of won-ton, and he had work waiting in his office.

"Oh, because," Gerard raised both hands, "Marielle lost her mind."

"Marielle? Ellie? The calmest, most composed, and one of the ablest young women I know?"

"I don't understand it either. Something has bothered her lately, but she did her usual excellent job. I trusted her to tell me in her own time if anything was wrong. Last Friday morning, we reviewed the speech. Then while I went to a meeting, she was to finish typing it and put it, and the reports, in my briefcase. After the meeting I found a note telling me that she had received an urgent call–her mother ill and she was off to Halifax. I had to go too–the train, you know?"

"Still not keen on air travel?"

"Lord no. Maybe I jumped out of one too many planes over France. Or because one of those jumps was the last time I saw Ray." Gerard looked over his shoulder as if his old friend might walk in the door. Michael gave him a minute. "McCandless took it hard, but he was the proudest father of the bride when Marcella and I married."

"Twelve years now, isn't it?" But no kids. He and Lou waited ten years for Georgie, but time was running out for Gerard and Marcella. "About Ellie and the report? Does that explain why you're here? In Regina?"

"Yes. I was on the train when I discovered I had the brochures and other folders in my briefcase, but no speech and no report. She must have been really rattled. I could scribble up a speech on table napkins, but I wired Liz from Sudbury and asked if she could find me a steno. At least temporarily. Does Mrs. Kerr know about this?"

Michael shook his head. Lou hadn't said anything about her sister feeling poorly. "Perhaps its not as dire as Ellie understood?"

R. Rigsby

"I spoke to Liz this morning. She may or may not know what's going on, but she said she would let me know if she finds out. More like she'll let me know if she thinks I need to know."

Michael nodded. "That's our Liz."

"I'll find out eventually, but I wanted to review the report on the train, and now I must rewrite the speech. I hope Liz has a girl who can take dictation and type. This speech is important. It's the first time the conference directors have asked a Pinnace executive to speak. I don't want to read from table napkins." He grinned.

Michael raised his coffee to him. Nothing much phased Gerard. Lydia or Georgie might know about Ellie. He would ask them tonight at supper. He waited. Gerard had two questions.

Gerard cleared his throat. "Before Dad died, we talked about when we lived here in that house on Reynolds. He said those years when I was a kid and he and Mum were full of vim, he called it, were the best of his life. She was the prettiest teacher in Horner, and he hadn't given up until she married him.

I said I loved helping them in the shop and those were my best days. He became quiet and said it was hard to give it up, but he had principles, by God. If the wars had taught him anything, he knew violence, breaking promises, and ignoring laws only produced more violence, lies, and murder."

Michael stared into his coffee and concentrated on disciplining his face.

"He had a coughing fit then, and more pain, so I gave him his pills. I held him up so he could swallow, and he rested against my shoulder. 'It was Birch that caused it,' he said, 'nobody told me so, but I knew. His rotten temper. Paddy saved my life when he hauled my sorry ass back to the trench.' I put it down to the ramblings of a man drugged and in pain. God, I hope I don't get cancer."

Michael's throat tightened, but he disguised his croak behind a cough, and clanked his cup into the saucer. "Sounds like an old war story to me. Lots of guys called Patrick or Paddy. Lots of things happened which we would rather forget. Your dad was one of the good guys. Best to remember him that way."

"Oh, I do. Always will. I didn't think of it again until Regan talked to me last week. Do you hear from him?"

"We've written each other, but it's been a while since I've had a letter. I haven't seen Regan since he left in 1939."

Regan too, within days of the declaration of war, had signed up. Michael had thought the recruiters would discover his condition. He could finish his degree and come back and sort things out with Liz. Marry her. The spirits of both Abe and Paddy would have been pleased. But no, Regan went to war and somehow his disorder escaped notice. He was wounded and spent over a year convalescing in England. When he was released, he returned to Toronto and found Gerard, who immediately gave him a job. He never came back to Regina.

Gerard poked at a coffee stain on the tablecloth. "The other day, Regan asked if I remembered his father's death. I said yes, barely, because I was only eight." Gerard nodded at the waitress who appeared with the coffee pot. He stared into his brimming cup as if a memory lurked in its depths. "I was in the stockroom with a comic book. The door opened, and a man talked to dad, then left. Mum was painting the front counter, but she came down the aisle to where Dad had opened a cask of nails. I went to the door. Dad bashed the keg on its edge and dumped the nails in the bin. 'Bloody evil business,' he said, 'and I know Birch pushed him to do it.' That's when my mother spotted me and gave him one of those looks. Anyway, Regan asked me again if I knew of a man called Birch."

"Again?"

"Yes. He wrote me after his mother died and wanted me to ask Dad. Dad said he knew nobody who went by that name. Regan never mentioned it again until the other day. I said I didn't know anybody called that, which is true. I wondered if you might know this Birch and why Regan is asking? He was intense about it."

Michael too, looked toward the door, but nobody hailed him from the doorway. Unless it was Fred's ghost begging him to look out for Gerard. Michael rubbed his forehead. Regan. It had been over twenty years since he had misconstrued that Fred Bakker was Birch. Fred died. But Regan's obsession hadn't.

"You know about Regan's condition? Or the condition he used to have?"

"Still has. He takes medication, but once he keeled over in my office. He had expected a promotion, but I said he wasn't ready. Slept on my couch for the rest of the night and woke up with no idea what had happened. Liz warned me years ago. We were good friends before my folks moved to Vancouver, and I was delighted when he returned from England. He was devastated that my dad had died. I was touched at his concern. He worked at Pinnace while he got his business degree, then came on full time."

"Ten years now? From shipping to a production manager."

"My right-hand man, and well-liked by everybody. But he's never been the same with me as when we were kids. Yet, none of us are the same after the war. The bullet in the head didn't help." Gerard sat back and waited.

"Ah, Regan." He needed to call him. If he was planning a reprisal against Gerard as a stand-in for Fred, he needed straightening out. And it was certainly time. How much longer could he go on burying the lie? Why couldn't Regan just let it go? Liz hadn't thought he would, and she was right.

Even so, he had worked over ten years for Gerard. Had he waited for the right time? Could he do something to the business? Sabotage machinery? Not likely. This was personal. What harm could he do to Gerard, who didn't deserve whatever grief Regan schemed?

He and McCandless had to tell Regan about his father's accident, and what lead to it. To give him perspective on the times. Would Regan, once he knew the truth, be content with that? No. Regan would want to properly bury his father's body. Would a half-lie do? Just tell Regan that McCandless was Birch, but his father had made his own decision to run the border? He would call Regan and set up a time to talk to McCandless.

"What about 'Birch'?" Gerard prompted. "I asked Liz, but she said if I needed a typist, she didn't have time to discuss Regan's delusions."

Michael looked Gerard in the eye. "I know who Birch is, but I can't tell you the whole story yet. Let's just say that Regan deserves an explanation first. But your father is blameless."

"Then I'll leave it to you. I like Regan and I hate seeing him disturbed. I trust you to make this work out."

Toronto, Mon Oct 5: Regan, A Blueprint for Vengeance

Regan strode the production line of cooktops. They were the sunshine yellow that buyers loved as much as the aqua. He returned the smiles and nods from his crew on the floor. All good guys, some of whom had worked with him, and for him, for years. The serene smile on his face gave no hint of the vortex in his mind. Where was Ellie? Enroute to Halifax? Or on the train with Gerard? With the confidential report? Secrets he needed to make the plan work.

On Friday, he'd waited for her, and the secret report, in the York's lobby for as long as he could, with Wilf hiding behind his newspaper. Then believing she hadn't got away as planned, he returned to the office. But she wasn't there. One of the girls in the steno pool said she had left before lunch. Gerard was gone too, his office locked.

Gerard. The liar. Like his father, Birch. Gerard knew perfectly well his father was Birch. Yet again he had lied. He should have acknowledged that his father was Birch, and said he was sorry for whatever had happened. But no, he pretended he didn't know. Gerard had missed his last chance. Regan had turned away before fury warped his smile. The rage that had risen in his mind almost overwhelmed his self-control. The new prescription *was* better.

He had thought his years of planning had come together. The timing was right and the conference a perfect place to achieve justice for his father–Gerard, instead of Fred Bakker, would be disgraced and humiliated; he would lose his position with Pinnace, and maybe even more. But then a glitch with Ellie. He needed that report.

He had gone home and spent an anxious weekend. He packed on Sunday and took a long look at the object in his bottom drawer. If the original plan was a washout, there was one thing he could do. He picked up the object and stroked its smooth metal barrel. Could he do it? If he had to? He had once thought so. Thought it would be easy. That was before the war. He closed his suitcase.

He had come in to work as usual that Monday morning, but still no call from Ellie. She had to be on the train. He continued walking, nodding to the men working the line. None of them had any idea what he was thinking. A skill perfected while working for Gerard. And seeing Marcella.

Before leaving to catch his flight to Vancouver, he met his floor supervisor and reviewed the instructions for the week's production. He returned to his office and hung his shop coat.

Regina, Mon Oct 5 1959: Michael, A Stranger Calls

Outside the Cecil, Michael buttoned his coat and watched Gerard continue up the sidewalk weaving among other pedestrians. Off to stroll about his old neighbourhood and look at his old home. He walked just like Fred, that straight back and sure step, touching his hat as he stepped aside for two ladies. Every bit a gentleman. Like Fred. Birchmann Bakker. Who, like Paddy, was dead. People still remembered Fred and Paddy, but at least Kesey was long forgotten. Michael looked at his dragging feet, but instead of crossing the street to his office, he veered left up the stairs to The Arms.

"Quiet afternoon, eh, Jon?" He stared at his reflection in the bar's polished surface and gripped the foam-topped glass Sorensen placed before him.

Jon wiped drips of beer and shrugged. Jon never quite got that, as proprietor, it was prudent to maintain a respectful distance from guests, but as bartender, he should encourage friendly rapport. The more his customers enjoyed the bonhomie, the more they drank. The Arms had its regulars, none of which were in place, but as the only watering hole for many blocks, it should have more loyal patronage. Or the lack was the decades long curse on The Prairie Arms.

"How long you had this place now, Jon?"

"Close on ten years. Sold the farm when Dad died."

Michael thought of saying something about his advice, dear God, that was thirty-two years ago. He rarely thought about Kesey. And Paddy. Until this morning. And now Fred looked at him from the foam on his beer. Worried about Gerard. If he looked in the mirror, would he see Abe's long face appear over his shoulder? And David too? May as well summon them all.

Jon continued. "Couldn't get off the farm fast enough. I should have stayed away after the war, but my mother begged me to come back. Another five years of eating dirt. Course, I had to sell the farm to buy this place. Got a good deal. Old owners fed up with it."

"Right. We did the contract. Doesn't seem that long ago. You planned some changes."

R. Rigsby

"Yeah, when I worked here before the war, I dreamed about it. Wrote notes and sketched floorplans. That dream kept me going while chasing back and forth across France."

Michael nodded and sipped, amazed at Jon's loquaciousness. And he wasn't done.

"I've spruced up some of the rooms–the better ones facing the street. But every time I have money to improve the service or look of the place, somet'ing comes up." Michael smiled. Jon's accent still there after all these years, especially when he was worked up. "Last year it was the roof. This year it's that boiler downstairs." Jon flipped a towel over his shoulder and set clean glasses on the shelf. "I'll get a new oil furnace put in, but first I want to level the floor and pour cement. That dingy hole has always bothered me. Might have to dig down a bit. I've got a couple of guys coming in on Wednesday."

The pitter patter of icy feet ran up and down Michael's neck. Paddy's face and blank eyes formed in his own reflection. He had seen a lot of those eyes during the war, but none haunted him like Paddy's.

"Your niece, Lydia, talked to some of my guests at Ho's. They said the rooms were nice, but too cold. Smart girl, your niece."

Michael drained his glass and slid it forward. Lydia. Who would have thought such a twig of a lass could lever momentum on a boulder the size of The Arms?

"There was a guy in here looking for you earlier. I sent him to your office."

"Missed him. Who was he?"

"Dunno, but here he is now." Jon lifted his chin toward the door where a tall man wearing a hat blocked the lobby light. He was in silhouette so Michael couldn't make out his features. Yet, his innards tightened. The man walked forward and held out his hand.

"Michael Kerr? I'm Joe Mason. I'm looking for one Calvin Kesey."

Jon placed a polished glass on the shelf and looked at Michael's face in the mirror.

"Now there's a name I haven't heard in a long while." Michael put down his glass and swiveled to look at the stranger. "Should I know you, Joe?"

"No. I'm from Vancouver. I've been engaged by Robert Kesey to find out what became of his brother whose last known whereabouts were here in Regina. In this hotel."

Michael concentrated on showing polite interest and thought of a thirty-two-year-old conversation. "I've always understood that Mr. Kesey went to Toronto."

"Yes. That's what the police were told when my client first lodged a missing person report, in, let's see," Mason pulled a small notepad from his pocket and flipped pages, "January of 1928. Seems that Mr. Kesey, Calvin, no matter where he was, and it's true he moved around a lot, always called his mother at Christmas. That Christmas, no call."

Michael saw Jon staring at him and picked up his beer. He raised an eyebrow at Joe and glanced at his watch.

"I'm a lawyer, Mr. Mason, but Mr. Kesey wasn't one of my clients."

"Let me explain. The 1928 investigation petered out. The man on the case was told Calvin went to Toronto. Nothing turned up there. Dead end. Then, earlier this year, Mrs. Kesey died, and while going through her effects, Robert found a letter that Calvin had sent early in October of 1927. He thinks the housekeeper might have placed the letter on a book Mrs. Kesey was reading, but the book was closed and replaced on the shelf. The letter was never opened."

"Why that's a shame." Michael slid off his stool and downed the last of his beer. Kesey was literate? Joe reached out and gently for such a big man, grasped his forearm.

"The real shame is that he wrote his mother she would see him in a week. He would take the job with his brother and bring a friend." Jon Sorensen's head jerked, but Joe continued. "He said The Prairie Arms job hadn't worked out like he hoped."

"Mr. Mason, Joe." Michael sighed. "From what I recall about Calvin Kesey, he was a good man, but one that had his demons."

"And I have heard that too, even from his own brother. But my question for you, is, what kind of job did Calvin do for The Prairie Arms? I know you were one of the owners back then."

Michael didn't hesitate. "I was, but as a silent partner. The majority owner, as you must know, was Bertram McCandless."

"I do know. Courtesy of the city property archives, which is where I found your name. He was interviewed in 1928, but the investigator failed to interview you."

"He probably knew I had no say in the day-to-day business. That only lasted until 1934. Fourteen years of bad luck. Two lots of seven years; enough for anybody. McCandless sold the place." Then because it might send Mason on a wild goose chase, he said, "But I guess hotels are in his blood. I believe McCandless has an interest in a place called The Sylvia. In Vancouver." Joe blinked.

"I know The Sylvia. It's near my office. I also found out that a Paddy Fitzroy was listed as an owner of the Prairie Arms in 1927, but the investigator simply made a note that he was deceased at the time of his inquiry."

R. Rigsby

Michael stared into the mirror amazed that the torment in his heart didn't show on his face. "Paddy too had little to do with the daily operations. He was a good friend of mine."

"Did you know Calvin Kesey?"

"I knew *of* Mr. Kesey. Most people in this neighbourhood did. Now, I must go."

"Are you still in touch with Bertram McCandless?"

"Of course. He's the Chairman of the Board of a company called Pinnace. I'm on the board too." Michael almost smiled at the looks on their faces. Neither was expecting that information. Well good luck making something of it. "Now, I must go."

Michael straightened his coat and saw Mason and Jon exchange glances. Jon thought he could add to the story, but whatever he thought he knew, he also knew he should have shared it long ago.

Regina, Mon Oct 5 1959: Lydia, Street View

With seconds to spare for her three-p.m. class, Miss P clattered up the outside stairs and disappeared through the door, leaving me to my contemplation of her father. He sounded like a caring dad, and a trusted friend. Uncle Michael thought so.

I shouldered my purse and holdall and gripped the handrail. One could use the inside stairs, but students usually climbed the outer staircase which, never painted in its life, looked as though it was attached with thumb tacks.

I passed classrooms in which throbbed typewriters, dictating voices, and a discussion on telephone manners. In Miss P's office, I pulled pencils and my unused secretarial pad out of my holdall, and just because I liked how it looked on the desk, my new notebook. Dark red Moroccan leather embossed with my initials: LJP: a graduation gift from Uncle Michael. Ellie and Georgie had each received patent leather handbags when they graduated from Miss Primnase's school, but I had sighed in relief when I unwrapped my notebook.

It had an open slot inside the front cover, but I discovered a hidden pocket disguised by the inner fold and the loop for a pen. Inside: a five-dollar bill. My uncle had not only supported me for most of two years, but he had also given me a lovely gift, one that put a dent in my aunt's grocery budget and added one more item to my guilt list. When Aunt Lou hinted that I hadn't paid board for weeks, he had said, "It's alright, Lou. Our Georgie spent a lot of time with my sister when you were sick; it's the least we can do."

I opened my notebook and fingered the empty pen holder. One day I would treat myself to a fine fountain pen like Uncle Michael's. My notebook was much too fine to use for work, not that I'd yet had the opportunity to make the distinction.

I finished the list within forty-five minutes which gave me fifteen minutes to consider my new job. I should tell Mother and Dad I was going to Vancouver. I could phone, but I didn't want to answer questions. I should have asked more questions myself. I pulled a piece of note paper from a pad on Miss P's desk. Instead of the school's logo on top of each page, there was a queer little emblem: a family herald of the Primnase family? I wrote a few sentences, then put the note in my purse. Miss P could give it to Uncle Michael this evening. Aunt Lou would be miffed having cooked for four instead of three, but I didn't want to telephone her either. There was one call I had to make.

"Miss Kerr speaking."

"Georgie, it's Lydia–"

"Are you nuts? Why are you calling me at work?"

"Sorry, I told your supervisor it's urgent. And it is. First, have you heard from Ellie? She missed getting on the train with her boss."

"A letter two weeks ago. She has a charge account at Eaton's–can you believe it? She probably just caught a later train. What else. Make it quick. I'm being watched."

"And you'll never guess, Miss Primnase got me a job. I'm going to Vancouver. A secretary for Mr. Bakker. Ellie's boss; probably temporary."

Georgie squealed but immediately cut it off with a throat clearing, "Ah, yes, thankyou so much for letting me know. We'll be in touch soon." Her lurking supervisor must have moved away because she then whispered, "Way to go, Lydia, I'm sure Ellie's fine," followed by, "goodbye."

I had no idea what explanation she would give her supervisor, but surely the granddaughter of a former bank manager wouldn't need to be too creative.

I sat at Miss Primnase's desk enjoying its massive expanse and her leather chair. My feet didn't reach the floor, but if I lowered the chair, I wasn't sure I could raise it to where Miss P had it set to accommodate her long bony legs. I leaned back with my arms behind my head. This could be me in a few years. Miss P's office had a good view of the street and late afternoon shoppers. I leaned my arms on the window ledge and looked toward Uncle Michael's office. *Was he there?* It was too far to see the sign, not that it meant anything.

He was known to walk out and lock up without changing the sign or turn it to 'Closed' and keep working because, "People just dropped in to pass the time of day, including that André guy, who never seems to have anything else to do."

He had laughed, and so did I. My father was the last person in Saskatchewan who would run out of things to do. The farm usually kept him home, but when he went to town, he had a list in mind. As methodically as ploughing summer fallow, he followed his list, except for having a coffee or lunch with his friend and brother-in-law. Usually they went to The Cecil, but my father wasn't above a beer at The Prairie Arms.

Mother often accompanied Dad, but she would have a list of her own like buying yard goods at Spencer's or picking up a parcel at Eaton's. On no condition whatever would she cross the threshold of The Arms and wasn't sure The Cecil met her respectability requirements.

She wasn't happy when I took the job there, but Uncle Michael said Mr. Ho ran a clean and proper establishment. However, mother wasn't a prude. After kissing my father and wishing him a nice talk with her brother, she would join my Aunt Lou for a ladies' lunch at the Royal.

I doubted I would see Mother or Dad, but my heart skipped a beat when I saw a lady with red curls go into the pharmacy across the street. She was much too 'broad in the beam' as Dad would say. How a prairie farmer who never set eyes on an ocean learned nautical terms I blamed on the books he read about sailing ships and naval battles.

Then Uncle Michael came out of The Prairie Arms. He jaywalked diagonally across the street toward his office. Another man followed him and jaywalked on the other diagonal. I looked down at the man. Apart from the hat, which not so many men wore, he had a 'hitch in his get-along,' an expression that was pure Uncle Michael. Not a limp, but not a smooth stride. I didn't know the man, but *heavens, Lydia Jane, you don't know everybody, no matter what your mother says*.

But Uncle Michael knew him. Just before the man reached the curb, he touched his hat to my uncle who nodded back from his office door. Well Uncle M has lunch, or beer, with a lot of people. *Good grief, I could run over and tell him I have a job and give him the note*.

I drummed my fingers on the windowsill still wondering if I had time to dash across the street. Or just phone. The little clock on Miss P's desk dinged four. No time. I saw the man with the limp reappear in front of the pharmacy, and after a glance up the street, he jaywalked again right into The Prairie Arms. Must have forgotten something. I picked up the list, then gathered my pencils and stuffed everything in my holdall.

Regina, Mon Oct 5 1959: Lydia, Platform Pas de Deux

Outside Miss P's shorthand class, I leaned against the wall, one leg bent with my foot braced on the wainscotting. I'd seen this pose in a show at the Broadway. A cigarette holder would complete the look. Except I didn't smoke. *Congratulations, Lydia, you finally applied your skills in telephone research and etiquette.*

I had booked the hotel and had left a message for 'Davis' whose number I deciphered from the list. Davis didn't answer the telephone himself; it was a man though, with a deep voice, who said that Davis was out, and could he take a message? He was probably an underling of some sort. I advised him of the Vancouver arrival of Mr. Bakker's train and impressed upon him that it was *very important*. Mr. Bakker would be much inconvenienced if Davis were not informed. I thought the man chuckled, but he coughed. He excused himself and assured me he would inform Mr. Davis directly he returned home.

It was a good thing I knew the conference was in Vancouver or I would have had a much harder time finding the number for The Sylvia Hotel. I had placed my first long distance phone calls and dealt with fussy operators, an obtuse desk clerk, and a diffident aide. Pleased with my competence, I fizzed at the prospect of taking a train ride west to a city that really was a city and having a job that would require more than having ten fingers and knowing my ABCs.

I had thought of going to Calgary in search of work, and, if I admitted it, as an evasive maneuver, but with my luck I wouldn't have made it to Moose Jaw. But now I was going to Vancouver, and I had a real job. The dozen or so girls in Miss Primnase's class filed out. Did I once look that young and inexperienced?

I followed Miss Primnase to her car. She didn't ask me about the list and whether I'd had any trouble completing it. Or she had something else on her mind. She chewed her lip and kept both hands on the wheel.

I added a few lines to my note to Uncle Michael. I asked him to please let Mother and Dad know that I would write soon, with more details. *What details, Lydia?* I had no idea how long this job would last. I was as good a stenographer as Ellie. We wrote each other in shorthand. But if my new employer wasn't thrilled, I might find myself on the return train without setting foot in Vancouver.

"Miss Primnase, would you please leave this note for my parents with my uncle? If convenient?" She looked at me sharply.

"Yes, Lydia. If you hadn't written it, I would have advised you to do so. I'll drop it off after I lock up tonight."

That sounded like perfect timing. That train would be well down the track. We found Mr. Bakker pacing the platform and looking at his watch.

"This is Lydia Perrault," Miss Primnase said. He shook my hand, shot me a quick smile, but then turned to Miss Primnase.

"A word, please Liz, before you rush off. But here, ah, Miss...," he handed me my ticket, "Please, go find our seats. I'll join you in a minute."

Seats in first-class. I'd taken a train with my parents but that was to Moosomin to see my sister Jeanette's new baby. I was fourteen so had no appreciation for how one should conduct oneself on a train, and our seats hadn't been first-class. I wished I had worn my pumps, although the loafers were best for walking. And I'd done a lot of that.

From the aisle, I saw Mr. Bakker and Miss Primnase. Miss Primnase stepped sideways and shook her head, while Mr. Bakker stepped after her and flung a hand around. She was almost as tall as him and he leaned forward with his face close to hers. She didn't back away, just stuck out her chin like the bulldog I had seen in a travel advertisement.

Regina, Mon Oct 5 1959: Michael, The Whirlwind

Michael called Regan's boarding house, but the landlady said he had moved when the former owner retired. An operator said there were over twenty R Fitzroy's listed; could he tell her the name of the street? He had no idea where Regan lived. They had lost touch more than he thought, poor lad. It was hard to think of him as a man, when he was hardly more than a boy that morning at the station in 1939. Paddy, not he, should have been there to see Regan off on a new chapter in his life.

He remembered his aching throat as he said goodbye. And the conversation with Liz the next day when he learned that Regan had a rage on about Fred Bakker. He remembered his deflation on realizing that Regan hadn't forgotten about finding Birch. He had thought about calling Fred, but the relief, yes, he had to admit it was relief that Regan was leaving Regina, probably for good, if Liz was correct, soothed his fretting conscience better than the best rye.

Then distance and more distance yet when war broke out, and the temporal distance of twenty years had made it easy to believe that Regan now lived in the present. Which was apparently wishful thinking. Birch had said years ago that once an idea got into Regan's head, it had no way to get out, and maybe he was right.

He placed a call to Pinnace, praying that a ringing phone would be heard above the racket of machinery stamping out oven doors. A harried supervisor answered. Mr. Fitzroy had left to catch a plane. He was not expected back until next Monday. After the conference. Gerard hadn't said Regan would attend, but of course it made sense. Gerard was safe enough on the train until Wednesday. He had time to think this through.

He saw two possible scenarios. They tell Regan about his father's role in the rumrunning, and that McCandless was Birch, and that his father chose to run the border. If Paddy remained buried in The Arms basement, it might be enough. In the other scenario, Paddy's body would be discovered, and everything would come undone. His career and reputation would be ruined, and he would lose the respect of his family, his friends, and Regan, who would suffer the ultimate betrayal.

Well first things first. He would call McCandless and tell him about Jon's project in The Arms cellar. Then McCandless could meet Regan, and he could join in on the phone. They would tell Regan that Fred Bakker wasn't Birch, and Gerard didn't deserve whatever mischief he had cooked up.

Tomorrow. But tonight, he would go home and have supper with his family. Lou or the girls might know about Ellie, his other worry. He opened the bottom drawer.

Insistent rapping accompanied, "Mr. Kerr, Michael, I know you're in there!"

Michael lifted his feet off his desk and swallowed the dregs in his mug. Liz. No doubt who belonged to that voice. He unlocked the door, letting in a blast of cold air, a flurry of snow, and the wild woman of the west. Liz rotated into the room and whirled to face him; at thirty-eight she put the spin in spinster. Her frizzy hair, never tamed by the most stringent permanent and her flapping couture gave one the impression that she was in perpetual motion. Liz had no idea that her one good feature, a sunshine smile, redeemed her sharp features.

"Liz, what a nice surprise." He sat on the edge of his desk and glanced at his empty mug. "What brings you to see me?"

"A man accosted me. I was locking up before going to The Cecil for my dinner."

"Good heavens, isn't this a job for the constable?" Liz stared at him. "I'm sorry, Liz, you are flustered. Please. Sit down. Tell me why this man caused you to rattle my locks after six in the evening." Liz flapped into the chair. Her hands clasped her purse in her lap, and her skirt draped over sharp knees. Michael's mind flashed a vision of Abe. He shook off the whiskey haze and sat in his own chair.

"He asked me what I knew about Calvin Kesey's disappearance and Paddy Fitzroy's death. He thinks they're related.

"Joe Mason. Thanks to Jon, right?"

"Yes. He said he talked to you, but I don't think he liked your answers. I said I was a child when Mr. Fitzroy died and that my father died over twenty years ago."

"Good answer. Now about Ellie. What do you know about her missing the train? And her mother's illness? Or Gerard's missing report, for that matter?"

Liz looked at her purse, and again Michael saw a spectre from the past.

"Only what Gerard told me. I haven't heard from Marielle."

Michael bit back further words on the subject. As for the report, it was probably in Gerard's safe. He would mention it to McCandless when he called him. He leaned back in his chair.

"And Mason asked about Lydia," Liz said.

Michael sat forward, his chair squealing at the sudden movement. "Lydia? Why?"

"Jon told him she was my student and to ask for her at the school. Mr. Kerr. Michael. Sometimes Jig Kesey stayed with me when Dad delivered those temperance pamphlets he used to print. I was only six when he disappeared."

Michael nodded as if this wasn't news to him. Kesey the neighbourhood drunk nobody would miss was also a beloved babysitter. How ironic that a man with a drinking problem babysat so teetotalers could read temperance pamphlets.

"I didn't tell that to Joe Mason."

"I have always valued your discretion, Liz."

"And I didn't tell him where to find Lydia."

R. Rigsby

Regina, Mon Oct 5 1959: Regan, Turbulence

Regan looked out of the window of the thrumming aircraft. He fancied he saw the line of a railroad far below, and a moving train swallowing the glint of moonlight on the tracks. He thought they were past Regina, a place he hadn't seen in over twenty years. When this was over, he should visit. He hadn't seen Mr. Kerr since he left, and when he thought about it, he realized he hadn't sent a letter in a long time either. He still owed much to Mr. Kerr, and to Mr. McCandless. He now understood the nature of partnerships and how, unless otherwise stated in the partnership agreement, only living partners received the proceeds of the partners' business. But his father's partners had ensured that he and his mother had all they needed. He wouldn't be where he was now if it weren't for their generosity. He massaged his temples.

He had taken his prescription when the headache came back and had dozed for a few hours. The headaches had been getting worse lately, and he supposed he should see a doctor again. But he hadn't had a blackout for a long time. That medication was doing its job, but it had taken a long time before his condition had been discovered.

He never got around to seeing a doctor when he first went to Toronto for university. He'd been too busy settling into his boarding house and getting familiar with the campus. He had met up with Gerard, only because it was a good way to keep tabs on Fred. He had learned to wear the mask of friendship and to restrain the urge to scream at Gerard that his father was a murderer.

He hadn't paid much attention to world events, but when Canada declared war in September '39, he presented himself at the nearest recruitment office. Gerard had been unhappy that he wouldn't go to Vancouver with him so they could join Ray, and all sign up together.

The war had been more of a nightmare than he expected. And longer too. Near the end, he was wounded and was eventually transported to a hospital outside of London. The abdominal surgeries, a series of infections, and the operations on his skull kept him bedridden for more than a year. He'd spent what felt like eons swathed in bandages, half blinded by those wrapped around his head. On one occasion, he awoke knowing he had had an episode, which brought on more doctors. When they discharged him, he was advised to see a doctor as soon as he resettled in Canada: to follow up and monitor his condition, and to check the bullet in his head. As time went on, that doctor had said, medical improvements might make it less dangerous to remove.

He had intended to see a doctor, but was so glad to be back in Canada, he wanted to forget the years of convalescence. In Toronto, he recovered his possessions from his former landlady who had stored them in her basement. She gave him back his old room and was with him the day he tipped over and spent the night on her living room floor. The next day, she drove him to her doctor, and he had since diligently followed all medical advice.

He had boarded in that good woman's house for years but moved to an apartment when she retired and sold. He had never lived alone in his life. Was that why Gerard kept inviting him for dinner? The plane bucked and dipped in bumpy air over the mountains.

He leaned his head back and closed his eyes. Soon he would be in Vancouver. Ellie, and the secrets, had to be on that train with Gerard.

Regina, Mon Oct 5 1959: Michael, The Medium

Michael lifted his brows at Liz. Lydia should be at home helping her aunt and cousin make dinner, like mashing the potatoes or stirring the gravy. Or more likely setting the table. Lou said Lydia shouldn't be allowed in a kitchen. Michael leaned across his desk.

"So just where is my niece, Liz?"

"On this evening's train to Vancouver. With her employer, Gerard Bakker."

Michael whistled as he sat back. Jean was going to kill him. She and André granted that Lydia should take the secretarial course, find a job, and see a little of the world prior to a sensible marriage. Their proviso was that she had to do it on her own, since they hadn't been able to do it for her sisters. Sisters who had all dutifully married. Henri had stayed on the farm, as was expected, and Mick, being a young version of himself, just left and went east. But he was a boy. Man. Lydia was, was…a definition eluded him.

He, as their doting uncle with only one child, was expressly forbidden to assist Lydia or Mick either. He pushed that boundary by letting Lydia 'board' with him and Lou. Lydia, the spunkiest Perrault niece–that filled out part of the definition–now had a job that would take her miles from Saskatchewan if it lasted after Ellie returned. He would have to tell André and Jean their little brown bird wasn't typing memos for a kindly boss in Regina. At the library, preferably. Not that Gerard wasn't kindly. And he wasn't a stranger. But Vancouver? Toronto?

He emerged from his contemplation. "Why Lydia? You must have other girls?"

Liz too seemed lost in thoughts of her own. She looked up with that set to her chin that told him she wasn't likely to tell him. "Because she needs a job. And she's very good."

"I know that. But she's also young and inexperienced. Never mind. The train won't back up. I talked to Gerard this afternoon."

"I know."

"Of course you do."

"This Joe Mason wouldn't harm Lydia?" Liz, apparently on an entirely different thought track, gripped her bag. "I saw Dad's letter in the files ages

R. Rigsby

ago. I was surprised you kept it. I think she read it. And if she did, she might put it together with, um, other things she has heard."

"You mean like when I drink too much?"

"I didn't say that. But she asked about a Kesey family. If Mason presses her, she might reveal more than she intends. Or realizes. Michael, you know more about what happened to Paddy and Jig than you have ever told me, and you have your reasons. I don't want anything to ruin the good memory of my father."

Michael sat back and looked at his ceiling. He recalled taking the letter from Lydia, but he hadn't put it away. Sloppy. Or fate had decided.

"Lydia wasn't even born when Kesey left town. If Mason questions her, and if she has read the letter, she's smart enough to keep mum." But he didn't want Mason finding Lydia before he could talk to her. He had wondered for a while how much Lydia had learned of past sorry events. She was always eager for stories, and he wasn't certain how much he had revealed during his afternoon intermissions. He would tell Lydia everything. In Vancouver. Now he would have to go there. She should find out the whole story from him, not from consequences, if there were to be consequences, of his conversation with Regan, or from what lay buried in The Arms.

Strange, he always knew that one day the ghosts would rise, but he never thought Lydia would be the medium. Who was now on her way to a conference where…

"Have you talked to Regan?" Michael said, "He still believes Fred killed his father. And what if Lydia is with Gerard if Regan does something? Regan isn't capable of violence, is he?"

Liz's already firm features cemented over. "I haven't spoken to or seen Regan in over twenty years. I don't write him, and he has never written me. I told Gerard that. But Marcella and I write each other. She thinks Regan should be more grateful to Gerard for giving him a job and…"

"What?"

"Nothing."

"Tell me."

Liz sighed. "Regan always mooned over Marcella, but he has always given her the creeps. She's never been one for tact. She said Regan used to stare at her, but when he came for dinner, he stared at Gerard as if he'd sprouted horns and a forked tail. The truth is we don't know what Regan is capable of."

Michael inhaled.

Liz looked up. "We need to fix this."

"We will. I don't want Lydia caught in something that has nothing to do with her. I assume Gerard will stay at the Hotel Vancouver?"

"Oh. No. He stays at The Sylvia, because–"

"McCandless says he should."

"Well no. He and Marcella prefer it, although she will stay at her parents' house, because the hotel is too busy. Because of the conference."

"Great. I told Mason to go chase up McCandless at The Sylvia. Exactly where Lydia will be. Not that she's likely to run into him. Could this mess get more complicated?"

"Oh, here." Liz handed him a folded piece of paper. "Lydia would like you to tell her parents. And just so you know, you might have a word with Richard Pulaski."

R. Rigsby

Vancouver, Sat Oct 12 2019: Lydia,_Worlds

I gulp the last of my cold tea. Janey hasn't taken her eyes off me and although her eyes widened and mouth opened many times, she didn't interrupt. As for Rennie, judging by the number of times she has glanced at her bag, she is impatient.

"I'm sorry, Rennie, but I started telling Janey this story and I'll soon get to the part that interests you." She has the grace to grin, and my heart flips over. Lachie again.

"It's a wonderful story," she says.

I credit her with being kind to an old lady. I look up to see Mick, followed by Gordon, coming into the lounge. Is it really that late?

"Dearest Auntie." Gordon leans wayyy down to peck my cheek. He doesn't resemble Mick but is a resurrection of our father. Snapping brown eyes, white teeth, dark hair with a few streaks of very becoming silver at his temples. "Have these two kept you talking all afternoon?"

"Gordon, you look more like your grandfather every day." I put my hand on my forehead. "I can't believe I said something so inane. I'm more drained than I thought."

Gordon and the girls laugh, but Mick just stands there like the Cheshire Cat.

"Then I'll take these two off your hands." He nods at Janey and Rennie, who take the hint and pick up bags and coats. "You and Dad will have the evening to recover. Kelsey sends hugs. She wanted to come but had a call. Maybe she's a few turkeys short." He says it as a joke, but if that's the case, Kelsey is brow-beating every turkey supplier in town to come up with the missing birds. Like her mother, she's a dynamo of energy and efficiency. So serendipitous that she and Gordon hit it off. Ellie and I couldn't be more pleased.

Gordon and the girls go out the door.

"Mick, let's walk." A few minutes later, we cross Beach Avenue without getting run over and stroll in shadows as the sun drops behind the headland. "Tell me what you and Gordon discussed that put that smirk on your face." Mick grins at me and tucks my hand under his arm.

"Gordon and I walked as far as Jericho Beach and back. We visited the Marine Museum and had lunch."

I let it go. There's no point pushing him do something before he's ready. Our father never understood that.

When a farm came up for sale, Dad wanted to buy it. He had the money, but he wanted Mick to farm it. And eventually it would be Mick's. Mick had never wanted to farm, but he didn't know what he wanted to do either. This made no sense to Dad, but Mick had always been the unknown quantity of the family, especially after we lost David.

David had been closer to Mick and me than Henri or our sisters. He taught us to ride and swim and read to us on winter nights. His death changed all of us, but afterward our parents and Henri and our sisters went back to being more themselves again. But not Mick. After that contretemps with Dad, Mick went to Toronto. And not me. David's death was my fault.

Unlike Mick's strained relationship with our father, Mick and Gordon get on well. Mick and Dad found a way to agree, but disagree, but Mick and Gordon have never disagreed on anything. They miss each other, and I have missed Gordon's family too.

Jasper and Desirée, and their kids still at home, welcomed us. Despite Des' clucking, I have never felt in the way. Within our limits, Mick and I help with the million jobs a farm requires. I again drove a truck this harvest. Working in the fields suited me fine, leaving Des to her kitchen, which has never been my best room. Mick and I weren't the only geriatrics in the fields. Our old neighbour, Richard, now eighty-four, exhorted his nephew from his pick-up.

Earlier in the year when green shoots glazed the fields, he had invited me for lunch. I hadn't been in his house since we were kids, when his mother ruled her kitchen with an ever-present wooden spoon. Richard never married. His mother's reign on the homestead probably intimidated all candidates. His nephew and family have a comfortable double-wide mobile on the property, but Richard lives alone in the house.

We sat in his kitchen. He had replaced the ten-foot table, making room for a bookcase and armchairs beside the ancient wood stove, in which a fire crackled. A crockpot of soup bubbled on the counter. His niece-in-law, if there is such a thing, delivered a coffee cake, but Richard, a dab hand in the kitchen himself, had a round of biscuits in the oven. We reminisced, but avoided some topics, keeping to more recent events–recent being anything in the last sixty years.

He looks good for his age. Still tall and lean. That day during harvest, I gave over the truck to Jasper who said I'd done enough and went and sat with

Richard, sweat and all. He poured me a mug of iced tea from his thermos and steadied my hand on the mug. He didn't let my hand go.

Later, Mick and I laughed at the irony: we were back in the world we couldn't leave fast enough years before. Neither of us had thought that would ever happen. But when Mick's lovely Noreen died, and I too had losses, in addition to my house's plumbing disaster, our return to the farm on Jasper's invitation was the balm both of us needed.

"I'm not looking forward to winter on the farm," I blurt, and I have no idea why. Not why I'm not looking forward to winter on the farm, but why I said it out loud. I look at Mick thinking how ungrateful I sound, but he laughs. "Not that I can't cope, but even I will get tired of reading."

"I'm already fed up and they haven't had the first snow. If we were in the city, we could go to a restaurant, or to a show, or just for fun, the casino. Before nine o'clock, naturally."

"More like the seniors' centre. For a rousing game of Cribbage. With other old coots like us."

"Line dancing."

"Oh, you're hilarious. Let's go back. I'm hungry now." And tired. Talking for hours is exhausting. And so is opening all those musty mental file drawers. Some of what I found surprised me with restirred emotions. Richard, for instance. Later, I drift off to sleep dreaming of cotton-fluff clouds in an August sky.

Janey and Rennie wait at the foot of the stairs this morning. They must know I avoid the elevator. I carry my coat and wear sensible shoes. At my age, all my shoes are sensible. I'm also wearing corduroy slacks and a cardigan over a long-sleeved shirt.

"Oh, wow, Auntie, you're ready. You didn't forget about breakfast. Where's Grandad?"

"I never forget breakfast, Janey, but your Grandad is already up and out. He met some people last night and they've all gone to the park."

Rennie leads the way, and Janey walks beside me. We reach Denman and turn north a few blocks to a café. Or a bistro, whatever they call it these days. My blood congeals and I stare.

Different name, newer windows, but it's the same building.

I'm a zombie, but circulation returns to my limbs. Janey takes my sleeve and I follow her inside. The coffee smells divine: just its aroma is restorative, but people clog the order counter and those who don't have seats stand. Servers behind the counter shout orders at the cooks, clatter mugs and plates, and yell out numbers as they fill orders. There's good-natured jostling as people reach

R. Rigsby

for food and drinks placed on top of a glass showcase, showcasing, mmm, pastries and muffins. Alive again.

I trail the girls through an archway at the back and feel a prickle of melancholy. We settle into tub chairs around a low table in front of a fireplace. The electric flame glows with warmth. Our table has a 'reserved' card and I look up at a young man carrying a tray. I think we're about to get the bum's rush, but he smiles at us, reaches down to retrieve the card, and installs three brimming mugs and three menus.

"Aren't you the clever one."

"Rennie's idea. She works here." To which Rennie nods with a shy smile.

"We can stay as long as we like," she says.

I sink into my comfortable chair. A warm room, and enough chatter and clatter from the front to remind me that there is another world out there, to which I can return any time. So many worlds, worlds within worlds, and I had no idea to which world that train in 1959 carried me.

Regina, Mon Oct 5 1959: Lydia, Escape

The train slid away from the station as Mr. Bakker joined me. He dragged his briefcase onto his lap.

"Miss, ah, Lydia, I need to check some figures for the speech."

His briefcase was so full it could have sprung its hinges. He shuffled papers then settled on a sheaf which he frowned at through glasses pulled from his inside pocket. Brow furrowed, he read.

Flurries of snow blew by the window. It might not amount to anything, but at this time of year, one never knew. I pulled my cardigan closer. The rail yards and the fair grounds rolled by under lowering dusk. Barns and windmills appeared and receded, but my parents' farm, although close to the city by Saskatchewan standards, wasn't within sight.

Everybody would be sitting down to Mother's shepherd's pie, or chicken stew, or the tourtière she learned to make for Dad. Henri and Natalie and their kids, four of my nine nieces and nephews there too. Their faces glowing. The kitchen stifling, and Mother checking a spice cake in the oven.

My nose tingled and I dug a hanky out of my purse. Must have been the conjured scent of nutmeg and cloves. My stomach ground out a reminder that I hadn't eaten since breakfast, not counting my coffee in The Cecil. Mr. Bakker looked up.

"I'm sorry. You must have your dinner. I had a late lunch, so I won't bother. Once you are sufficed," he smiled, "we will start."

The steward showed me to a window seat and, while forking roast beef and mashed potatoes into my mouth, dark engulfed the land. I passed on dessert, thinking of Mother's cake, and rejoined Mr. Bakker.

He put his papers in his briefcase, removed his glasses, then crossed his legs, elbows on the armrests and fingers together. I opened my holdall and placed a clutch of sharp pencils on the seat beside me. Every one of them vibrated onto the floor before I opened my steno-pad.

"Oh dear!" I bent to grab escapee pencils and knocked over the briefcase. He had only closed one catch, and the other sprang open releasing a torrent of paper.

"Wait!" Mr. Bakker bent over too, as I, on my hands and knees, scrabbled under the seats, grabbing pencils and paper. I came up between his knees.

"Ow!"

My head smacked him in the nose. Mr. Bakker sprang upright, and I looked up with my hair in my face when the attendant walked by. His eyes widened then rolled skyward.

"Miss, ah, Lydia," in a nasally voice. Gerard had his hand over his nose. "Please sit down."

"Oh, Mr. B., so sorry; can I get you something?" I wasn't sure what would help, but he motioned me to my seat. He held down the pile of sheets in his lap and pulled a handkerchief out of his pocket.

"I'm fine." He laughed and blew his nose. "It was just a slight bump. We can find the rest of your pencils later." I pushed my hair back knowing my pink cheeks clashed horribly with my raspberry twin set. I had bought it at Sweet Sixteen as a graduation present to myself when I expected to have a job soon. I wasn't sure how far the ten dollars in my purse would take me. And there was only $1.57 in my bank account. And if I kept this up, Gerard would fire me before I had earned fifty cents.

"I'm sorry. I, I, I, …I'm ready now."

"We have a whole train ride ahead of us. Slow and steady, right?" He smiled, but I wouldn't be surprised if he booted me off the train at the next stop. Moose Jaw.

"Lydia, I'm president of Pinnace Appliances, and this is an important speech."

Me, a farm girl working for the *President* of a company?

"The conference is an important opportunity for Pinnace." He showed me their logo: a slim sailboat. *Dad would love that.* Something about it tripped a memory, but it wasn't because I knew anything about boats. Gerard's voice was warm and modulated, as if talking to a skittish horse. I sat up straight, pencil ready: bolting was the last thing on my mind.

"Let's begin, shall we?" he said.

In my best Pitman shorthand, I wrote as he dictated. He would give this speech the day after we arrived in Vancouver. Shouldn't such an important speech be ready? Did Ellie have the speech and it too missed the train? If she did miss it. Miss Primnase, if she knew, hadn't seen fit to tell me. Nor Gerard either, if that's what the tango at the station was about.

Mr. B, Gerard, dictated until my hand cramped and my pencils ran down.

"Lydia," he said, "May I ask you something?"

"Of course." I flexed my hand.

"How old are you?"

"I'll be twenty-two on the fourteenth. Nine days from now. I know why you asked. You should have seen me opening my bank account. I had to threaten to get my uncle."

"Well, these are modern times. Young women are striking out on their own. Good for you for standing up for yourself. My wife says Pinnace should hire women for positions other than secretarial."

My ears perked up. Aside from Miss Primnase, my only experience with women who worked, outside of clerical, like Georgie's job in the bank, or in shops, was with nurses or teachers. Or librarians. Most of those worked until they got married. Although certainly my mother, like all farm wives, worked every day of their lives. Worked hard every day. But that's not why I didn't want to marry a farmer. Entirely. "Does Mrs. Bakker work for Pinnace too? Or does she look after your family."

"No. She is very committed to several charities. We don't have children. Let's continue."

I easily kept up with his meandering dictation: a diatribe about fridges, stoves, and laundry machines. The speech was far from cohesive, despite being the story of the company, an introduction of the latest models, and random comments on the industry.

"A break, Lydia? Oh, and you took care of that list?"

I stretched my fingers "Yes, no problem. I left a message for Davis and made a reservation."

Gerard pointed to a stack of brochures on the seat beside him. "Good. Good. Take a minute to read a pamphlet. You're an employee of the best in the business."

Guilt prodded my bubble of hope. I had Ellie's job, but I wanted the bubble to last longer than a train ride to Vancouver; we were well past Moose Jaw. I reached for a brochure. My hand jerked with a movement of the train and every glossy pamphlet glided to the floor.

We bent for them, and our foreheads smacked together.

"Sorry, sorry," we harmonized as we shot upright with hands on heads like a pair of bookends. Gerard reached once more, and I put out my hand.

"I'll do it. My fault. Again. I can't believe I keep doing this."

"I'll take a walk." Gerard sidestepped my latest disaster. He disappeared and I built a neat stack on the floor. So much to know about stoves and refrigerators. I read until Gerard reappeared. I thought he might have gone for a drink, but he didn't smell like Uncle Michael after communing with his bottom drawer on a slow afternoon. Grinning, Gerard said he had found a newspaper and a vacant seat where he had read in safety. He dictated for another hour, and I read it back to him, word after dull word.

R. Rigsby

"Great work, Lydia. We'll do more tomorrow, and you can type it up at the hotel. You did ask for a typewriter?"

"Yes, yes." I beamed efficiency. Typewriter? Was that the scrawl on the list? How would I get one now?

Gerard retrieved one of his reports and resumed reading. I looked out the window. Blacker than the inside of a cow. I let my eyes wander the coach and met Gerard's over the top of his glasses.

"Third Quarter Financials. They at least made it into my briefcase. Lots to check, but no surprises. You may as well know. My secretary, Miss Tremblay, received an urgent phone call about her mother. She went home to Halifax. It must have flustered her immensely, because not only did she not put the speech in my briefcase, but I'm missing another report which is probably in the safe. No matter, I'll get a copy in Vancouver. Nor did she confirm the items on your list."

"Would the report be useful?" I had no idea, but the speech was mind-numbing.

"I would like to include items from that report, but the board is conservative on sharing developments ahead of a finished product." He sighed. "It's an ongoing battle for me, but," he saw my yawn, "we can talk tomorrow. Here's the steward to make up the beds. Goodnight, Lydia."

I crawled into the overhead bunk. A long day. What had happened to Ellie's mother? Unlike Aunt Lou, she was one of the most robust women I knew. Georgie would find out. Ellie had to be okay. Like Georgie and me, she too had learned some fancy footwork to get herself out of trouble. Like that time at the Broadway. We hadn't noticed Henri and Natalie sat behind us. We had no idea the smell of beer could carry that far. Natalie giggled, but Henri tapped me on the shoulder. In the lobby, I said that we took it from Auntie Lou's fridge, but we thought it was root beer. Blink, blink.

I thought I would be awake all night worrying about the typewriter but fell asleep right away. All night the train rushed across the prairie, the whistle wailing a warning at every crossing.

Regina, Tues, Oct 6 1959: Michael, Sun on Water

The sun hovered at the skyline as if hesitant to launch the new day. Michael drove the rutted road to the Perrault farm, the long shadows suspended, waiting for the reluctant sun. He wished all things could be suspended, but as he pulled up in the yard, the sun cleared the horizon and rays refracting from the slough blinded him. He shaded his eyes and saw Jean in her kitchen window. Henri opened the door. André stood behind him.

"Uncle Mike…," Henri said.

Michael thought he must have leached doom, because Henri then said he had to go feed the stock. André lifted his brows and led Michael into the kitchen. Natalie wiped toast crumbs from her children's faces and hustled them upstairs.

"What is it, Michael?" Jean said. "You're not here this early for coffee. What has happened?"

André pulled up a chair and sat across from Michael.

They were, as Michael had predicted, stunned that Lydia was on her way to Vancouver. He put the best possible spin on the news, as if he were a criminal lawyer appealing to a jury of skeptics. That Lydia had taken a job with Gerard Bakker helped. Jean's eyes sparked when she read the note, but tears dampened her lashes.

André took her hand. "Well, Michael," he said, "we have only met Gerard once since he left Regina, but he was a good boy. We trust your opinion of him as a man. As for Lydia, she might appear otherwise, but she has her mother's brains."

"She does," Michael said, "but she was hired because Marielle missed the train. The job might be temporary."

"Marielle missed a train?" Jean said.

Michael relayed the details. "Lou called her sister. She twisted her ankle, but she didn't call Ellie. She thinks her husband might have done so as a surprise for her. Lou said train connections to Halifax are dismal, and it might take Ellie a few days to get home."

"Does Georgie know anything?"

"Lydia called her just before she left."

Jean just nodded. "I understand. I wouldn't have called my mother either. At least she wrote a note."

André followed Michael to the car.

"You have more to tell me, don't you my old friend? Shall we walk?"

André took the path along the slough and Michael trudged behind him, the sun again in his eyes. He would tell André everything. As he should have done years before.

They stood looking over the limpid water and across the fields on the far side. A drift of smoke rose from the Pulaski's chimney. Next stop, thought Michael, then returned to the present.

"Thirty-two years ago, I lied to you. About what happened to Paddy Fitzroy and Jig Kesey."

"I know you did. But I knew that one day you would tell me the truth."

"How did he get that name? Jig, that is." Why ask that now?

André grinned. "Dad said somebody had once asked Kesey, when he was very drunk, if he was doing the 'Whiskey Jig.' It stuck."

"Well Jig Kesey is buried in that grave with Paddy's name on the stone."

André shook his head. "So mon père had it wrong. It's not Kesey's ghost in The Arms. What happened?"

Michael told him.

"You've carried this load too long. You should have told me. You changed after Paddy's death. The war didn't change you much. You were more thoughtful, but you were the same guy who played ball with me and my sisters. But after Paddy died and Kesey disappeared, you changed. More cynical."

Michael shoved his hands into his coat pockets. "I'm not a hero for telling you now. Paddy's body will probably be found this week."

André tilted his head back and closed his eyes. "Yes, Jon's new heater."

"What's really ironic is that he made the decision because Lydia told him his guests complained."

"Ah, our little brown bird has a way of making things happen." André's mouth smiled but his eyes did not. He headed back to the house.

Michael followed. *He's thinking of David.* He thought of David too, but said, "I'm going to Vancouver." He then told André about Regan's apparent obsession to avenge his father's death.

"Regan?" André turned around at Michael's car. "We've not seen or heard from him in twenty years. Is he dangerous?"

"He won't be once McCandless tells him he's Birch. I'll deal with whatever turns up in Jon's cellar when I get back." He leaned on the fender. "And André, another thing. When I get to Vancouver, I'm going to tell Lydia as well. I think she read a letter that Abe wrote to me just before he, he…the fire. Liz knows about it too. Even so, I think Lydia's worked out a few things on her own. It's your right to tell her, but I would like to do so."

André hesitated and looked toward the house. "When we think of Lydia, we see our baby girl running to catch up with her brothers and sisters. But she is a grown woman. You must tell her yourself."

"I wish I'd told you long ago."

"Michael, you are the brother I've never had."

Michael hugged André, and over his shoulder he saw Jean watching from her kitchen window. He waved to her and got in his car, knowing that brothers or not, his friendship with André would never be the same.

R. Rigsby

Calgary, Tues Oct 6 1959: Lydia, Mixed Messaging

My eyes cracked open to a band of light in my upper bunk cradle. The train had stopped, and I missed its gentle rocking. I pulled on the outfit de jour, which was the same as the outfit of the day before. In the bathroom I combed a little water through my hair and pinched my cheeks. Our car was near the end of a station where a sign declared 'Calgary.'

I grabbed my purse and hopped onto the platform. In luck for once, I found the telegraph office right away. On my way in, a beautiful set of matched luggage on a cart diverted my attention and I bumped into Gerard on his way out.

"Good morning, Lydia." He took my elbow and steered me through the doorway. "Meet me in the dining car when you are done."

"Oh, Gerard, this won't take long." And it didn't. I'd never sent a telegram, in this case two, in my life, although the two messages reduced my capital. Gerard hadn't said when I would see a cheque.

The train shunted forward as I teetered down the aisle to the dining car. Gerard stood, smiled, and pulled out my chair. He poured coffee and asked the steward to bring me bacon and eggs, cocking an eyebrow to make sure this was okay. He laughed at my head-bobs. So cheerful this morning. Perhaps he had worked out problems with his speech.

He watched me scoop eggs and bite toast, probably wondering why I ate so fast, and in the next few minutes I told him.

"Lydia, I'm sorry, I was only half listening when Liz introduced you. Did she say your last name was Perrault?" I nodded and kept chewing. "I knew some Perraults when I lived in Regina."

I took a swallow of coffee. "Really? When was that?"

"My folks had the Bakker's Hardware Store next to Primnase's Books, but we left for Vancouver in 1934. Still know a few people in Regina though." He lifted his coffee.

Of course! Mr. Ho told me the café had once been Fred Bakker's store. "My father is André Perrault, but if you know him, you must know my uncle, Michael Kerr." It might have been the train veering around a lump in the landscape that caused him to splutter into his cup. This time I was quicker on the draw and pressed the napkin into his groping hand.

"Your father, your uncle," he choked out. "Yes, I know them both."

Later, I read to him everything he had dictated, word for word, and each word for word, his frown deepened. I glanced up while reading and at the initial frown decided that my delivery was monotonous. I injected more expression. It hadn't helped.

"Something wrong?"

He cleared his throat. "It's even duller than I thought. I'm speaking to industry leaders and major buyers."

I looked at the creased pages of my steno book. Would I ever keep my mouth shut? Mother always said I couldn't keep my opinions to myself, but Uncle Michael always asked what I thought of everything. We discussed the opening of the Seaway, hula hoops, and whether television would change family life. Auntie Lou said she had read that a television damaged a person's eyes, and she wouldn't have one in the house. When I looked at Uncle Michael, he winked. A television was on order. Georgie only commented if the conversation veered around to the new fashions like stiletto heels and pencil skirts. We had that in common with Ellie.

Ellie, Georgie, and I spent the whole summer together when Auntie Lou got polio. Georgie came to the farm, and because Ellie's mother nursed her sister, Ellie came too. Ellie and Georgie were already twelve, and I was eleven. When Mother didn't have us hoeing and watering the garden, or churning butter, we caught frogs in the slough or stuffed our faces with Saskatoon berries or rode our two plodding, and retired, work horses. Sometimes Mick joined us, but the next thing Georgie and I knew, both Mick and Ellie disappeared in what we thought was a game of hide'n'seek. They were always in the loft, so no big effort to find them. I figured out why the loft when I was fifteen. Richard Pulaski said we should hide there from his nephews, who were all of four. When he kissed me, I bit him, kneed him, and took off. My opinion of lofts changed after that.

I didn't know if Gerard wanted my opinion or not, but he was going to get it.

"Mr. Bakker–"

"You may as well call me Gerard." He sighed. "Tell me what you think."

"It's as dull as dust on the slough. But I don't think it's your fault and it's only the first draft." I searched my brain for something that Miss Primnase would suggest.

"Maybe consider what you want your audience to do after they hear the speech. I understand the company story is important, but that's history. Could you emphasize what's in the future, and why your stoves and fridges are the leading edge in design?" I bit my lip.

Gerard nodded. "I have given dozens of speeches over the years, but they all say the same thing. Let me think about this."

Gerard scratched a few words in his notebook. I looked out the window at rolling hills. Seeing that he, too, had given up writing for watching scenery, I thought it a good time to change the subject, or reopen an old one.

"How do you know my father and my uncle?"

"Ah, yes," Gerard sat back and crossed his legs. "Well of course I watched your father play ball when I was a kid. He could sizzle a pitch like nobody in the league. He coached my team, but as your grandparents aged, and he had his own family, he didn't have as much time."

"I don't remember my grandmother, and Grand-Père died two years ago. Dad can still whiz a ball. He had all of us kids playing as soon as we could walk. My oldest brother, Henri, is good and played in the league. My sisters are good too, but my brother David was the best." I could never stop the catch in my throat when I spoke of David.

"David? Yes. Vehicle accident, wasn't it?"

Putting the memory of my brother back in the box, I smiled and said, "That's about where the talent stopped, because my brother, Mick, and I are pathetic. I can throw a cow pat farther than a ball, but at least I can run. Mick just never cared. He's in Toronto, working in an insurance office." He was, last I heard. "How do you know my Uncle Michael?"

"He was my father's friend. They went to war, the Great War, along with a few others including my wife's father. They came back with just a few wounds between them. Your uncle got his law degree and did a lot of work for my father, probably for free. Not that it helped. He lost the business anyway. Mr. Primnase, a good man Dad said, was his landlord, but when the depression came, Dad couldn't keep the store going. Lost the house too. Primnase's bookshop did okay, God knows how."

Gerard sat back in his chair and looked at a point far away above my head. I kept silent. Mr. Primnase admitted in his letter that he made money from the whiskey business. Did Gerard know?

"Most people had no money for potatoes, let alone books." Gerard, back on track, continued, "We went to Vancouver to my mother's family. My grandfather had an appliance repair shop and sold washing machines. He had the franchise. He paid for my education, but I had to work in the shop. I liked it. Got my start in this business." He uncrossed his legs and rubbed his eyes. "And you must know your uncle owns shares in Pinnace. Is on the board in fact. We should get back to work, Lydia."

I sharpened a pencil and Gerard added more comments, but in my mind, I heard Gerard's voice droning to a room full of dozing heads. He paused for a moment, and I waited for him to resume, which gave me time to think about

Uncle Michael. He had money in Gerard's company. If he owned a piece of Pinnace, wouldn't he receive reports? I hadn't filed one piece of paper with that name. I didn't file for him every day, or even every week, but he had never mentioned it.

The scenery flashed by. I thought the foothills were intriguing but now we were into the mountains. I kept gawking out the window but catching Gerard's wrinkled brow zipped my face back over my work. Gerard looked at me with head on one side and then burst out laughing.

"You've never seen mountains before, have you? Okay, Lydia, feast your eyes and we can pick this up when it gets dark. I'll walk." He laughed again. I should have been embarrassed, but I was grateful and beheld mountains, deep valleys, and rushing rivers until it was too dark to see anything but my own reflection and the filmy print from my nose.

Gerard came back and led me to the dining car, where I purposefully ate more slowly and tasted every bite. I had my pencil and pad ready while Gerard sipped his coffee and rattled on with his speech. Then he stopped.

He smiled. "We have made excellent progress, Lydia."

Regina, Tues Oct 6 1959: Michael, Lightening the Load

In the early afternoon, after calling his office and then his home, Michael finally tracked down McCandless. Bertram listened without interruption while Michael disclosed Mason's snooping, Jon's renovations, and Regan's belief that Fred was the Birch who killed his father.

"He thinks *Fred* did it?" Disbelief in McCandless' voice.

"Has thought so for years. And because Fred died, he's after Gerard."

"Do you know how he plans on evening the score?" In his usual tone of confident authority. "Does this have anything to do with Gerard's telegram about his R&D report that may or may not be missing?"

"I don't know." Michael refrained from adding that he didn't care. "I'm flying to Vancouver. We, you and I, need to tell Regan you are Birch. And decide what we do if Paddy's body is found."

"Look, Mike, let's work on one thing at a time. I'll warn Gerard. And yes, we'll deal with Regan, body or no body. Don't worry, we'll get through this."

Michael put down the phone. *We'll get through this.* He supposed they would. Regan might be mollified by Birch's fiction, Paddy's body might not be found, and Mason and his quest to find Kesey might come to nothing. For some reason he had never thought to find Kesey's family and make restitution for the use of Kesey's money. And Jon's.

He had returned to the day's work when a telegram arrived: Lydia asking him to find Ellie. He called Liz.

He told her what Lou had said about her sister and train travel to Halifax. "If Ellie isn't already home, she could be sitting in Fredericton waiting for a train, but Lydia doesn't know that."

"I had hoped to hear from her by today, Michael. It's just not like her. There are telephones at train stations. If she wanted to tell me anything."

"Let me deal with this, Liz."

That evening, while Georgie walked with her young fellow from the bank, Michael used the telegram to reopen the talk with Lou.

"Those two girls would make a saint weep," she said. "Our Georgie has learned sense. Especially after that silly business in the Broadway." Then Lou waited. Put down her knitting and waited, knowing there was more.

R. Rigsby

Michael told her everything he should have told her over three decades before. A good woman, Lou, practical, caring, and competent in her realm as wife of a lawyer. One always knew what to expect from Lou. He wasn't sure she always knew what to expect from him. He wasn't sure of that himself.

Fraser River, Wed Oct 7 1959: Lydia, Knowledge

Breakfast was a repeat of the morning before, but I poked at my food. The train had reached the Fraser Canyon, and I looked straight down at swirling brown water. My head swirled too, but I couldn't make myself not look. Gerard suggested we return to our seats on the opposite side of the car. I must have looked green and for sure, the sausage omelette I did swallow was making its own peculiar rotations in sync with those in the river below.

"Lydia, look at me. Tell me why you enrolled in Liz Primnase's school."

"Oh." He was trying to distract me, not asking for my life story. "The year after I finished high school, I took a part-time job at The Cecil Café. I liked it, and Mr. Ho wanted me to stay, but my family needed me on the farm for harvest. I was stuck there all winter and thought I would go mad, despite the Perrault family library. I wanted to work. In an office, using my mind. In the spring, I asked Mr. Ho for my job. I stayed with my Uncle Michael and Auntie Lou. To save money."

I wasn't about to share what else I did to get the money. After over a year at The Cecil, I still didn't have enough to pay for a course in pencil sharpening let alone stenography. Girls I knew graduated and got jobs. Like Ellie and Georgie. Gerard waited and I thought I should stay on point with him.

"I already knew about Miss Primnase's school from my cousin and almost cousin."

Gerard laughed. "How could somebody be an 'almost cousin?'"

Reveal that I knew Ellie? No. "Oh… just had to think it through. She's one of my aunts-by-marriage sister's daughter, so not a real cousin, but we were all kids together." I hoped he wasn't that familiar with my family. Other than Auntie Lou, I had no other aunts-by-marriage. Dad had sisters, no brothers. "I'm feeling better now; I'll go powder my nose and find a drink of water."

In the bathroom, I splashed water on my face and dug through my purse for my lipstick. In the bottom, my fingers felt not a smooth metal tube but crinkled paper, and I pulled out the envelope I had picked up on my way out of the house. I had forgotten all about it. I opened the envelope to find Ellie's shorthand note written on sheets from her steno book. It was dated over a week ago. I sat on the toilet seat.

Dear Lydia,

I have worked for Mr. Bakker for a year, and he has been kind and patient. But now I am shocked. A person I trust told me that Mr. Bakker has been selling company secrets to the competition.

I didn't believe it at first, but I witnessed the proof. Can't explain here. My friend said Pinnace was once Mr. Bakker's family company, and it was taken from him under false pretenses. I can barely look at him. And he thinks there is a confidential report of secrets that is in danger of being leaked.

My friend warned me not to share what I know because it's not clear if Mr. Bakker is acting alone or not.

My stomach is in knots. I don't expect you to do anything, but I had to share this or burst. I will let you know as soon as this is resolved. Yours, Ellie.

Oh, dear. This wasn't about her newest ensemble or latest favourite restaurant. Who was her friend? Was that why she missed the train? Because she couldn't work for Gerard for another three days?

She was convinced that he, her friend, I assumed it was *he*, was correct about Gerard, and I understood her shock. Gerard was so concerned that his speech set the right tone and present the interests of his company in a positive light, a company he was proud of. He didn't seem like a man who would sell it out because of its loss to his family years and years ago. Besides, he was president of Pinnace, not the janitor. And a president scheduled to deliver an important speech.

Did Ellie have the speech? Is the report in danger of being leaked the one that Gerard is missing?

Was it a good thing I hadn't told Gerard I knew Ellie? I needed to talk to her. *Think, Lydia, think.* If she had the secret report, she probably wouldn't take it to Halifax. If that bit about going to Halifax wasn't balderdash. Would she give it to this trusted person? And how could I behave with Gerard as if nothing had changed?

Somebody rapped on the door. I crammed the letter in my purse and opened the door to a plump lady with a perplexed expression. I didn't think I'd sat there that long. Gerard hadn't missed me, being engrossed reading paperwork.

I took out my leather notebook and rubbed the red leather surface as if a genie might arise pronouncing the solution to my predicament. When we got to Vancouver, I would call Uncle Michael. Ellie didn't want me to tell anybody, but Uncle Michael was good at fixing tricky situations. He saved me from Richard's insistence that I uphold the deal we made. Richard agreed to a year's grace, but that would be up in, *dear, dear,* on my birthday, in seven days. Except I had a job.

"Lydia."

My head snapped up. "Yes, sir?"

A frown flitted over Gerard's face. "I have a few more thoughts to add to the speech. And really, Lydia, there's no need for such formality. Hardly anybody calls me 'sir.'" Then he grinned his funny lop-sided grin. "The only person who ever calls me 'sir' is one of my managers, Fitzroy. And then only when he feels the need for me to give him a 'yes' to something he wants. You'll meet him at the conference."

"Oh, has he worked for you very long." I didn't care to know, but not telling Gerard that I knew Ellie, and what she had said about him, had become a big, fat, wodge of guilt. The last thing I wanted was any more conversation on my 'almost cousin.'

"Why, yes he has." Gerard prattled on about Fitzroy, while I dug in my holdall. With steno pad and professional smile in place, I took more notes. The trip was almost over.

R. Rigsby

Vancouver, Wed Oct 7 1959: Regan, The Set-Up

Regan strode into the conference room at the Hotel Vancouver and was pleased to see that the rest of the appliances for the Pinnace display had arrived. They were still in cartons and not properly grouped, but it wouldn't take long to finish setting up. The new models would look stunning under the Pinnace banners. He checked himself. By next week, he wouldn't work for Pinnace as a mere manager but would have an executive position with Empress. Ellie would be his secretary. Ellie and the report were on the train with Gerard. She would find a way to give it to him.

He had said so to Wilf, after it was clear last Friday that Ellie wouldn't show. Wilf said he would also go to Vancouver where he could receive the package as soon as Regan had it.

Regan pulled open a carton but looked up when a mammoth blocked his light. Wilf.

"Busy, busy, are we?" Wilf wheezed, thumbs in a belt overshadowed by his belly.

"Ah, you made it then." Regan eyed Wilf. His whiskey nose shone more than usual and sweat beaded on his forehead, although the room was cool. "Good flight?"

"No. They ran out of Crown Royal. Any sign of your boss and the Ellie gal?"

"Shhh. Not yet. He should have arrived late last night. He could walk in any minute. Wilf, you shouldn't be here."

"Why not? I'm a loyal Empress employee just shooting the breeze with the competition. There's my boss now." He lifted his chins to a thin man across the room, who only scowled. "But you're right. Here's where I'm staying." He handed Regan a limp scrap of paper with a number. "You call me as soon as you get that package. If my man over there," and again Wilf waggled his chins, "doesn't get what he wants, then your deal is off."

"Tell him not to worry. Ellie has that report."

Vancouver, Wed Oct 7 1959: Lydia, The Wrong Foot

We walked out of the magnificent Canadian Pacific Station, and I nearly fell over while looking up at the Marine Building soaring in art deco glory to the clouds. I once read a travelogue on Vancouver attractions, but never believed I would see Vancouver, or any other city, despite my fantasizing about moving to Calgary.

If Miss Primnase hadn't found me, I would be packing to go back to the farm. And deal with Richard. Mr. Ho had hired a widow with three kids for my job, and I couldn't live at Uncle Michael's for free all winter. Uncle Michael didn't mind, nor Georgie either, although she shared her room with me. But Auntie Lou? She told her sister she couldn't believe how much a scrap like me could eat. That surprised me. Not that she complained to her sister, but that she thought I ate a lot. She only had the one sister, so she had no idea what it was like being the youngest at a table set for nine.

Still awed by the Marine Building, I followed Gerard through criss-crossing masses of people; he lugged his suitcase and briefcase and had thrown his coat thrown over his shoulder. I carried my coat, purse, carpetbag, and holdall with the umbrella sticking out. I thought it constantly rained on the west coast, but streaks of watered blue showed between high clouds.

Gerard suddenly stopped and bent over. I bumped into him, but he caught himself with a hand on the fender of a blue car. He fished under its front tire and produced a key. At the look on my face, he said, "My father-in-law's driver, Davis, parked it here."

Davis was a chauffeur? Who had I spoken to?

"It's a Buick Riviera. Just off the lot. My father-in-law bought it for my wife and me," finished Gerard, misinterpreting my expression.

"It's lovely." Then I really looked at it: dark blue, the most amazing fins, white wall tires. The enormous steering wheel made my palms tingle, but Gerard threw his bags in the trunk and opened the passenger door for me. I heaved my carpetbag onto the back seat and wondered at the man who would buy his daughter and son-in-law a brand-new car. I was also wondering if I would get a cheque before that son-in-law was arrested. And if he wasn't, could I keep working for him? I could go home, I guess. Go home? Now that I was here?

Gerard braked in time to miss rear-ending a taxi at a red light. I held my breath for the rest of the drive that ended under the portico of a grand building. The Hotel Vancouver. I had reserved at The Sylvia. I must have looked like a horse with its tail on fire.

"We'll check into The Sylvia later." Gerard jerked the car to a halt. "I want to see how Fitzroy is doing, although I'm sure he's almost finished setting up. He doesn't know about my delay in Regina." I looked at him, relieved and a little confused.

"Fitzroy flew out. I, um, prefer the train." Then he grinned. "You may as well know–I hate flying. My wife loves it. She will fly out tomorrow–her father lives in Vancouver, but she too is a Regina girl." I wasn't about to correct him. I wasn't really a Regina girl–more like a farm-north-of-Regina girl.

The valet took the car, and we crossed the lobby to an elevator which whisked us to the conference floor. Gerard pushed open a door and stepped aside to let me enter a ballroom, identified by its bronze plaque as The Magnolia Room. No Magnolias, but a blooming array of appliances shone from semi-arranged displays and opened cartons. The man who strode toward us neither shone nor bloomed. A stern face shadowed by a lock of light brown hair. He bee-lined for Gerard, hand out.

"Gerard, glad you are here." The bared teeth under the close-clipped moustache didn't look like any smile I'd ever seen. He was about Gerard's height and age, but his eyes glowed rather than twinkled.

He ignored me until Gerard motioned me forward and said, while looking around the room, "This is Lydia Perrault, my new secretary. Lydia, meet Regan Fitzroy."

"Your new....?" Gerard, looking at a refrigerator, didn't see the remarkable range of expressions that flashed over Fitzroy's face, before they settled into a rude stare. I smiled and lifted my chin. *Did I have crumbs on my cheek?*

"Yes, Marielle went to Halifax. An emergency with her mother." Gerard pulled apart the cardboard on a stove. "She must have been terribly distraught. You wouldn't know if her mother has been ill, would you?" Gerard paused and looked at Fitzroy. "You lunched with Marielle last week?"

"Yes, Gerard, but sorry, we talked shop."

"Excuse me," I said, "I'm just going to…" then pointed across the room to an exit.

I found the ladies behind a spring-hinged entry door where I washed my hands and splashed my face. When I left the restroom, the spring-hinged door closed more abruptly than I expected, catching my holdall. I freed it then turned and smacked into Fitzroy.

"Oooo, excuse me," I said. Why was I apologizing to *him*? I expected something along the line of 'Oops, wrong door,' but instead he pushed me none too gently against the wall. I gasped, more with surprise than fear. I had been on the receiving end of many sibling rough-housings–all six of them at one time or another.

"We need to talk." He placed one hand on my shoulder and the other on the wall beside my head.

Getting over my surprise, I tensed my back. "Kindly take your hand off me." I jerked my shoulder sideways. Balanced on one foot, I thought it was a good thing I wore my pleated skirt. But he stepped back, with a sixth sense for the family jewels. At least one of my brothers hadn't been so quick. I held my holdall with both hands in front of my chest. I could mash it into his face.

"Where's Marielle?"

I don't know what I expected, but it wasn't that, so all I could stammer was "Who?" So silly. But I was beyond annoyed. "How should I know? Mr. Bakker hired me in Regina. Now kindly step back and let me pass."

"Regina?" he said as stupidly as I had said 'Who?' "From Primnase's school? Did *she* say anything?"

I stepped sideways, still ready to slam his face with my holdall, but he grabbed my arm. Already in motion, I staggered, stepping on his foot.

"Owww, shit!" He twisted my arm.

"Owww," I said, wishing I could also say *shit*.

"Here now, what's going on?" A voice that sounded as officious as the gold braided and befrogged uniform he wore. He stood at the end of the hall, at the door marked 'Private.' A doorman? I didn't care. Fitzroy leaped back and I made off to the Magnolia Room, not stopping to argue his lame excuse of assisting the lady when she tripped.

"Oh, there you are." Gerard closed the oven on a shiny stove. "What have you done with Fitzroy? Oh, never mind, there he is. We still have setting up to do, so here, take a seat." He overturned a metal waste basket and dusted the bottom. "In case I think of more for the speech. Fitzroy, man, why are you limping? There are still cartons to open."

I sank onto my improvised steno chair, but not before I caught the look of thrown daggers from Fitzroy.

"I'll be with you in a minute, Gerard," Fitzroy said, "I have to make a call."

I put my steno book on my shaking knee. Why would Fitzroy, whom I had never met, and only heard of on the train, think I knew the whereabouts of Ellie? What on earth had gotten into the man?

This man? And Ellie? Couldn't be. He'd worked for Gerard for years. *Think, Lydia, what did Gerard tell you on the train?* I should have asked more questions, but I was taking notes for his speech, not his biography. How did Fitzroy know Miss Primnase? His name, Regan, a nice name, chimed a distant bell in my memory. It would come to me once my liver quit leaping about.

Fitzroy returned and he and Gerard opened more cartons and checked each sleek appliance for scrapes or dents.

"I can finish if you want to go check in?" Fitzroy said.

"Yes, thanks, Lydia and I must finish the speech." Gerard didn't see Fitzroy's eyebrows shoot up.

"Oh, Gerard," he said, with the smile of a ferret, "Shall I meet you later in the lounge? We could review the customer list?"

"Excellent idea, Regan," although Gerard looked surprised.

Vancouver, Wed Oct 7 1959: Lydia, Grace and Mystery

We travelled a delightfully treed street beside sparkling water and sandy beaches. Gerard had ground gears as he steered into traffic and forgot to signal. If he thought pilots flew airplanes like he drove, no wonder he was afraid of flying. The large man stepping into the crosswalk didn't know how lucky he was that Gerard saw him. Gerard drummed his fingers on the steering wheel while the man puffed across.

I looked ahead. The Sylvia. Not at all what I expected. Such a graceful and enigmatic building with its vine shrouded windows. It had to shelter more than late season tourists or businessmen in town for Gerard's convention. It looked like the perfect retreat for weary celebrities or secret couples. Not that I would confess to Mother I knew about such things, but while working next to The Arms, I had seen interesting comings and goings.

No celebrities unless they were in disguise. And lost. No celebrities visited Regina on purpose. Unless they were politicians. Dad said they didn't count as celebrities. The Queen and Prince Philip had visited, but they were royalty passing through.

"Ah, here we are." Gerard pulled in behind a cab and bumped the curb. I had leaned forward to look up at the hotel and nearly hit my nose on the dashboard. I had never been in a real hotel, and today I had been in one resplendent hotel and was about to enter another that looked equally promising.

Regina had hotels, but I had only been in The Prairie Arms, briefly, when I rescued Uncle Michael. Its lobby had a square of green linoleum over plank floors, a dark wood registry desk, and dreary wallpaper. The place was spotless, but despite Jon's scrubbing, it smelled of fermentation and smoke. In the beer parlour, I was too busy keeping Uncle Michael upright to notice anything but surprised looks and loud guffaws. I never did tell Mother about that. And here I would stay in my own room in a lovely gracious inn. What would Mother think? She and Dad would know by now I had left Regina. *Should I expect a phone call ordering me home?*

I opened my door and glanced up. Gerard, his head in the trunk, didn't see the woman, and I didn't get to see much of her either. She came out, spun on her heel, and went back in. Fair hair frothed from under a pill-box hat. The retreating figure was clad in a dove grey suit, which I wished I could see close-up. I was sure I would look dead in grey, but the cut was superb. The same suit in, say, aqua, would look stunning on me. If I were a bit taller. And owned black stiletto heels like those that clicked up the stairs.

Gerard shut the trunk and looked at me, eyebrows raised. I grabbed my coat and carpet bag from the back seat and joined him on the steps, where I tripped because I was again looking up. Gerard stuck his briefcase under his arm and took my elbow. I made it into the building without falling on my face.

The tiled entry lead onto plush carpet that swallowed sound. The modern décor surprised me with its spare uncluttered and unadorned style. A refined hum of subdued conversation emanated from the lounge to the right, and the elevator emitted a dignified chime. I smelled lemon-scented polish. I could hardly wait to see my room.

We approached the desk where the register lay open. I turned to watch a man in a white jacket rush past with a tray of rattling glasses and a tall bottle in an ice bucket.

"Lydia!" In my ear.

I swung around. A middle-aged man, with very slick hair that seemed much too dark for his face, fixed narrowed eyes on me and indicated the register where I should sign.

"Mr. Bakker you, and your, uh, *secretary*, are booked into suite 501–a *one* bedroom suite as was requested," confirmed his disapproval. I stared at him.

"But the person I spoke to said it was a suite with two beds, so I thought that meant two bedrooms." Heat rose in my cheeks.

"No indeed. One bedroom with twin beds. However, the living room has a fold out couch. And we are fully booked, so I have nothing else to offer you." His tight little smile became a full-blown smirk. My mouth fell open.

If I'd known Gerard to be gentlemanly under all circumstances, I mightn't have gulped like a bullhead yanked from the slough. But I didn't know him. He was apparently a thief. I looked at a lobby chair. How comfortable was that?

"This is ridiculous, Albert. My secretary will have the bedroom, and I will take the couch. Tomorrow I will stay at my father-in-law's, so for one night I'm sure such an arrangement won't compromise this fine establishment's reputation? Even with the esteemed patronage of Mr. Errol Flynn? And given that you know me, my wife, *and* my father-in-law you do understand discretion?" He glared into the desk clerk's face which melted into a mask of fawning placation, even as his shoulders stiffened.

I wrote the first initials of my name, LJ, but the clerk whipped the register away as if my signature tainted it. An illegible scribble followed the J in my name, but the clerk plucked the pen out of my hand.

I shrugged and caught sight of a large man who dropped heavily into one of the upholstered chairs. The man from the crosswalk. He raised his paper in front of his florid face but looked at me over the top of his glasses.

"Oh, and I am sorry Mr. Bakker, I almost forgot. Your father-in-law would like you to call him, Mrs. Bakker left a message for you, and we have something in the safe too." Albert held up a finger, disappeared for a minute and then reappeared. His phone rang, but he pushed forward a bulging manila envelope, a folded piece of paper, and a key.

Gerard took the note. He looked at the envelope but didn't pick it up. Stamped on top was *'Confidential.'*

"Ah, the miracle of modern communication. My report. Bring that Lydia if you please." He snatched the key. The red-faced man in the chair peered at me over the top of his paper. Gerard hoisted his briefcase and marched toward the elevator. Over his shoulder, he said to the clerk, still on his phone, "Have your man bring the baggage up. Come along Lydia."

I grabbed my holdall and the bulging envelope. I trotted after Gerard, ducking into the elevator in his wake. I couldn't help myself and stuck out my tongue at the desk clerk just as the doors closed.

R. Rigsby

Vancouver, Wed Oct 7 1959: Regan, Plan B

Regan shifted the aqua refrigerator so that it angled to its matching stove, a pattern that helped draw buyers' eyes around the corner of the space and on to the next set. Now to place the posters and hang streamers before going to his room for a shower.

Not two hours ago, Gerard had come in with a mousy twit of a girl and no Ellie. And possibly no report. When Gerard took the brochures out of his briefcase, he hadn't been quick enough to see if the report, with its red lettered warning of 'Confidential' was there too. He couldn't ask. Gerard was obtuse, but not as obtuse as that.

The twit had no idea about Ellie, so he had called Wilf. Told him to get to The Sylvia. Ellie gave Gerard the cock-and-bull story about Halifax, but did she then come to Vancouver with the secrets? Maybe she couldn't face sitting on a train with that criminal all the way from Toronto. She might be on a later train. Or flew.

Ellie believed every word he had told her. And she should. Gerard was a fraud who had killed his father. Well, no, Regan rubbed his forehead. That wasn't right. Gerard's father had done that. But he was dead, so Gerard had to pay. And for Abe too.

He would get the secrets for Empress. Then the Pinnace board would blame Gerard for losing vital secret material. Regan would then resign saying he couldn't work for such an incompetent. Empress would reward him with a vice presidential position, at least. He paused with a few yards of dark blue streamer in his hand. And if Gerard was found dead, it would look like suicide. Gerard. Well, it couldn't be helped. He shouldn't have lied.

"Mr. Fitzroy?" A hotel page. An urgent call, he could use the courtesy phone in the hall.

"Have I got news," said Wilf. "A girl with your boss, a Lydia, not the good looker, she has the report! I saw the stamp on the envelope."

"Her name is Lydia Perrault." Regan said, distracted by a stocky man in a grey suit who passed him and then went into the Magnolia Room. Her name sounded familiar, but it couldn't be important. He gave Wilf instructions, then decided he had done enough for the day and went up to his room.

R. Rigsby

There on the nightstand was the photo of him and his parents. The photo went everywhere with him, a constant reminder of what he had lost, and who was to blame. If his father had lived, he might have made his mother accept treatment and she too might have lived.

When he asked Gerard to meet, he had intended to buy him a drink, find out if he had the confidential report. He had the report, but his speech wasn't finished. That drink for Gerard would really be useful now.

He put a hand on his forehead. The headache was back, but he had time for a lie-down before meeting Gerard. Birch. Or son of a Birch. He snorted at his joke and closed his eyes.

Vancouver, Wed Oct 7 1959: Lydia, Enter the Ghost

The elevator door whooshed sideways. Gerard, frowning, had read his note, and I wondered if it was unwelcome news. He picked up his briefcase and waved me ahead of him.

"Look!" I froze.

Gerard's envelope under my arm tilted, bursting the gummed flap. Everything in it slithered floorward. I grabbed backwards. My fist thumped Gerard who hadn't stopped. "Shoot!" I bent over to grab paper and lost sight of the opaque figure I had seen sliding around the corner at the end of the hall. "Did you see that?"

Gerard in my ear. "All I ssssee is this messsss on the floor."

Did I hit him that hard? When the cow kicked Mick, he rolled around for ten minutes. But no, Gerard, still upright, hissed, "Hundreds of pages here. Good grief, right in front of the elevator."

Gerard and I kneeled together, and our cracking skulls would have exorcized apparitions on every floor.

"Ow…" He rocked back on his heels. "Lydia, here's the key. I'll go to the lounge. Could you get those papers together and keep them safe until I can see straight?" Not bothering with the elevator, and still hunched, Gerard lurched down the stairs, rubbing his forehead.

I rubbed mine too. I had never seen Gerard so discombobulated. But I'd only known him two days. Just because of the silly envelope. And well, popping him in the …I refused to say the word even in my mind, hadn't helped. Was it the room mix-up? I was sure that a double suite meant two bedrooms. Or was it his message from Mrs. Bakker. Was her flight was delayed?

I kneeled, then giving up on ladylike pretense, sat on the plushy carpet, and gathered the pleats of my plaid skirt around my legs.

"I might as well sort these papers here, while I'm picking them up," I said out loud to myself, or I said it to the, what, strange form I had seen? I looked down the hall. He, or she, wasn't there now. Probably slid under a door. I picked up pages and tapped them into place. The plaque on the wall indicated rooms 501 to 505 to the left, and 506 to 510 to the right. The key Gerard had tossed at me: 501.

R. Rigsby

Voices and a maid pushing her cleaning cart into a storeroom alerted me that all rooms would receive guests soon. This would look great: me sprawled on a hallway floor in a fine hotel, surrounded by papers, holdall, and an umbrella. An unnecessary umbrella so far. A short cough interrupted my papers-and-woolgathering.

A young man had come up the stairs, or sneaked, because I hadn't heard him. Now on eye level with me, he smiled through the rails on the balustrade. He wore the white jacket, which was undone.

"Hello, looks like you dropped something."

I could have made a scathing remark and ignored him, but the quirky smile and bright blue eyes left me no choice. I laughed.

"Not at all, this is a perfect place to sort paperwork. I think it's background material for my boss's speech. See?" I held up a sheet full of diagrams. He leaned forward and squinted.

"I hope he can read it. Is he the guy who almost pushed me backwards on the stairs? In a hurry to get to the bar?"

"I've never seen him drink. Shouldn't you be in the bar yourself?"

Still amassing wayward sheets, I looked up at the young man. He glanced down the stairs behind him, then at me and grinned. "Just taking a break. I like to–er–check the upper floors. To make sure everything is okay." He grinned again.

I was only half listening being engrossed in putting papers back right side up and in order. Fortunately, some were numbered, and some, thank goodness were stapled together. The brochures I read on the train had been geared to convince appliance dealers their customers clamoured for Pinnace Appliances–the best their money could buy. The papers now in a semi-sorted piles were technical details, and diagrams.

Oh, really, Lydia, you are so dense. It was a copy of the report that Gerard left in his safe. He had sent a telegram.

"Hey, you didn't happen to see anybody else on this floor, did you?"

"Just a ghost." I hadn't meant to sound flippant, but I was sorting pages. I didn't care why he chose to wander around the upper floors on his breaks. I looked up at his gasp and caught the momentary look on his face. As if he had seen a ghost. Then he grinned.

"My name is Lachlan. Lachlan Flynn Jones. Or just Lachie. Where did you see this ghost?"

Did he really believe I'd seen a ghost? "I don't know what I saw." I pointed down the hall to where the figure, person, spook, or phantom had turned into the hall to our room. "When we got out of the elevator, I thought I saw somebody turn the corner there." Speaking of the elevator must have inspired a summoning of sorts, because the light flashed, and the arrival bell dinged. "Why do you want to know?"

But my new friend spun around and scampered down the stairs.

"Well goodbye then," I muttered under my breath. The doors stood open on emptiness for a few seconds, but then closed and the elevator descended. How odd.

R. Rigsby

Vancouver, Wed Oct 7 1959: Lydia, Presences

I slipped the remaining pages back in the envelope. Sitting on the hallway floor finally struck me as undignified and I didn't want the desk clerk to see me if he too was in the habit of wandering the upper floors on his breaks. Gerard had left his briefcase, but I shoved the envelope into the sleeve of my coat, then with my coat under my arm, I had two hands free to grip my holdall and the briefcase. I stuck the fob of the room key between my teeth where it dangled against my chin. I rounded the corner into a short hallway: our suite 501 on the right and 502 on the left.

I stuck the key in the lock and wiggled it up and down, back and forth. It wouldn't turn either way. It was just like Uncle Michael's office key, I thought, remembering the night I took him from The Arms.

After dinner on the same day I had read that letter from Mr. Primnase, Georgie and I washed dishes. Uncle Michael hadn't come home, but a plate waited in the warming oven. Auntie Lou was at her bridge party. I was about to tell Georgie about the letter when the phone rang. Georgie answered. Jon Sorensen, who spoke like the first mate on a Viking ship, said her father was propping up the bar and to come and get him. There was nobody left who could take him home, and Jon couldn't leave.

Georgie sputtered, "Noooo, I couldn't," and looked like a cow going to auction. "I can't go in there," she said to me, "what if my supervisor sees me....?"

I took the phone and told Jon I was on my way. If window-shopping, the walk would have taken about twenty minutes, but I made it in under ten. I puffed through the lobby and pushed open the door to the beer parlour. Ignoring grins, I rubbed my twitching nose. Uncle Michael on a stool. Jon leaning over the bar listening to him.

"Ooohh, Marg'ret," my uncle said, staring at me with unfocussed eyes. "Been a long time."

How he could confuse Marguerite and me was more than I could figure. Marguerite was tall, red-headed like our mother, and would never in a million years darken the door to The Prairie Arms.

"I'm not Marguerite. Let's go."

He draped his arm around my shoulder, slid off his stool and would have dragged us to the floor if Jon, who had probably seen this before, hadn't come around and taken his other arm. He helped us out the front door.

"Where's your car?"

"I walked. Auntie Lou has the car."

"His office then. You can call a taxi." Jon yelled to the clerk on the desk to mind the bar for a few minutes, while we performed a parody of a three-legged race and shuffled Uncle Michael to his office door. I dug in his pocket for his keys and found the flat silver one. It stuck going in and took a bit of wiggling before the door opened. Jon dumped Uncle Michael in his desk chair.

"He's had a lot. I would have cut him off an hour ago, but I got called upstairs. My clerk didn't know how much he'd had. When I came back to the bar he was going on about old times, as he sometimes does. Don't pay any attention to his yarnings…" Jon hesitated but didn't say anything else and left.

I went to the back and plugged in the kettle. When I came out, Uncle Michael sat with his elbows on his desk, his hands supporting his head.

"So, sorry," he said. "I never meant for that to happen, damn Birch. I should have let him leave when he wanted to. My fault."

My stomach hollowed out and a lump came to my throat. David, he was talking about when David died.

That day, Georgie had called me to go to a show at the Broadway and stay overnight. Ellie was grounded. Dad was fixing the combine and Mother, pushing soggy sheets through the wringers, flatly refused to drive me. I sulked. Henri helped Dad, and Mick was off with his friends, as usual. Christine said I should help pick the tomatoes. Couldn't I see there was a storm coming? It could hail. Those tomatoes needed picking. I sulked some more. Christine had always bossed me around.

David, who had come in with an armload of wood overheard. He dumped the sticks in the wood box and said, "I'll drive her." Christine clucked her tongue. At sixteen she thought she had the right.

But Mother, like everybody who ever laid eyes on David with his red curls and magnetic smile, said it was kind of him to offer. We drove off in the pick-up, and yes, big clouds billowed, but in late July, they could blow right on by and amount to nothing. We slowed at the Pulaski's lane where their tractor was stopped on the road. Richard lay on his back looking underneath.

"Need any help?" David asked.

"No, thanks. I thought I heard something let go, but it looks fine." He came over and rested his forearms on David's window. He had to bend down to talk to David. He smiled at me, and I sat up as straight as I could for my not yet fourteen years. He was sixteen and Georgie said he was a dish.

When we arrived, Georgie and I dressed. I brought my full-skirted blue seersucker that Marguerite had sent from one of her sisters-in-law. Georgie, who never wore hand-me-downs, said I looked very grown-up. She had borrowed her mother's lipstick from her purse. We came out and found, to our surprise, that David was still in the kitchen with Uncle Michael, who's eyes didn't focus. It had begun to rain. We would be soaked by the time we reached the Broadway. I moaned. None of my escape plan had gone right.

"You two look gorgeous," David said, "too pretty to walk in the rain. I'll drop you off."

As Christine predicted, the rain became a deluge followed by hail, and the dirt roads became the famous prairie gumbo. It was like driving on a bar of soap. But Georgie and I were already inside the theatre buying popcorn. On his way home, on a curve around a low hill, David met Richard on the tractor. David swerved. Richard too cranked his wheel but instead of turning, it crashed straight into the truck and both tractor and truck slid off the road. The truck rolled and smacked into the only stand of trees in the whole five-mile stretch. Not one of them a birch.

"Marg'ret, I'm so sorry. And Keshey too." Uncle Michael's arms had slowly subsided until they became a pillow on the desk. He snored, and the kettle squealed. I sighed, thinking that coffee really wouldn't have been much help anyway.

I gave the key another wiggle and it turned. David's death was a constant presence in my mind. But why Marguerite? She wasn't even at home; she and her husband lived south of Assiniboia. And nobody had ever called Marguerite, 'Margaret.' But there was a Margaret mentioned in that letter I shouldn't have read. And that Kesey name. Unless Uncle Michael hadn't been talking about David?

Shaking off ghost-shadows of long-past history that couldn't matter now, I opened the door to a light-filled corner suite with windows facing east and south. My heart lifted, and I dropped a curtain on memories of my brother's death.

A bedroom to the right, and sure enough two twin beds. In the sitting room, I rested my palms on the window ledge. Late afternoon sun skimmed beneath a layer of cloud, promising a magnificent sunset. Long shadows striped the pavement below. On a desk under one of the windows, a note sat propped against the lamp and 'typewriter' caught my eye. One had been set aside for Mr. Bakker and was at the front desk. I sighed in relief. So, they had received my wire from Calgary. My other message had likely been delivered too.

Vancouver, Wed Oct 7 1959: Lydia, Blonding

Not bothering to lock the door, I punched the elevator call button. The third-floor light remained lit but no hum behind the doors indicated imminent arrival. No elevators in Regina had given me such an odd feeling of apprehension. Down the stairs I went, and presented myself at the desk, regretting sticking out my tongue.

Nobody was there, but I caught a whiff of familiar perfume. At a whispered "Lydia" I whirled and stood gaping.

"Ellie!"

"Shhh for heaven's sake. Quick, follow me." She, the lady of the frothing yellow curls, grabbed my arm and towed me out the side door.

"What are you doing here? And when did you go blond?"

"It's a wig. Come *on*." She turned into the lane and stopped beside two overflowing garbage cans. I shifted my feet to avoid a banana peel and a soggy newspaper.

"I got your letter," I said. "Gerard thinks you missed the train because of your mother, soooo why are you here and not in Halifax? Or I'm guessing there's nothing wrong with your mother and you're here because of something else?" A long gray cat slunk by and stared at me as suspiciously as I stared at Ellie.

"I'll explain that in a sec. Why are *you* here?"

"Gerard needed a sten–a secretary. He stopped in Regina and Miss P gave me the job. Do you have his speech?"

"No. Shoot." I'd rarely seen Ellie flustered. "It's on Gerard's desk. I didn't put it in his case." She looked at me as if we hadn't known each other since babyhood. "Oh. I see. Miss P is a lot sharper than we think, isn't she? Anyway, forget what I said in the letter. Gerard isn't selling secrets to anybody, but that rat, the man I trusted, is framing him."

"Let me guess. Regan Fitzroy."

Ellie didn't blink. "You always were quick. Oh. The Magnolia Room."

"He wasn't thrilled to meet me. I didn't say I knew you. Or what you were up to. What are you up to?"

"I've been had, and I was on my way to see Gerard at the Hotel Vancouver. That's the reason for the wig. I didn't want Regan to recognize me

R. Rigsby

before I talked to Gerard. I had expected him to stay in the Magnolia Room until every stove aligned perfectly."

I pictured Gerard doing that with no trouble at all. "Regan said he could finish on his own."

"I nearly fainted when he drove up with you in his car, but the front doorway wasn't the best place to explain everything to him, or the best time to give you a big hug."

"What happened to make you change your mind about Gerard? What happened in the first place to make you think he was a thief?"

Ellie inclined toward the brick wall, then looked at it, and straightened. "I met Regan when I started working for Gerard. I'm such a baby. He was so flattering."

Well, who wouldn't be? Even in her natural brunette, Ellie was a stunner. Regan had taken her under his wing. He was also from Regina and in fact knew many of the people she knew. Miss Primnase for one.

"They went to school together," Ellie said, "but that was in the thirties."

"How old *is* Regan Fitzroy?" He looked at least forty to me. Old.

"Never mind that, I'm not marrying him, just listen! A few weeks ago, he took me to lunch and asked me to keep a secret for the good of the company. Our table was at the back, but he looked around as if Pinnace private eyes hid behind the draperies."

I snickered.

"I know. It was so melodramatic. Then he told me Gerard was selling confidential information to the competition."

"Surely you didn't believe that?"

"I was doubtful, but soon after Gerard asked me for a design proposal from the safe, which I pulled out. Then he said I was free to go home. I got as far as the elevator and missed my coat. When I went back in, his door was open. He had his back to me, but he was on the phone and reading from the proposal."

My face showed my skepticism. "That's your proof?"

"Don't look at me like that. I'm not a complete simpleton, and yes, he could have been discussing them with a Pinnace employee, but I overheard him say 'you Empress people need to show your appreciation.' Empress Domestics is a major competitor. I slipped away, but I met Regan in the lobby. He said I shouldn't worry; he had a plan, and a board member was aware of the situation."

"He must send out hypnotic rays if he took you in."

"No really, he's very sweet and good company. He's polite to everybody and has been proper with me. It's not been easy working for a man I thought was a thief."

I stared at my shoes. "What happened next."

"Last Friday morning, Regan said there was a major breakthrough in technology and circuitry. He was certain Gerard would take the report to Vancouver and hand it over to Empress. He would then assume a new position with that company. Regan told me meet him at The York before noon with the report. He told me to leave a note for Gerard saying I needed to go to Halifax. He said he would call me when Gerard had been dealt with. When Gerard went to his usual Friday morning meeting, I wrote the note and went to The York. Never mind the rest, but that's when I found out I'm a fool. *Regan* is selling secrets and is trying to disgrace Gerard."

"Okay. Gerard isn't a traitor to Pinnace, isn't about to jump ship, ha-ha, for Empress, but he was talking to somebody from Empress. What do you think that was about?"

"I don't know. I'll ask him when I see him."

"One thing." Actually, there were several things. "So, Regan is trying to frame Gerard, but there might be somebody on the board helping him? Somebody who doesn't care if Pinnace sinks, ha-ha, if Empress gets the secrets."

"You have to quit with the dopey jokes."

"Then you came here with the report. You flew! Wow! And you left the report at the desk!"

"Yes."

"Well, Gerard got it, but he seems to think it was left by somebody else."

"Oh. I'll sort it out with Gerard. I might go to Halifax when he fires me."

"I'm sure he isn't like that. He's been incredibly kind and patient with me, despite his worry about the secrets, and when I would knock him on the head again."

"What?"

"Never mind."

"What about Miss P? Now that you know Gerard isn't a thief, and you still haven't told me how you found out, she might help. Oh, Regan knows her too."

"Yes, and I have no idea if she's complicit. You know she has shares in Pinnace? She's a director."

I thought of the notepad on her desk with the emblem like the logo on Gerard's brochures. Would she help Regan frame Gerard? Why? She said he was an old friend.

"Lydia?"

"Gerard said that Uncle Michael has shares in Pinnace too.

"I know. I take minutes at board meetings."

"Would he have a reason to sabotage Pinnace and discredit Gerard."

"Uncle Michael? Our Uncle Michael doing something illegal…" Ellie's voice trailed off.

"I know. Ridiculous." Except that he did once, long ago. Was that such a terrible experience that he had been scrupulously honest since? "Oh, I sent him a telegram about your disappearing act. You better call your mother."

"I will. I didn't want to explain anything until this business with the report was over. Where's the envelope now?"

I blanked. "It's in our–er, my room…in my coat, but," and then I choked, "I didn't lock the door. I was coming down for a typewriter. Shoot! I ran."

"You go and…"

She called something else, but I dashed inside and not bothering with the elevator, ran up the stairs.

Vancouver, Wed Oct 7 1959: Lydia, Lounge Lizards

My coat with the envelope stuck in the sleeve was where I had tossed it on the coffee table. A typewriter and a ream of white paper sat on the desk. And our luggage on the floor. Before I could gather my scattered thoughts, the phone rang.

"Do you have the report? I'm calling from the courtesy phone in the lobby, and–"

"Yes, yes," I cut Ellie off, "They're here. Gerard should be in the lounge."

"He is."

I replaced the phone and immediately picked it up again. Uncle Michael. Ellie was fine. He needed to know. He wasn't in his office, and nobody answered at the house. Georgie would be finished at the bank; she could be shopping. *Think, Lydia*. I called The Arms and waited six rings. So unlike Jon.

"Hello!" He panted like he'd run up a flight of stairs. "Uh, Prairie Arms."

"Jon? It's Lydia Perrault. Is my uncle in the beer parlour?"

"No, sorry, we've closed for the day."

Closed? Early evening on a Wednesday? "I see." I didn't see at all. "Jon, could you please give my uncle a message? He's not in his office and nobody's at home."

"Sure. I can't leave right now. I have a crew taking out that old boiler. Tomorrow, they take out the brickwork and level the floor."

Jon had listened to me about the cold rooms.

"What do you want me to tell Mike?"

"Ellie is with me. I'm in room 501 at The Sylvia Hotel. In Vancouver."

"Sure. I'll tell him." The phone clicked off.

And goodbye to you too Jon, have a fine evening. Five seconds and the phone rang again.

"Sorry about abandoning you, Lydia." Gerard. "I have some business to take care of for the next hour. Why don't you take some time for yourself before joining me in the lounge? I would like you to meet somebody. Then we can have dinner and work on the speech."

R. Rigsby

Time for myself? A long hot bath? With a shot of brandy to sip while soaking. I'd never had brandy, but in all the books I read, it was the preferred prescription for shock. Or, in this case, relief. Gerard selling secrets. Ridiculous. Ellie would talk to him and sort everything out. And dear Mr. Fitzroy would get his comeuppance. Gerard might need two secretaries. Or a secretary and a stenographer/typist. One who was happy to wash socks.

I hung my clothes. My butterflies settled while I smoothed a scrunched blouse. Why would Regan want to frame Gerard? What would he gain? Unless framing Gerard wasn't the goal but getting his hands on the secrets was. For what? Would he desert to Empress? Was it that good an opportunity? But he and Gerard were old friends since school. Whatever had happened to make him turn on a friend? What a mess. But Gerard could take care of Mr. Fitzroy. Then we would eat and finish the speech.

I gazed at the marble floored bathroom but turned my back on the shiny tub. At the typewriter, I opened my steno-book; the speech would be easier to rework from typed sheets. It was just as dull as when I read it on the train, but I typed away, humming to myself, and occasionally looking out the window at the view: as predicted, a fine sunset. I rolled another page into the typewriter.

I jumped when the telephone rang again. Oh, gosh. Gerard. I grabbed the phone, "I'm coming now Gerard." I heard an 'ahem' at the other end.

"Miss, um, this is Mr. Santos, the acting manager." He didn't know my name. "Could you come to the lounge immediately?"

I'm fired. "Yes, of course."

Not waiting for the elevator, I dashed down the stairs and into the lounge crowded with guests. I expected to find an impatient Gerard facing me across a table for two. Instead, I found a facedown Gerard lifted by two: Mr. Santos and the ghost-chasing young man, Lachlan. I had seen that pose before but couldn't believe it of Gerard.

Santos, wide eyed, muttered an apology to a nearby patron enjoying a cocktail, and the entertainment, by the look on his face. Which looked familiar. At first glance, I took him for Mr. Fitzroy, but then realized the man sipping from his glass, his eyes crinkling in amusement, was older. I couldn't think why I thought I should know him since I knew nobody in Vancouver. The young barman, now with jacket buttoned, and grin in place, winked at me. Mr. Santos scowled at him. Lachie's expression sobered, but his eyes still sparkled. Before I could ask questions, the potted palm on my right spoke.

"Drunk? We didn't even order, but he had just met with somebody. He's tired from the train ride, and I know he hasn't eaten."

Then I realized that a woman sat on the other side of the plant. Hatted and gloved, she held an unlit cigarette in a holder.

"I'm afraid so, Mrs. Bakker. Will you take him home with you?"

"No. He must be on the conference floor early tomorrow. It's important."

I stared at her, my mouth open. Mrs. Bakker? What was she doing here? Gerard said she would fly out tomorrow. And probably first class. I noted her coat's mink collar, although I had never seen a mink. Aunty Pearl had a coat with a sable collar, but this looked much finer.

"And who is this, Albert," she said, slicing a glance at me. The sparkly bracelet on her wrist flashed with every jab of the cigarette holder.

I stuck out my ungloved hand. "Mrs. Bakker, we haven't met. I'm filling in for Mr. Bakker's secretary until she is back from Halifax." Big smile. Unless she wished to appear unschooled in social graces, Mrs. Bakker had to take my hand. I expected a limp reluctant grasp, but she transferred her cigarette holder to her left hand and crushed my fingers like a farmer gripping a monkey wrench. Or farmer's son. I knew that from the mistake of arm wrestling with Henri when I was twelve.

"Ah. I see." Mrs. Bakker stared at me, but a slow smile lifted the corners of her mouth. "Then I'll give you custody of Gerard. Would you help these gentlemen get him to his room?"

His room? That was my room too, but it wasn't the best time to explain those arrangements. Then rising and sweeping–one could only describe such composure as sweeping, although I doubted she had ever in her life swept anything–she glided to the door.

"Off you go, Albert. I didn't get a chance to tell him why I flew in early, but I expect he'll be more attentive tomorrow. Please tell Davis I'm ready to go. It was a long flight and I'm fatigued. We'll not mention this to my father."

"I can manage, Mr. Santos," said Lachlan. Lachie. Albert off lifted his share of the mumbling burden and scurried out after Mrs. Bakker. I looked at Lachlan and shrugged. Lachie and Gerard, who seemed able to keep his feet with help, followed me out of the lounge.

R. Rigsby

Vancouver, Wed Oct 7 1959: Lydia, Room 502

I jiggled the key in the lock, opened the door, and stepped aside while Lachie waltzed Gerard to the bedroom. I had seen that dance before. It was much like the version in which Jon and I took Uncle Michael out of the Prairie Arms. Gerard's mumbling caused that incident to pop into my head twice in one day.

Uncle Michael had muttered the name of a man I never knew. A name that didn't die with Grand-Père. And mentioned in that letter. Had Georgie come across it too? I would ask the next time I saw her. A pebble hit the bottom of my stomach. I didn't know when I would see Georgie or my uncle or my parents again.

"He'll be out for a while." Lachlan leaned against the door, hands in pockets. I sat on the desk chair where I expected to spend some quality time. I took a good look at Lachie: slight and trim, but nicely put together with square shoulders and slim hips. My cheeks warmed. I wasn't at a stock auction.

"We didn't finish our ghost conversation." He grinned. My heart dipped and stepped up its rhythm.

"We did not. But I have a speech to type." Which sounded harsh, so I smiled. "But I have a minute."

"Did you see who was in the lounge this evening?"

"If you recall, I was busy taking custody of my drunk boss. So strange. He didn't drink a thing on the train ride here."

"Yes." Lachie frowned. "The other waiter said he only had one, but he did take some pills. The guy he sat with before his wife came in gave them to him. He said something about a headache."

Three times Gerard and I had clonked heads and that last one outside the elevator was a good one. Not the first time I had given somebody a headache.

"Who was he with?" I rubbed my own goose-egg.

"Didn't see. The other waiter served them. Mr. Bakker had his back to me, then I was called to deliver an order. I just saw hands cross the table."

"He might come around tonight, but I do need to get to work." This time Lachie took the hint and with a touch to his forehead, he left. *Hmmm. When might he go off duty? Tomorrow. Who in the lounge had so excited him?*

R. Rigsby

Burbling snores from the bedroom interrupted my thoughts on mysterious strangers. So much for me having the bedroom. I looked at the couch and at the pile of paper and my steno pad and the typewriter. It would be a long time before I and that couch met. My stomach rumbled its own observation. I wasn't going to do this on an empty stomach was I?

Albert himself delivered my sandwiches and extra-large pot of coffee.

"Sorry, Miss," he said without a trace of the derision of earlier, "we're a bit understaffed downstairs."

Was this the same man? He looked for a place for the tray–the coffee table being submerged under my holdall and coat, and the desk similarly in service to speech writing.

"Here." I pointed at the deep window ledge above the desk.

"Is Mr. Bakker okay?" He looked around.

"Yes. If you can call sleeping like a pole-axed ox okay."

"Ah, yes. So unfortunate. Mrs. Bakker asked me to leave these for him." He held up a bottle of Aspirin. "I should look, just to make sure."

Was he deaf? In addition to snores, a cough had echoed from the bedroom. I swallowed half a sandwich in one bite. I hadn't eaten since getting off the train. Stuffing egg salad in my face, I poured coffee.

Albert emerged satisfied that snores and coughs evidenced sufficient proof of life. He paused at the door to which I had followed him sandwich in one hand and cup in the other.

"Oh, just a moment." My purse. I hadn't watched every movie played at The Broadway and not learned something about hotel manners.

Albert held up his hand. "Not necessary, Miss. I'll send somebody up for the tray later."

Why on earth did he want to check on Gerard when he heard him snoring and saw his feet, shoes and all, on the bed? That was weird, even if he was delivering Aspirin which was hardly an antidote for inebriation.

I had seen a few people drink to excess and pass out. Never at our place. My mother didn't allow a drop in the house. Nor did she dance, but she loved to go to dances where she could listen to the music and chat with her neighbours. Such events entailed the whole family. As each of us kids became tired, we simply lay down on the pile of blankets and coats. I had more than one memory of friends and neighbours, who had overindulged, also taking up space on the floor. I also knew that such overindulgence led to a miserable morning after. Once, Henri and his friends demolished a bottle of rye. My mother sent him to the barn to sleep, but the next morning made him one of her tonics for headache and queasy stomach.

Gerard would need tonic. Unless Lachie was wrong about how much he'd drunk. He must have been with Regan. What did he give him for the headache? Did Ellie speak to him? *Should I try to find her?* But the speech was a long way from finished. I would get up early and find her room. If she hadn't talked to Gerard, they could meet tomorrow before the conference.

I shoved the last sandwich in my mouth, wiped my fingers and began typing and retyping. So much more could be done with a talk on stoves and refrigerators. From the material in the envelope, I found references to ovens that could sense when a roast was fully cooked and refrigerators that would set off an alarm if the temperature dropped. Wonderful stuff and into the speech it went.

A few hours later, I stood up to pop the kinks and pour the remainder of the coffee. Between gulps, I read the speech out loud, with emphatic hand motions and knowing glances at my imaginary audience. Miss P had insisted we practice public speaking. In my crowd of buyers, all faces expressed rapture at the future of household appliances.

Gerard snored in the background as I read, but we had competition. I stopped mid-sentence and heard voices, and a clatter, in the hallway. So inconsiderate. I went to open the door to tell them to knock it off, or rather, to kindly keep the racket down. I'd chained up the door after Mr. Santos left, so had to shut the door and unchain it.

The light in our little hallway flickered as I poked my head out in time to see a filmy shape disappear around the corner. The hair on my neck stood up. Across the hall, the other suite's door stood open. I stepped out nearly tripping over a tray holding a greasy plate, its upside-down dome, and a tipped over glass. I bent and righted the glass and pushed the tray to the wall. I could hear Mother tut-tutting at such carelessness.

"Hello?" I peeked in the door of 502. No answer. It wasn't a suite, just a room with a rumpled bed on the right and a bathroom on the left. I called again. A light shone under the bathroom door. Did somebody need help? I pushed the door open: nobody sprawled on the floor, and nobody stuck in the tub like great Aunt Deirdre, who my mother described as corpulent, but my dad snorted and said she was downright f–, until he caught the look on Mother's face. But no, the bathroom, except for a pink robe, and the tub were empty. On the bedside table an empty drinking glass lay on its side beside a key. A pair of dark rimmed spectacles had fallen on the floor and beside them just under the bed, a bottle. Empty.

So silly. Whoever was here just ran out for some reason. I didn't see a ghost at all, just some poor person who received shocking news and left in a hurry. I straightened the glass and placed bottle and spectacles on the table. The spectacles were at odds with the pink robe, but spots danced before my eyes, and I just wanted to lie down. I went back to the room, made more red marks on the typewritten sheets, and started retyping.

R. Rigsby

Regina, Thurs Oct 8 1959: Michael, Buried Lies

Michael stood at his office window, knuckles braced on the ledge, and blind to the familiar street. It had been an eventful week.

On Tuesday, after his walk with André, and his conversation with Bertram, he had attended to the day's appointments, and rescheduled everything else to the following week. He booked a flight, Thursday being the earliest possible.

He still marvelled at Lou's response when he had told her the truth. She said that yes, he should have told her everything all those years ago, because it wouldn't have mattered. He was the only man for her.

He must have looked shocked, because she then said, "Oh, really, Michael. I do wonder about you sometimes. It was an accident, and yes, you should have called the police. But not Mutch. I know being a lawyer was your dream, but you could have turned to another profession, and I would have stood by you. Dad too. Yes, he knew about the 'enterprise' as you called it, but believe me, he knew of others doing the same thing." She had then taken his hand and said that she wouldn't tell Georgie anything until they both knew how things would turn out. The back door opened and shut, and Georgie stood in the hall hanging up her coat.

Yesterday, Wednesday, he had visualized Jon's crew in the cellar dismantling the old boiler. He had no appointments, but had pulled a document from the cabinet, made some notations, then crossed the street to The Arms. He found Jon behind the lobby desk, catching up on his own paperwork. On hearing Michael's request, Jon called one of his workers up from the cellar to co-witness Michael's signature. Michael passed on the offer of a beer and returned to his office. He had one more item to take care of: Mrs. Croft had died, and her son had inherited the house.

Then he had filed. Which made him think of Lydia, who should be safely checked into The Sylvia under Gerard's care. Gerard should have received Bertram's warning, or better yet, both Gerard and Lydia would be safe in Bertram's house. And while he was on the subject of best-outcomes, perhaps Bertram had spoken to Regan who had accepted his apology and explanation. Regan. A sensitive child who never accepted his father's death. Maybe deep in his subconscious, he knew what happened that night.

Just before he was ready to go home, Jon had jogged across the street and relayed Lydia's message. Ellie was fine. In Vancouver. He allowed himself a moment's alarm for Ellie's safety, but surely she would have contacted Gerard, and he would have tucked her under his wing too? He called Liz, who was relieved, but then said, "That doesn't fix everything though, does it?" and said goodbye without further comment. Michael went home and during supper told Lou and Georgie about Ellie's re-emergence. Only Lou had seemed surprised.

Michael looked at his knuckles on the window ledge. For decades he had buried the truth, and it might have gone on for years, if it weren't for Lydia. She had no idea the havoc her helpful suggestion had raised. Or the ghosts it had mustered. The faces of Paddy, Kesey, and Abe faded in and out of his mind, all waiting for him to help them find rest.

He got up and went to the window. The Arms had been closed since yesterday afternoon, not that it ever looked much different, open or closed. Jon's guys in the cellar had removed the brickwork. Today they would dig down and level off the whole floor before pouring cement. How deeply had Birch buried Paddy? They might not find a thing.

"We'll get through this," Birch had said.

God, he hoped so. When this was over, he would return to Lou and Georgie and pick up the pieces. He may never lawyer again, but he could still be a husband and father. And one day a grandfather. He glanced at the clock. He should wind it before he left, but there was the cab.

Michael locked his door and turned at a beloved voice at his elbow.

"Daddy. I had to talk to you before you left. I came home early from my walk Tuesday. I overheard you talking to Mummy, but I already knew most of it. From that old letter in the files." Michael stood paralyzed, but Georgie went on. "This Regan guy sounds like a first-class fruitcake. And whatever happened all those years ago doesn't matter to me either." She wrapped her arms around his neck, and he kissed the top of her hat.

"I must get back to work. Give my cousins hugs."

Vancouver, Thurs Oct 8 1959: Lydia, Speechless

In the night, the couch and I became acquainted. I awoke stretched out on it with my notebook on my chest and my cardigan over my stomach. I swung my feet to the floor and took stock. Small brown birds in the vines outside cheeped to the rising sun. On the desk, stacks of paper beside the typewriter proved last night's industry wasn't a dream. The tray held a plate of sandwich crumbs and the empty coffee urn.

"Nobody came for the tray." My voice croaked.

"What's that, Lydia?" A light flashed on, making me blink. Gerard emerged from the bedroom, knotting his tie. Freshly showered and dressed, he looked impossibly clear-eyed for a man who should have the world's biggest hangover. Still in the clothes I wore when we checked in, I did not possess clear eyes and my hair had to be flat on one side.

"I'm sorry about the couch. I had a quick look at the speech. Excellent typing. I'm going down to the lobby. I'll use the office phone to call my wife." He grimaced. "Last night wasn't the introduction I had in mind." I must have looked dazed. "Can you get a move on, Lydia? The conference doesn't start until ten, but I want to see Fitzroy before then. And I want you to listen while I read the speech–catch anything we can change at the last minute. I'm finished here. It's all yours."

I had stood up, but the mention of Fitzroy froze me in place. Ellie hadn't spoken to Gerard. How could she when he was comatose all night? Where was Ellie? I assumed she had a room here at the hotel, but she hadn't called again. And why did Mrs. Bakker fly out early?

Gerard snapped shut his briefcase, and I snapped out of my stupor. I had put the mass of secret papers in a neat stack on top of the manila envelope. He picked a sheet and frowned as he read it, then pulled another sheet from the pile and gave it a similar frown.

"Hmmm, some good stuff in here. I'll read it later. When you come down, could you drop this off at the front desk and see that it goes in the safe?" This to my back as I dashed for the bathroom and a rummage through the closet for a fresh outfit.

A few minutes later, I stood in front of our suite, again fighting with the lock. The tray was gone and a 'Do Not Disturb' sign hung on the doorknob to

502. Whoever ran out had returned, and now enjoyed a cozy lie-in. Maybe with breakfast in bed.

In the elevator, I fluffed my hair in the mirrored wall and checked my teeth, my holdall at my feet. I hoped breakfast was on the agenda, but Gerard was nowhere in sight in the lobby. A clerk, not Mr. Santos, stood behind the desk, sorting a stack of mail.

I leaned over and spoke quietly. "Could you please tell me the room number for Marielle Tremblay?"

"Nobody by that name registered here." He didn't look up. I blinked.

"Do you suppose you could please check?" I kept my voice low and neutral and tried to smile.

"I don't need to check because I was asked the same question last night. Nobody has checked in since then, so, again, nobody by that name registered here. And before you ask, we don't have an Ellie Tremblay either."

Before I could shut my mouth, he went on. "If you're Mr. Bakker's secretary, he said he will wait for you at the car. I think he's in a hurry." I jerked away like a puppet on strings. If Ellie wasn't here, she must be at the Hotel Vancouver. My stomach protested at the change of direction, but I pushed open the glass doors. Gerard waited by the car, reading his speech.

"Could you drive? I'm a little fuzzy headed." He handed me the keys. At my gape-mouthed surprise, he said, "You do know how to drive, don't you?"

Yes, I did. With my brothers' instruction, I drove the tractor when I was twelve, and then Dad taught me to drive the pick-up and Mother's station wagon when I was fourteen. I had driven all over the farm, through mud and snow, and in our nearest village. With its single four-way stop sign. I had never driven in Regina.

"Of course, I can drive." *Really how hard can this be?* If I could keep the tractor between the rows, I could keep the car in its own lane. The Buick purred to life at the turn of the key. I gave it a minute to warm up, let out the choke, depressed the clutch, and with the barest hesitation we were off. Signalling and looking, I eased into the line of traffic on Beach Avenue. I shifted into second, then followed Gerard's directions to the Hotel Vancouver.

In the lobby, Gerard took my sleeve when I goggled about looking for Ellie. The Magnolia Room had been transformed from a depot for misplaced domestic devices to a magnificent series of displays bedecked with hanging posters and crepe paper. The Pinnace exhibit's bright blue banners lifted in the draft.

Gerard straightened a poster then disappeared behind a fridge and stove combo, as Fitzroy appeared in front of it. His surprised expression became more fixed. I made a pretense of opening my holdall in search of my steno pad.

Blast, the secrets envelope. I looked up to see Fitzroy diverting his glance to the watch he pulled from his pocket.

"Did you finish the speech last night?" He looked at his watch as if making polite conversation at a cocktail party. Not that I'd ever been to a cocktail party.

"Yes, why wouldn't it be finished?" I smothered my stammer under annoyance which added inflection to: "It only took a short time last night to type it up. We were both able to get a good night's sleep."

"I'm glad to hear it." There was no mistaking the single raised eyebrow. My cheeks warmed, but before I could jabber something more idiotic, Gerard poked his head from the other side of the refrigerator.

"Ah, Fitzroy, help me shift this just a bit. I'd like it to line up better with the matching stove, and then we'll step into the hall for a minute."

Regan didn't mean for me to catch his eye-rolling, as he turned away. While Gerard and Regan shifted and shoved appliances, I opened doors, investigated refrigerator drawers, and twiddled knobs and dials. Mother could really use a refrigerator. Or a new washing machine. No chance for an electric stove though. The farm just got service a year ago but not enough juice to power a stove. Not that she would give up the massive wood stove in the kitchen that not only cooked our food but kept one room in our drafty house livable in winter. What had Regan the Rat really asked when he mentioned the speech, and why was he surprised to see us?

I hadn't noticed that Gerard and Regan had gone out to the hallway until I saw them return. I did notice Fitzroy's flushed face and lips in a firm white line.

More people had entered the Magnolia Room, and some had come into the display. Fitzroy went to two men in suits, each of whom held a brochure, and Gerard spoke to a blond lady. Not Ellie. Where the heck was Ellie? Should I tell Gerard? Using my handkerchief, I made myself useful wiping the tops of appliances, while keeping an eye on the entry. A side door opened from where I caught an aroma of roasting chicken. Lunch.

"Lydia!"

I swung around.

"Come, Lydia. Fitzroy can handle the buyers while you and I find a place to run over the speech." I followed Gerard down the hall and into a small meeting room; a good place to tell him about Fitzroy.

"The speech, Lydia, if you please."

I stared at him. "I don't have it, Gerard. You were reading it, then you shut your briefcase."

Gerard opened his briefcase. He fanned through a report and flipped folders. No speech. He rubbed his brow. Maybe there was some residual effects of the evening after all.

"Dammit, Lydia, it's not here. It must be in the room. I don't speak until after lunch. Drive back to the hotel and get it. Hurry, please."

Vancouver, Thurs Oct 8 1959: Lydia, Collisions

I inched the Buick through traffic. It stalled once. My fault. Half an hour later, I rounded the corner to The Sylvia, but there were no spaces in front. I said a word that would flabbergast my mother. Would my use of the word shock her more than knowing where I had heard it? One can learn a lot working next to The Prairie Arms. I parked the car way up the next street and ran for the hotel.

Nobody was on the desk when I flashed through the lobby and pushed the elevator button. Nothing happened. No movement on the dial. Stuck on the fifth floor. Great. Why now? Stairs then. Head down, minding my feet, I stepped as fast as I could. At the turn for the fifth floor, I ploughed into a person coming down.

"Oof!" The explosion of breath over my head matched the impact that sent me reeling.

"Dear God woman." In a strangled breath. My head butt had caught him south of his belt buckle. "Don't you look where you're going?"

He must have been looking up the stairs if he hadn't noticed that my rapidly clicking heels bore me on a collision course.

"I was looking at my feet. These stairs are slippery. Where were you looking?" I straddled two steps and gripped the railing with both hands. My holdall had slipped off my shoulder and dangled from my arm. Hair hung in my face. I flicked it back and stared up at the man looming over me.

A beige topcoat over a dark brown suit and a similarly dark brown fedora pulled well down over his forehead. A nice wide forehead, under which were grey eyes, a forthright nose, and a mouth set in a firm line that might have held a nice smile in other circumstances. He had recovered and stood erect, again glancing up the stairs behind.

Okay, this was kind of my fault. Dad said when I had something on my mind, I could walk into the slough up to my eyebrows. I didn't know what kind of a slough this was, but I might swim out on an apology.

I held out my hand. "I'm Lydia Perrault, and I am so sorry. You're absolutely correct. I really should look where I am going."

"Lydia…?"

His brows lifted, and his mouth opened, but his face resumed its neutral expression.

"Lydia?" he said again. "Lydia, I'm Joe," his hand engulfed mine. "Mason."

Yes, he did have a nice smile even though it wasn't a full, delighted-to-meet-you-smile, but a quirked you-leave-me-no-choice smile.

"Now Miss Perrault, Lydia, why are you in such a hurry?"

Not bothering to point out that it was none of his business, I blurted, "My boss's speech–he forgot it in our room…well not our room, our room, just that the…never mind, I have to go. Very nice to meet you, so sorry."

I pushed past him and resumed my upward momentum.

"When you're not in such a rush, could we chat?"

A picture of Gerard pacing the Magnolia Room, pushed aside visions of a leisurely cocktail under the view of those grey eyes. Well almost, but it certainly left no room to wonder why a suave, good-looking man would want to chat with an accident-prone bubblehead.

"Sure." This time envisioning Gerard looking at his watch. I puffed around the corner at the top of the stairs and rammed into another man. Lachie. He had a hand underneath his jacket but fended me off with the other palm on my elbow.

"Oh, hello. A little early for a delivery from the bar, isn't it? Or are you hunting the ghost?"

His eyes widened, but his mouth crinkled into his wicked grin. "I do whatever duty requires." Lachie saluted and left.

I stuck the key in the lock. I clamped my teeth together and growled. That worked.

Inside, I scrabbled among the papers on the coffee table, looked under the cushions on the couch, and under the typewriter cover. No speech. This was nuts. He said he'd read it. I found it on the bedside table beside a half-empty glass of water and the bottle of Aspirin. *He might need these.* I took both bottle and speech and threw them in my holdall along with the–dear God, I still had the envelope. I sprinted for the elevator just as a maid, 'Lorraine,' by her nametag, pulled her cart out of room 505, blocking my path. She set her chin and made no move to give me right of way. Beyond the cart, a man in a grey suit stepped out of the elevator and the doors closed right behind him. No chance to catch that.

I U-turned to the stairs. If I was to keep galloping up and down stairs, I needed a lot more calories. I hoped lunch was still on when I got back. I leaned over the front desk. "Hello!?" Nobody came running. *Shoot.* The report was safe enough with me. In the rack of pigeonholes, I saw a piece of paper in 501. I ducked around the counter, grabbed it and after a quick look, dropped it in my holdall.

I jogged to the car. A delivery van blocked the street ahead and somebody had squeaked a motorcycle in the space between the Buick and the next car. After tacking back and forth I turned the big boat in the street and again drove past the hotel, where of course, nobody parked. I heard the siren before I saw the police car, lights flashing. In my rear-view mirror, I saw it pull up in front of The Sylvia. Such relief. It was nothing to do with me. Gerard's speech overrode any conjecture on what had happened.

I missed lunch and handed Gerard his speech just as he took the podium. He looked at the pages in front of him, smiled at the tables of attendees, some of whom continued conversations in whispers. After the predictable beginning, Gerard continued with pronouncements that raised eyebrows and elicited 'ahhhs.' Nobody whispered, and he too seemed astounded by the future of Pinnace appliances.

I stood off to the side, ready to dash in to refresh his water, but he seemed in no danger of running out of saliva. Fitzroy sat very straight at a nearby table. Gerard came to the parts about the recent advances in circuitry. All eyes were on him, but Fitzroy's found mine. He glared. I squirmed. Instead of running for my life, I smiled and waggled my fingers. He didn't smile back. I wanted to see his expression when Gerard learned the truth. Where was Ellie?

The applause brought me out of contemplation. Some men stood up. Wow, a standing ovation. A triumphant success. Gerard bowed his head to the crowd, then left the podium. The master of ceremonies tried to speak above the voices and concluded the afternoon's agenda. If anybody had further questions for any of the speakers, they could approach now. Gerard was already mobbed.

He looked happier than I had seen him in days–well I had only known him for a few days. I moved closer. Fitzroy stood at Gerard's elbow, rapidly scribbling in his order book. He should have learned shorthand. Shorthand? I dug in my holdall for the note.

Lydia, I can't believe what has happened. I'm in room 502. We must talk as soon as you and Gerard are back from the conference.

No kidding we must talk. Talk about her getting in front of Gerard. Room 502? She must have checked in later this morning. I had assumed she was already registered at The Sylvia. Maybe she had simply changed rooms.

The crowd around Gerard thinned, and many headed to the private bar, no doubt to discuss the future of kitchen stoves.

One man stood unsmiling across the room from Gerard's fan club with his arms crossed. He wasn't looking at Gerard though, he was watching Fitzroy, and when he caught his eye, he jerked his head to the side exit and walked out. I buried my face in my holdall and let a lock of hair fall forward. I watched Fitzroy as he handed his order book to Gerard, and with a quick gesture toward the washrooms, left. I started to follow thinking I could use the same excuse.

"Lydia!"

My master's voice. I spun on my heel and when in range Gerard grabbed my elbow and quick-marched me out of the Magnolia Room.

"I want to talk to you," he hissed in my ear, but not here. "Get the car while I finish up. And if you see Fitzroy, tell him to meet us in the lounge, before dinner." Dinner, yes, please. I hoped I was included in that plan, but I would have welcomed a bowl of day-old mush. And if Ellie got a chance to see Gerard, we might toast Regan's, what? What would Gerard do with Regan? Or would he have to involve somebody on the board?

And that Joe guy. Why did he want to talk to me?

Vancouver, Thurs Oct 8 1959: Lydia, Bodily Harm

Gerard stood on the sidewalk waiting for me. The big car didn't lurch to a halt nor drive over his toes. I was really getting a feel for this buggy. My pleasure withered at the look on Gerard's face.

"Drive," he said.

Two police cars took up the spaces in front of the hotel and an ambulance was parked across the street, no lights flashing. Gerard didn't comment, but instead of babbling my wonderment about what was going on, I bit my tongue, and parked around the corner, complimenting myself on some nifty parallel parking. Gerard hadn't spoken a word to me. Because of the speech? But if the man hadn't been passed out, he could have finished his own damn, sorry Mother, speech.

Gerard got out and marched to the entrance. I followed him through the lobby to the elevator.

"Wait! You can't go up there." Albert's normally slick hair looked like he had run his fingers through it a few times, his face gleamed, and the rasp in his voice stopped us in our tracks.

"Why ever not?" Gerard said.

"Because, because, the police are here. Or up there." Albert's eyes jigged toward the ceiling, and he didn't seem to know what to do with his hands.

"Police? You mean it's not you-know-who drunk and causing trouble?"

"No, not this time. No…Lorraine went to clean a room." Albert retreated behind the desk and placed both hands on the blotter. "She found a body. Dead. Room 502."

I jerked and gasped but disguised both with a grab for my holdall which fell off my shoulder.

"Who," Gerard said, Who?" like a confused owl. Albert shifted and his brow wrinkled.

"The police said not to say anything to anybody. I shouldn't even tell you, but–"

"My father-in-law is a loyal patron. Never mind then. Lydia, give me the car keys. You may as well make yourself comfortable here in the lobby

R. Rigsby

until the police say you can go up. And Lydia," his eyes narrowed. "I'll see you when I get back."

My knees wobbled, I flopped into the nearest chair and clutched my holdall in my lap. Room 502? Ellie? I stood up and stepped into the hall. Lachie came down the stairs behind a policeman standing guard.

"Sorry sir, everybody is supposed to stay where they are. Didn't my colleague up there tell you to stay put? Nobody to go up or down until they say so." He pointed vaguely upwards.

Lachlan shrugged and looked uncertain, even a bit daft. "I told the officer what I knew. Nobody said I couldn't leave. And nobody is on the stairs up there." He shrugged again, and then seeing me, winked.

The policeman peered up the stairs as if he could see through solid marble. "What, hey there Howard," he said and took a few steps up.

Lachie made his escape, but not past me. I grabbed his arm and steered him out the side door.

"Who is dead? Tell me what's happened."

He shook off my arm and looked back over his shoulder. "I don't know. For sure. Why do you want to know?"

"My friend is in room 502."

"Your friend? Lydia Perrault?"

My mouth must have looked like Ali Baba's cave, but he continued.

"That room is registered to Lydia Perrault."

"But, but…" I sat down on an ash can. I knew the lid had to be disgustingly dirty and would for sure leave something icky on my pale blue skirt. I dropped holdall and purse and leaned forward holding my head in my hands.

"Here now, you're not going to faint are you? Or puke? Come on." He dragged me down the lane to a door propped open with a brick. "Staff entrance. We're supposed to keep it locked, but a pain for anybody who wants a quick puff." Inside, a short hall lined with lockers, and through a door, a small lunchroom. He picked a glass off a shelf and filled it with water at the sink.

"She's dead?" I pulled a hankie out of my skirt pocket and held it to my face.

"She? No, it's a guy. Old guy. Somebody said heart attack. Cuz he's fat and couldn't keep up with this Lydia dame."

Well thank God it wasn't Ellie. I drank, and hiccupped.

"Here, here." Lachie put his arms around me. "Don't cry, it's okay." And because he felt so good, I pressed my face against his shoulder and hiccupped again. He held me closer and stroked my back. I leaned into his chest and then with a sigh I pulled back, wiped my nose, and smiled.

"I, I'm better now, thankyou." He stepped back but held my elbows while staring into my face.

"You sure?" And grinned at my nod. My liver flip-flopped and even while I hoped Lachie and I might have time to get to know each other, I thought of Ellie. Why would she have some old fat guy in her room? She would never ask any man into her room. Lachie watched me.

"You better tell me what's going on."

I handed him the empty glass, squared my shoulders, and said, "I'm Lydia Perrault."

Lachie leaned back against the sink and whistled. "So, who's the bimbo in that room?"

"Ellie is no bimbo. I don't know why she registered under my name. She didn't tell me so…" But I supposed that she had wanted to and would have if she'd been able to talk to Gerard last night and sort everything out, like we planned.

"Okay. I don't know what you and this Ellie not-a-bimbo gal are up to, and I don't want to know. I got troubles of my own. And I'll have more if I don't make an appearance in the bar quick. Even if a body is found in every room up there, the drinkers in the lounge still want service. You should go back in." He took my elbows again, then kissed me. Like a promise.

Giving Lachie a few seconds head start, I retraced my steps to the lobby in time to see a pair of white coated attendants manhandle a gurney from the elevator to the door. The sheeted figure bulged up in the middle. Definitely not Ellie. The officer still guarded the stair, and I glanced around the lobby, empty except for a lady in a floppy brown hat. Eyes framed in wire-rimmed glasses squinted at me over a magazine. Mr. Santos fussed behind the counter, then disappeared through a door in back.

"Lydia!" whispered the lady in the corner, but she kept her magazine well up in front of her face.

"Ellie!"

"Shhhh. We need to talk." That was an understatement. "Here." She thrust a scrap of paper at me. We were sure keeping our shorthand skills sharp.

R. Rigsby

Vancouver, Thurs Oct 8 1959: Lydia, Benched

A few minutes later, I found Ellie on a bench facing the bay. No longer blond, she had shoved her hair up under the hat that could have come from the Salvation Army. She wore a tatty coat over–her nightgown? Pale floral cotton covered her knees where the coat parted.

"You better tell me what's going on, *Lydia*," I said.

"I was going to tell you yesterday, but you took off in such a state. I thought we would catch up after I saw Gerard, but I still haven't seen him.

"What happened?"

"Regan came into the lobby just as I put the phone down. He went into the lounge and sat with Gerard. I slipped past to a corner table and ordered a drink. That young guy in the bar is too cheeky for his own good, by the way."

"Then you must have seen me and that performance with Gerard. Lachie said he saw a man, it must have been Regan, give him something for a headache."

"Lachie?"

"The cheeky young guy." One eyebrow rose. "I'll tell you later."

"Regan takes medication for something, but I've never seen Gerard take anything. I've never known him to have a headache."

"That was before he met me, wasn't it?" Ellie compressed her lips. She wanted to laugh. I glared, daring her to say anything. She sobered.

"I went back to my room and ordered supper. I decided to catch Gerard in the morning, but I couldn't sleep. I got up for a drink of water. Nobody had come for my supper tray, so I put it outside the door. I heard that guy, Wilf, wheezing around the corner. I stepped inside but didn't expect him to bash my door open. I fell on my butt."

"You knew him?"

"I saw him once with Regan, who said he was Wilf, an acquaintance. But last Friday, when I went to The York, I was early. I sat facing the door. Wilf came in. I thought then that his wheeze didn't sound at all healthy. Seeing him there felt wrong. I put my head down and looked in my purse. He went right past me to the other side of a screen of plants. I didn't know Regan was there. Wilf asked for the report and made a joke about his boss at Empress. Regan shushed him and said 'the girl' was late."

"So, Mr. Fitzroy, Regan, must have thought something happened, and you were on the train with Gerard. No wonder he was shocked to see me."

"I don't know how Wilf found me here; I was so careful. The wig, you know."

I saw Regan excusing himself and later, Wilf in the crosswalk. "He didn't. He was looking for me. He came into the lobby when Gerard handed me the envelope. Regan must have called him and told him my name. Then all he had to do was look at the register. Whatever possessed you to use *my* name?"

"I didn't know you were coming, did I? I just took the first name that came into my head."

"Like Jane Smith was already spoken for?"

"Funny."

"What happened after you fell?"

"He looked at me for a second, then said, 'You're not ...' He reached down for me. I had knocked the bottle of mineral water off the table, but when I scrabbled back, I felt it. I bopped him with it. The poor man was probably trying to help me up. I didn't believe I'd hit him hard enough to do serious damage but then he fell on the bed. He started to sit up, but I just grabbed my bag and coat and ran."

"*That* coat?"

"Yes, Lydia. I left The York in a hurry. My own coat is still in the cloakroom with my suitcase. I claimed this at the Lost and Found at the airport. I thought it rained a lot in Vancouver."

"Me too." Both of us looked aloft. Layers of cloud, but no rain.

"I was awake. The speech, you know. I heard the dishes rattle and shouting. I saw you. I thought it was the ghost."

"What ghost?"

I ignored that. "I went into the room. He must have rolled over onto the other side of the bed, out of sight." Gooseflesh rippled up and down my arms. I'd been in a room with a dead, or worse yet, a dying man. Poor Wilf. He must have been baffled when he saw Ellie and not the brown mouse who had carried the envelope to the elevator. And stuck out her tongue.

"Where did you go last night? After bopping Wilf?"

Ellie pulled her coat over her knees. "I expected Wilf to get up and leave, so I hid in the maid's closet down the hall. That's where I found the hat."

I refrained from further observations on her fashion choices, but I wouldn't let her live this down. Imagine, Miss Marielle Tremblay in a stolen hat and coat.

"I heard somebody go by, Wilf, I thought, but found my room was locked. I thought Wilf locked it."

"I saw your key on the nightstand. Why not go to the front desk for another?"

"And raise a fuss in the middle of the night? No. And I couldn't knock on your door in case Gerard answered. I wasn't about to talk to him in my nightgown, and I had no idea you were awake. I decided to wait in the closet and catch you this morning. I dozed more than I thought. I just missed you when you went into the elevator. I left the closet just before ten when Lorraine would want the cart. I went up and down the fire stairs, keeping out of sight."

Hmmm. Not entirely out of sight. Lachie might have seen her. He looked like he'd seen a ghost when I ran into him.

"I waited until Lorraine went to clean my room–so she could let me back in. Then I heard her screeching the house down. She ran out yelling 'dead man, dead man.' I couldn't believe I had hit him that hard."

"I don't think you did. He had heart failure, and from what I heard you couldn't have helped."

Ellie looked at her hands in her lap. "I could have stayed with him. Nobody should die alone."

"If only I'd been able to talk to Gerard. Lydia, where is he?"

"I don't know. He drove off. He's a tad cranky with me. I might be on the next train east. Good thing you're here to take over."

Ellie started to say something sympathetic, but I wasn't in the mood.

"I met Mrs. Bakker last night."

"I know. Marcella wasn't expected until this evening, unless she decided to spend more time with her parents, Mr. and Mrs. McCandless."

McCandless? I knew that name. It sparked a link to Fitzroy, Regan, Kesey, and Primnase. All names mentioned in that letter in Uncle Michael's office.

I had tried to forget it–Miss P would be appalled that I had read something private. I had asked her about the Kesey name, as if I'd just heard it mentioned by another student. Surprise overrode her usual frown, but then she asked me if I was ready for my dictation test.

I never thought too hard about what my uncle once did. It was over thirty years ago and seemed like it was a cottage industry in those times. But Regan was once a little boy who lost his father. But why turn on Gerard who treated him as a younger brother and a friend?

R. Rigsby

Vancouver, Oct 13 2019: Lydia, The Terrarium

The waiter tops up my coffee for the third time. I would call him a dish if anybody still uses that expression. We finished eating an hour ago. The girls haven't looked at phones, but now they glance at each other. Rennie tensed when I spoke about Lachie, her *grandfather*. Dear God, how can that be? In my mind he exists as a jaunty young man, with an impish grin. And intense eyes. He's never existed as a senior citizen, but then I still see myself as a pert and energetic young woman.

"Miss Perrault, this is wonderful," breathes Rennie, her eyes shining, but with a sad set to her mouth. She removes her glasses and wipes them with a napkin. Blue eyes, with that same fixed look, like Lachie's.

"Thankyou, Rennie. I hope you're getting a better picture of your grandfather from the little I can tell you."

"We should go," Janey says, and we all get up.

I set the pace, and Rennie tells me about her studies at UBC; she's majoring in anthropology, with a minor in history. How apt. The girls leave me at The Sylvia's entrance.

"Dad says he will pick you up around four," Janey says. "You can rest for a few hours."

I look in the lounge. Mick, at my favourite table, gets up.

"The girls look happy. The saga is going well?" To which I nod. "Isn't this brilliant weather? Just look at that view. I counted eleven freighters. I love the sailboats. We could book a ride and feel the wind and waves."

I stare at him. Is his penchant for sailing inherited? Yet on my first view of the open Pacific my heart leapt as if I too had inherited a love of crashing waves. Did one of our Perrault ancestors sail with De Champlain? "We're going home tomorrow."

He shrugs, chuckling. Is my brother losing his grip? We go to my room, which is bigger and has the better view. I stretch out on my bed to read, and Mick with his tablet settles in the armchair. His snores wake me, and the ringing phone rouses him.

An hour later, we are at Gordon and Kelsey's new house. I liked their old house. It was out of the city, surrounded by farmland. But this house has an ocean view. Gordon opens his front door and from down the hall, swathed in the aroma of roasting turkey, comes Kelsey.

"Auntie," she squeals and wraps me in a hug, and "Dad, favourite father-in-law! Come in, come in, dinner is almost ready, what a treat, I'm so glad you are here, it's been way too long." She throws coats at the rack and herds us into the living room.

I am stuffed. With stuffing. And turkey, potatoes, assorted vegetables. Kelsey kept handing me bowls and plates and how could I say no?

She brings out my birthday cake. With too many candles even if it is only one for each decade plus two. A flaming reminder of my mortality, but who will remember me twenty-five years after I'm gone? And if anybody, apart from Janey, remembers me at all, what will shape those memories? What will they remember me for? Other than being a prickly old lady who loves cake.

I laugh at the family rendition of the birthday song and make a big production of inhaling enough air to blow out the candles. Then while Kelsey slices, Mick presents me with an old-fashioned skeleton key to add to my odd collection of keys, some of which I've stolen. At least it's a collection that's more portable than say, rocks. Kelsey knit me a scarf in my favourite green and Gordon and Janey give me a little voice recording gizmo. I always carry a notepad, but Janey says this will help if I want to record more than a reminder to buy fish oil capsules.

Rennie hands me an oblong box. I slide it open to a wooden fountain pen with gold trim. She says it's one of the last her grandfather, Lachlan Flynn Jones, made. It was a hobby he took up after retirement. It's a lovely thing in bird's eye maple, and my unpredictable liver trembles. I take her hand and squeeze my thanks.

Mick and I take liqueurs to the living room. Gordon excuses himself to return a call about a broken retainer. Laughter and chatter emanate from the kitchen, along with rattling dishware and the refrigerator opening and shutting seventy-five times. I glance toward the hall. Uncle Michael's clock hangs there beside, yes, that really is his old coat tree. The clock's pendulum swings.

Mick raises his glass and looks at me through it.

"Hey, Little Sis, before you fall asleep, come with me."

We're halfway down a flight of stairs before I can think. He opens a door to a kitchen and living room with a view of the bay through an acre of glass. Janey must live here. Mick opens the sliding door to the deck, and we step out. Urban lights spray the headland across the water and ships' lights pinpoint the dark in between.

"Wouldn't you love to look at this every day?"

"Indeed." I catch on. Janey doesn't live down here–no hoodie draped on a chair, no books on the coffee table, no unwashed mugs on the counter. I'm saved as Kelsey and Gordon with the girls behind them squeeze through the door and join us on the deck.

"So, what do you think, Auntie?" Gordon's earnestness borders on anxiety.

"I think these girls are waiting for the rest of the story." Everybody laughs, and we go inside. Gordon opens his mouth, but Kelsey touches his arm.

"Why don't you and the girls stay here?" she says, "I'll turn on the fireplace."

"I'll listen in too." Mick settles in an armchair.

I've already ensconced myself in a glider rocker and footrest by the fire. Where were we? Ah, yes, Ellie in her nightgown and me in a mood sitting on a bench.

R. Rigsby

Vancouver, Thurs Oct 8 1959: Lydia, Lunch, Ladies?

A shadow fell across our bench. Joe Mason. His bulk could have blotted out two suns. He looked about ten feet tall. Would I ever be on eye level with him? I knew one way that could happen.

"Good afternoon, ladies." His pleasant rumbly voice distracted me from further thoughts along that line. "Well, if it isn't Miss Perrault. And Miss Perrault number two?" Ellie gripped my arm.

"You know darn well there aren't two of us. Why are you annoying people minding their own business?" That would shock Mother. I had shocked myself, but he had no business sneaking up on us like that. What nerve. But he did indeed have a nice smile.

"My pardon." He removed his hat and bowed slightly to Ellie. "My name is Joe Mason. But we haven't been introduced."

No point coming up with yet another name for Ellie. "Ellie, meet Joe, Joe, this is my friend Marielle Tremblay, who is in a speck of trouble." Ellie squeezed my arm tighter. "I think we need to trust Joe," not understanding how a smile and a relationship of thirty seconds assured me he was trustworthy.

"Yes, ladies, we need to talk, but not here. My car is at the curb." He replaced his hat and escorted, yes, that hand on the elbow could only be described as escorted, Ellie, while I toddled behind. *Lydia, you have seen that limp before.*

Twenty minutes later, we sat at a table at the White Lunch Cafeteria with trays in front of us. Joe picked up the tab. Ellie said she couldn't eat, and her tray held a cup of black coffee. Mine held a glass of milk, a plate of macaroni and cheese, tomato slices, a buttered roll, an apple, and two brownies on a paper lace doily. Joe had coffee and a ham sandwich. He looked at my tray and at me, biting my roll and stabbing macaroni. Ellie kept her coat wrapped close but removed her hat. Black shiny locks cascaded around her shoulders. Her green eyes had dark circles beneath them, and she wore no lipstick, but even so, she looked calm, sophisticated, and beautiful. I thought of my diminutive figure and the freckles across my nose and cheeks and felt ten years old. But a ten-year old who was finally getting a decent meal. I looked up to see Joe and Ellie staring at each other.

He cleared his throat. "Miss Tremblay–"

"Ellie. Please, call me Ellie. But who are you?"

"I'm a private investigator hired by the Kesey family to locate their relative, a Calvin Kesey."

Ellie looked blank. I stopped chewing.

"That's why I needed to speak to you." Joe turned cool grey eyes on me.

It was my turn to look blank. Good grief, the man died or disappeared a decade before I was born. And Grand-Père died two years ago. Yet, Dad would remember Kesey. Why ask me? Then a vision of a man 'with a hitch in his get-along' crossing the street outside The Prairie Arms. Where I had only been once–that night I rescued my uncle...and Jon had helped. Had Jon heard Kesey's name that night or other nights too?

I had seen Jon often while working at the Cecil. He would come in for a meal, and on slow days we chatted. I'd mentioned going to Calgary, and he said he once planned to go to Vancouver with his friend, Jig. A nice man. But old, past fifty.

"Lydia? I would like to hear what you know about Mr. Kesey, sometimes called Jig. Or rather I would like to hear what your uncle might have told you."

I opened my mouth to protest. No. I couldn't pretend Uncle Michael hadn't said anything. I bit into a brownie and smiled.

"I spoke to him, you know."

"I do know." Joe's eyebrows rose. "I saw you come out of The Arms last Monday. But I haven't spoken to him. I was on the train within the hour."

I looked at the brownie crumbs wondering if it was really bad form to lick my finger and pick them up.

Vancouver, Thurs Oct 8 1959: Regan, Final Plan

Regan slammed the door on the toilet cubicle and leaned against the door. He had barely kept his temper when Gerard confronted him about the pills. He had apologized. Just a mistake. And now this.

He couldn't believe his ears when Gerard revealed so much of the upcoming designs and concepts in his speech–designs he, Regan, hadn't known or even guessed at. Unbelievable. Gerard looked like he had found it unbelievable too, and it was obvious that, that Lydia, *girl*, he couldn't think of an appropriate name, wrote the speech. A speech that should have been as rambling and boring as any Gerard had given if it had been completed at all.

"Damn, damn, silly little twit," he said out loud. He couldn't think of her as a 'bitch;' she was way too naïve and young for that. Just a silly, silly, *girl*. 'Girl' being the worst name he could think of to call her.

The guy from Empress had had no trouble coming up with names for him, sputtering rage between epithets. The entire world, so he said, now knew what Pinnace had in the works. There was no chance of him joining if that report wasn't in Wilf's hands by midnight. He needed those specs. Empress would jump on the plans ahead of Pinnace. If no plans showed, Empress might have to tell the Pinnace board what Regan had been doing.

Damn. Regan loosened his tie. Where was Wilf? He hadn't heard from him all day. He should have got that report last night. Gerard would have been conked out on the couch and that, that, girl should have been asleep in the bedroom. The report would be in the room because he knew it hadn't been put in the safe. He had asked the clerk on the desk, who with a flash of a fiver, had been accommodating on that question and on the other as well. May as well go back to the floor and wipe fingerprints off the appliances.

Regan polished the chrome on a stove top and was surprised to see Gerard coming into the Magnolia Room.

"Hey, Fitzroy," he said, "you won't believe what has happened…"

Regan leaned against a refrigerator. Wilf. It had to be him.

Instead of helping, Gerard had been hauled away by the head of the conference committee. Then he came back, apologized, and said he had to get back to The Sylvia.

R. Rigsby

The time for subterfuge was over. he would get the report himself. It was probably still in that sack that Lydia carried. He rubbed his temples with both hands. And who was Lydia again? He thought he should know her.

Gerard had invited him to dine. He would go early. He had to get his hands on that report. Lydia would be blamed. Gerard? That plan was still in play.

Vancouver, Thurs Oct 8 1959: Lydia, White Lie Lunch

I stared at my brownie crumbs.

"I like your uncle, Lydia." Joe said. "From what I learned he's well regarded, but I know when I'm not getting straight answers. Which is why I want to talk to you. Robert Kesey is just a guy who lost his brother."

Me too. I lost a brother. I raised my head to Joe, but instead saw Georgie and me sitting in the darkened theatre. We giggled at two boys who threw popcorn at us. We looked up when the usher leaned over to whisper in Georgie's ear and without a word, she took my hand and led me to the lobby. If that hadn't been enough to make my stomach hit my shoes, Auntie Lou's face was. She wore neither hat nor gloves and her hair sported a few pinned curls. David was dead, but Richard had survived.

At least we had a body to bury. My face must have shown my misery.

"Later, then." Joe said.

What could I tell Joe? That night after I took my uncle from The Arms, maybe he was going on about David, like I first thought. *Nice try Lydia.* I had let the mention of a birch distract me. Birch was a name, a nickname for a person. Why would I need to tell Joe anything? The two incidents, Kesey's disappearance and Gerard's report, weren't connected. Were they?

Joe continued, "You two need to tell me about the dead man in 502. I heard the ruckus and stuck around. I was a cop in this town and still have friends. That room is registered to Lydia Perrault, and the police would like to speak to a tall blond. I knew it wasn't you," he nodded at me, "but I followed you to that bench, and the lady I presumed was the other Lydia Perrault, who might need some advice?"

I nudged Ellie's arm, drank my milk, and stifled a burp.

I half-listened while Ellie told Joe about the R&D report, Fitzroy's treachery, and Wilf's attack.

"Regan must have told Wilf I had the envelope," I said, "but he had the wrong room. And the wrong Lydia."

Joe sat back in his chair. The back legs creaked. He looked at Ellie. "I had a word with the coroner, an old friend of mine, and he's convinced it was a massive heart attack. The bump on his head wasn't enough to kill him."

"He fell on the bed with a hand on his head, but he started to get up. I didn't think he was badly hurt," Ellie said.

"Sounds like self-defence to me. Why didn't you call for help?"

"If Lydia came out her door, Wilf might have tried to get the secrets from her. Gerard couldn't have helped, being passed out. I had to protect Lydia and the secrets."

"Not secret now," I piped up, "I used a lot in Gerard's speech. No wonder Fitzroy glared at me."

Joe nodded. "So, he's more eager yet to get his hands on the report. Where is it?"

"Oh, in the safest of places." I had my holdall clamped between my feet on the floor. "Joe, why were you in the hotel this morning? Did you know I was there?" He must have been on the stairs for the same reason as me–that finicky elevator.

Joe shook his head. "I was hunting for Bertram McCandless. He wasn't at home, but Mrs. McCandless said he had business at The Sylvia, and would dine there. She didn't know when as she had another engagement. I went up to the dining room and he has a reservation for eight o'clock tonight. Do you know Mr. McCandless?"

Ellie answered. "I've met Mr. McCandless once or twice when he's come to Toronto. A pleasant man. He's Gerard's, Mr. Bakker's, father-in-law. What does he have to do with this Mr. Kesey?"

Click, click, click, went the pieces in my head. They were all rumrunners together: McCandless, Kesey, Paddy, Mr. Primnase, and Uncle Michael too. One was called 'Birch.' McCandless. And in 1927 a man died, and another disappeared. One was buried in the graveyard. And the other? A ghost? What happened? I had thought about another brownie, but not now.

Joe answered Ellie, but kept his eyes on my face, "I don't know that Mr. McCandless has anything to do with Mr. Kesey. Your uncle," I looked up, "said I might find McCandless at The Sylvia. It's just a line of inquiry. I'll go make a call."

In a few minutes he was back. "I'll take you to a friend." He drove us to the police station.

Afterward we waited on the sidewalk while Joe went for the car.

Ellie had told a sympathetic sergeant that she believed Wilf saw her alone in the bar and got the wrong idea. She had opened her door for room service to pick up her tray, and after the scuffle with Wilf, she had been so overcome with fright that she ran out of the room in her nightgown, although she had the presence of mind to grab her purse and coat and put on shoes. Joe, who sat in on the interview didn't say a word. The sergeant said it looked like a clear case of self-defence but would be pleased if Miss Perrault stayed in town until everything was finalized.

"You're still Miss Perrault?" I asked.

"Yes, nobody asked for ID. The sergeant must owe Joe a few favours because he didn't ask too many questions."

While Joe drove, I had a nagging question myself. Who had locked Ellie's room? I had pulled the door shut. I didn't see the 'Do Not Disturb' card, but I was tired. Did that door have a sticky catch and Ellie thought it was locked? I leaned forward to ask Ellie, but Joe pulled up at the curb and handed me his card.

"I still want to talk to you about Calvin Kesey."

Mouth still open, I saw Gerard coming out of The Sylvia. *Good grief.*

"Pull down your hat," I ground out as I opened the door, but Ellie had already scrunched her shoulders around her ears.

"I need to talk to Gerard," she said, "but not like this. I'm a mess. I need to get into my room."

Gerard spotted me half-in, half-out of Joe's car, so I gave him a cheerful wave.

"Take her to the side entrance, I'll keep Gerard busy here," I murmured, then louder, "why thankyou kindly for lunch, I'll see you later." And shut the door. Bright smile for Gerard.

"Where the devil have you been?" he said.

R. Rigsby

Vancouver, Thurs Oct 8 1959: Lydia, Advice from a Star

I felt like saying that I'd been to London to visit the Queen. Where had he been? Instead, I walked up a step, then dropped my purse, which I had unsnapped. I didn't carry a lot in my purse, but it was enough and my compact, lipstick, wallet, a few pencils, a roll of breath mints, and the key to my, our, room skittered downward and across the sidewalk.

"Oh, dear me." I put my hands on my cheeks. Slowly, I dropped my holdall beside me. I bent my knees and gracefully picked up my purse.

"Good Lord, Lydia." Gerard, probably remembering one of the times we had picked up things I'd scattered, went as far from me as possible to where my new Cherry Sunrise lipstick rolled in the gutter. "Here and here." He handed me lipstick, mints, and a pencil. Then he smiled. Then he laughed.

"We need to work on another speech. Let's go to the lounge and you can make notes while I think out loud. I don't understand what ails Fitzroy, though," to which I summoned my blandest smile. "I went back to help him tidy, but he was as edgy as broken glass. Mentioned the kerfuffle here too. I told him to come for dinner at eight. You too."

On the way in, I saw Joe exiting by the side door. He gave me a surreptitious thumbs up. Ellie, safe in her room, could refresh. And in a dress, not a nightgown.

Later, I sat alone in the lounge with a big silly grin on my face, even though my unfinished drink was a soft cider. Gerard had gone upstairs first, so I could have as much time as I needed afterward.

He had said he was infuriated with me for taking liberties with his speech, but because of the response, he had thought about it. It was high time the company showed the buying masses just what Pinnace had in the works. The number of orders proved it. The organizers wanted his closing words at the final luncheon tomorrow. Together, we had cobbled together dazzling prognostications for the glorious future of home appliances. It wouldn't take long to type. It should guarantee me a train ride back to Regina, if not all the way to Toronto. Ellie? Oh dear. I wished for something stronger than my cider.

I looked up to see the man I had seen last night, the man whose movie I had seen at The Broadway. He had aged since the film was made, which was why I didn't immediately recognize him last night, apart from being distracted by Gerard's supposed tipsiness. He emitted charisma, and it struck me that Regan's resemblance, at least in looks, was remarkable. The man winked at me.

"Can I tell you something?" Lachlan, leaning behind me. "It's about Mr. Flynn." Not at all what I hoped to hear.

A few moments later, per Lachlan's whispered instructions, I stood outside the staff entrance by the ash cans. This was getting ridiculous. Like the cat, I spent more time skulking in the back alley than inside the hotel. I had left my holdall on my chair in the lounge with my coat draped over it suggesting that I had stepped to the ladies. I pulled my cardigan closer and was about to give up when a hand reached out and grabbed my arm.

"In here." He hauled me into the lunchroom.

"For heaven's sake, what's this about?" But I hung onto his hand. He took my other hand and I leaned forward, not really caring.

"Will you ask Mr. Flynn something for me? I tried to talk to him, but Santos watches me. He doesn't like people pestering celebrities. Especially staff. Mr. Flynn likes pretty girls; I'm sure he'll talk to you."

"About what?" Why so hepped-up on Mr. Flynn when I was right in front of him? It was the reference to pretty girls that did it, so I listened.

Over twenty years ago his mother, Brenda Jones, went to Hollywood and with supreme good luck had been assigned as an understudy, or one of two or three, Lachie wasn't sure, to Una O'Connor. Miss O'Connor was then working on the film Robin Hood as the character Bess, a friend of Maid Marian. Brenda had an affair with Mr. Flynn, so Lachlan said, and he was the result. But of course, Mr. Flynn was married at the time and promised to meet her in her hometown of Vancouver before the baby arrived. He told her they would meet at The Sylvia. He never contacted her.

"Your mother told you this?"

"Well, some. Some I overheard and figured out later. But she did name me Lachlan Flynn Jones, and she told me about working in Hollywood and meeting Mr. Flynn. She hinted that they had a relationship, but I wasn't old enough to ask what that meant. She wasn't well most of the time and died when I was ten."

"You don't think she just liked the name?" I could understand Lachlan wanting answers, but the connection seemed thin. And a child overhearing a conversation? I stepped toward the door. Lachlan grabbed my hand, his eyes wide.

"Please, just ask him if he recalls Brenda Jones, for my mother, the ghost, so she can quit waiting for him."

"Your, your mother the ghost!"

"Yes, yes, I know it sounds crazy, but she came to me once when I was picking up trays on the fifth floor. I'd left the fire-door ajar, and a gust of wind blew by me. I heard her voice, '*find him, find him,*' and I saw her disappear around the corner. I've almost seen her a couple of times since then."

Little shivers danced across my forearms, but I remembered how he had trouble seeing a few diagrams on a page and wondered what he thought he had seen. Ellie in her filmy nightgown under a flickering light looked like a ghost to me as she spun around that same corner.

I was shivering when I picked up my coat and holdall, intending to go run a hot bath. I looked up and directly into the eyes of Mr. Flynn at the next table. He raised his glass to me.

"Mr. Flynn." I walked, reeled in on a line, "Please pardon my intrusion," not that he looked at all intruded upon, "I saw Robin Hood in my hometown a few years ago and I enjoyed it very much."

"A few years ago? Good heavens, the film is ancient. How big is your town? Never mind, please, sit. I must go in a few minutes, but I'm always happy to speak to a fan." He had risen slightly but sat again when I dropped coat and bag and sat with my purse in my lap. "May I order you something?" He signalled toward the bar. Lachlan, back in place, watched us with eager eyes.

"A mineral water, please." I hadn't intended to sit, or drink, but Mr. Flynn's allure as movie star, even though that star was fading, compelled me to sit back in my chair, sip my water, and smile. He looked every day of what I knew was about fifty years, but the youthful handsomeness remained in the lines of forehead and jaw.

"Now, Miss, er,"

"Lydia. Just call me Lydia."

"Lydia." He circled his glass at the room. "Tell me, what brings you to this fine old establishment?" So, I did. I told him about coming out on the train, and the conference, and, surprisingly, how I missed my family. I opened my notebook and showed him the smooth ruled paper and my diploma in the pocket. I told him how I wouldn't have a job if it weren't for my dear uncle, and I hoped that my boss would keep me employed when his regular secretary returned. I told him how much I enjoyed working and couldn't picture myself in a kitchen or hanging laundry. He laughed at that and told me of his 'past' as an actor, and his current desire to write. We laughed together and then I noticed Lachie hovering at another table.

"I have a friend who knew somebody who worked on Robin Hood. Do you recall meeting a Brenda Jones? She was an understudy to Miss O'Connor."

R. Rigsby

"Hmmm, not by that name." He wrinkled his brow. "Was that the name she used?"

"Oh. I don't know." I couldn't jump up and go ask Lachlan. Wouldn't he have told me if he knew his mother used a stage name?

"Lydia, there are always many people working on a film and sometimes if two actors aren't in the same scene, they might never meet. I'm sorry." He did look sorry, and I was sorry for asking.

"It's quite all right. It was just a passing thought." His expression brightened at that, while behind him where he wiped a table, Lachie's darkened.

Mr. Flynn glanced at his watch. "I am sorry my dear, I must run, but I have so enjoyed your charming company. Excuse me." He rose and bowed. I watched him walk away and was surprised that he had an aura, or it could have been the lowering sun slanting through the windows. Such a lovely man. And I really had loved him in Robin Hood.

Vancouver, Thurs Oct 8 1959: Lydia, Gerard in Charge

Mr. Flynn disappeared through the entry, then time resumed its onward march. Still under his spell, I sleepwalked to the elevator, where two arriving guests with a pile of luggage waited. I went up the stairs thinking I would soon have calf muscles like Harry Jerome.

"Lydia!" Lachie bounded up behind me. "What did he tell you? Did you write it in your book?" I stopped and he stepped up, his face eager.

"I'm sorry, Lachie, he doesn't remember your mother, at least not as Brenda Jones." I had to say something in Mr. Flynn's defense. "On a big movie like Robin Hood, some actors, and especially understudies, might never see each other if they're not in the same scene." How had I become the font of all knowledge on movie making? "Hundreds of people work on big productions, and your mother would have been–"

"Just one of hundreds?" Hot colour flooded Lachie's cheeks. "My mother was just one of *hundreds*? Hundreds of girls he slept with?" He clenched his fists and glared.

"Well, no, he–"

"Jones. Where do you think you're off to?" Mr. Santos stood at the foot of the stairs, hair and eyes gleaming.

Lachie didn't offer his usual cheeky reply. He brushed past Santos but looked over his shoulder at me. My liver didn't like that look one bit. Suddenly tired, I plodded up to the fifth floor.

I tapped on Ellie's door, and said, "Gopher, gopher, who's got a gopher?" A silly game we played as kids.

"Where have you been? I expected you an hour ago."

An hour? Was that all it had been?

"I'll tell you later. Obviously, you had no trouble getting in here. As Miss Perrault?"

"Yes, once they found another key. Joe said that after my nasty shock, for which he holds the hotel accountable, I had run out and called a friend, insinuating himself. He's very tall, isn't he? Then that odious little man on the desk couldn't have been more helpful. The police were long gone; the room was cleaned. I caught the elevator just as you and Gerard came in. Joe went to his office and will return to see Mr. McCandless after dinner. He still wants to talk to you."

Ellie had swept her hair into a sleek roll with a kiss curl in front of each ear. She wore a black shift and matching bolero and black heels. She looked like she had spent the day in a beauty parlour. I looked like I'd spent a week on a threshing crew. My pale blue skirt had a smudge near the hem and my white blouse rumpled over the waist band. I felt sticky and tired.

"Lydia? What's the next step here?"

"Let's go see Gerard."

"Good Lord!" Gerard, on the couch, dropped his sheaf of notes and almost tipped the coffee table when he sprang to his feet. "Where did you come from? You two know each other?" Which needed no answer. "Does Liz, Miss Primnase, know about this? Both of you, sit, explain. And it better be good."

"Mr. Bakker, I'm sorry. We've been friends since—"

"Miss Primnase told me about Ellie," I cut in. "I'm sorry I didn't tell you, but I didn't know why she missed the train. I do now."

Gerard sat down and tapped his glasses on his knee. Ellie told him everything. About Fitzroy, the theft of company secrets, the incident in the York, her flight.

Gerard interrupted, "Sorry, Ellie, just to clarify; the report I collected at the desk is the one you brought with you?" to which Ellie nodded. "And my speech is…?"

"Gerard, it's on your desk. I didn't put it in your case."

"It's fine," Gerard smiled at me, "Your stand-in has done a wondrous job, it turns out, but please go on."

Ellie reran the miserable tale of Wilf's demise. Except she omitted Joe's help and only said she had talked to the police who believed the bop on Wilf's head was self-defence.

Gerard leaned forward with his elbows on his knees and contemplated his linked fingers. "Ah, Regan," he sighed, "something has troubled him for a long while. I don't know what."

Me neither. Regan's father died when he was young, but Gerard was a little boy too. His father had the hardware store, which was now The Cecil. Fred, his name was Fred. The Fred mentioned in the letter? Of course. But he wasn't a rumrunner.

"Does Regan know you're here?" Gerard went on, and Ellie shook her head. "Well, you must join us for dinner. It'll be an interesting party, don't you think?" And grinned at our open mouths. "I'm going down to the lounge." He stuffed papers into his briefcase. "Lydia, you can have the bathroom."

Bathroom? Dear God, yes. I leaped up to see if I owned anything suitable for dinner. Ellie followed me to the closet. She flipped hangers.

"Go have your bath, Lydia, I'll find you something to wear." Had she brought her fairy godmother's wand? When I came out, towelling my hair, a straight green skirt and a matching sleeveless top lay on the bed beside a fuzzy cream coloured jacket with elbow length sleeves. Angora. Abracadabra.

"Close your mouth, Lydia. I arrived here with only my purse. I had enough money to shop for a few things. Oh, and on Tuesday I sent a wire to Georgie. At the bank. I figured somebody should know I was here."

"Not me?"

"I couldn't send it to the house, could I? Auntie Lou? Why we write in shorthand?"

I could only shrug. Besides, I was on the train. We rolled the skirt's waist band and snugged it with safety pins. Ellie's high heels in warm vanilla were too big. I didn't want to make a grand entrance tripping over my own feet. She buffed my tan pumps.

"Alright. Hair." She parted it on the left, combed it off my forehead and over to the right and clipped it with an emerald barrette.

"There," she pronounced helping me into the jacket. I didn't fill out the top as much as Ellie, but I could sashay into any dining room, which we would do in an hour.

An hour in which to type. I fed a sheet into the machine, opened my steno pad, and clattered away. Ellie left, I presumed to touch up her already perfect self.

"I'm almost done," I said when the door opened, "Let's eat!"

"Sounds good." Followed by a chuckle, but I had already whirled in my chair.

"Uncle Michael!" I ran to hug him. "What are you doing here?"

"A most helpful young man in the lobby told me where to find you."

"My friend, Lachie!"

"Then Gerard came out of the lounge and invited me to dinner. Does he carry that briefcase everywhere?" He held my elbows. "You look splendid, by the way. Georgie sends hugs."

"Thankyou, but what are you doing here. In this hotel?"

"You sent me a telegram, remember?"

It seemed years ago. "Yes, didn't Jon give you the message? Ellie is fine. Your other favourite niece had some troubles, but we have it worked out now."

"Jon gave me your message, but I had to make sure you and Ellie were safe. There are other developments which I will share with you, but not just yet."

My brain fizzed but didn't register the look on his face, or his mention of 'safe.' "Joe Mason wants to talk to me."

R. Rigsby

"Mason? You ran into him?"

"Quite literally. But, you should know–"

"Later, later, Lydia. For now, I'm looking forward to watching heads turn when you walk in for dinner."

I could have cried then. Instead, I laughed and said I looked forward to that. We had time. Joe wouldn't be back until after we ate. And I had a speech to finish. Uncle Michael said he would wait for me in the dining room.

I typed, humming, editing as I bashed away. I heard the door open as I whipped the sheet out of the machine.

"Would just like to proofread. Then we can go."

"Well, well, look at you, all scrubbed up. And so efficient too." Fitzroy closed the door behind him and stepped toward me.

I spun in my chair thinking the seat was well polished. *The nerve of the man coming in here without knocking. The nerve of him coming in here, period.*

"Gerard isn't here. And I'm busy."

"Well take a break and hand over that envelope."

"It's in the hotel safe."

"Is it?" He grabbed my holdall and dumped it out. The envelope hit the floor, but the flap held. He picked it up and stuck it under his arm.

Such a shame that although he resembled Mr. Flynn when looking pensive, he didn't at all with, what Dad would call, when Mother wasn't around, that shit-eating grin.

Vancouver, Thurs Oct 8 1959: Lydia, Regan Revealed

"I don't think so." Ellie, hand on doorknob, exuded icicles of elegant fury. Regan turned his head, grin gone. My head planted Regan about the same time she punched him in the nose. Telepathy. Regan and I flailed on the floor. He curled like a crayfish, grabbing nose and crotch. I rolled away with the envelope. Ellie shook her hand, then inspected her manicure.

Regan gaped at Ellie. "You *are* here!" He rolled onto hands and knees. "You didn't use your name, did you?"

"No, you insufferable weasel. I've told Gerard everything."

Regan balanced on his knees. His eyes rolled up and the red splotches on his cheekbones faded to washed out puce.

"Regan!"

Ellie and I jumped and goggled as Miss Primnase swooped into the room and settled beside Regan. She put one hand behind his neck.

"Look at me! Deep breaths, remember? Look at me."

"Miss Primnase!" Miss Primnase?

"Here you girls," she said, "help him onto the couch." Which of course we did.

"Liz, Liz?" stammered Regan. He wasn't expecting her either.

"I had to stop you, Regan, before you do something stupid. Whatever you are planning is wrong and Gerard is the wrong man."

The door opened, and there was Gerard.

"What the devil?" He looked from one face to the other. "Liz? And you, Regan? I know what you've been up to. I just don't know why."

"I finished your speech." My lame words prompted an outpouring from Miss P and Regan.

"Gerard, you just don't get it do you?" Regan.

"Gerard, Regan doesn't know." Miss P. "It's my fault. I should have told you at the station. But I had to talk to Regan first."

Gerard held up his hand and the gabble died off. Regan, steadier from whatever had struck him, glared at Gerard. Gerard met his gaze. "I'll get to you man; we'll sort it out. Marielle, tell him what you told me."

R. Rigsby

"You, you said Gerard sold secrets to the competition, and somebody on the board of directors helped." Ellie spat. "Then I overheard you talking to, to, that man…who died."

Regan hung his head. He knew about Wilf then. He looked at Gerard. His eyes bulged; his nostrils flared. "Yes. I've been selling information for years. But when the board finds out, they'll fire *you*!"

"Selling to the competition?" Gerard said. "What competition? That sneak from Empress? We leak misinformation to them all the time. Even with the real specs, they don't have the equipment or financing to build a better toaster. What were you thinking man? Why?"

Ellie and I stared at Gerard as if he had grown another head. Fitzroy sprang to his feet, fists in balls at his side, ignoring Liz who plucked at his sleeve.

"No, Regan, no," she whispered. Ellie and I met each other's glances. Was this the same woman whose voice rang from one end of the school to the other?

"Blast you Gerard! Or should I call you *Birch Junior*? Too late to make your old man pay, but I could ruin your life, just like your old man ruined mine."

"My father? My father ruined your life? What on earth are you talking about? We've known each other since we were kids. You never said a thing."

"Because I didn't know until after he left town–Fred *Birchmann* Bakker. The rumrunner. Birch."

"He was no rumrunner; I guarantee you that. Birchmann was his middle name, but he was never called Birch."

"Regan," Miss Primnase said, "Gerard isn't Birch, never was, but I know who is. I should have told you, but, but…" she took a big breath, "Bertram McCandless is Birch."

"My father-in-law? Bertram McCandless, who was a friend of our fathers, is Birch?" Gerard said. "Whatever did he do to you?"

I stared at Gerard. *Oh, no.* I got it. My uncle didn't do anything. It had to be McCandless, the old friend who saved his life in the war.

Regan looked like he'd been slapped with a fish. "McCandless? McCandless is Birch?" He put his head down and Liz rubbed his back, but I caught his fleeting look of recalculation. I added insanity to the list of whatever else was wrong with him.

"I'm sure my father-in-law can explain. He's been trying to talk to me, but we keep missing each other. Regan, I don't understand what you have against Mr. McCandless but perchance Liz can tell us."

As if all our heads were on invisible strings, we looked at Liz. She pursed her lips and opened her mouth. And then we looked at the ringing telephone. Gerard snapped out of the trance first and picked it up.

"Yes, my dear, we'll be right up." He replaced the receiver and stood up. "Regan, this story can wait until you're fully recovered." He placed the envelope in his briefcase. Regan, who still looked green stared at the snapping catches. "Liz, why don't you take Regan to…"

"Ellie's room," I said, "She can stay here with me tonight."

"Yes. Excellent. Liz, make him lie down and rest. You two," he smiled, "look lovely, but come along, I'm sure you can use, if not a good meal, a stiff drink. As can I."

Liz hauled Regan to his feet, Ellie rose in a graceful sway, and the four of them made for the door, Gerard carrying his briefcase. I looked at the speech. I hadn't reread it, and the way things happened in this hotel, I might not get another chance.

"Gerard, I want to proofread your speech."

"You're a good girl, Lydia." The door closed behind them, and I melted onto the couch.

Stiff drink? I could use one now. Thoughts jumped in my head like grasshoppers on a summer day. I wanted them to settle. Into nice orderly rows, not that one could expect 'hoppers to do so, but I could at least queue up some thoughts. Forget the speech. I opened my notebook and in shorthand wrote everything I knew: from my uncle's drunken mutterings, his sober anecdotes, and Mr. Primnase's letter.

Regan's father died at the border when he was young. Was his father's sudden death so traumatic that it still gnawed him? David's death was traumatic, and I still cried when I thought of him, but I didn't blame Richard. Or did I?

Or was there more to Regan's rage? What did he see before Uncle Michael took him home? Why so rabid to find Birch? Now revealed as Mr. McCandless who I wouldn't know if he delivered a Scotch and water to me right now. I had never had whiskey of any kind, but after these last days…*Good grief, Lydia. Only three nights ago you boarded the train.*

If offered, I would have drunk that rubbish they once sold to the Thirsty States. Dad called them that once. He was a young man during prohibition, but he wasn't involved. Unlike my uncle, the ex-rumrunner. Did he know Regan blamed Birch? But blaming was one thing, doing something about it was another. Ruining Gerard's company was a ploy to get even, but what now? What was that calculating look about?

I lifted my pencil. What else? Grand-Père's conviction that somebody died in The Arms. Probably learned from my father. A speculation in confidence, that as he became older, became fact? Dad always looked worried when Grand-Père mentioned le fantôme in The Arms. Uncle Michael was there the night a man disappeared, and another died at the border. And Joe Mason was trying to find out what happened. He was coming to see McCandless after dinner. And my uncle would be there.

The phone jangled, much like my nerves, and I scrawled the last figure on the page. *Answer the phone Lydia.* It was probably Gerard.

"Hello, Miss, er, it's Mr. Santos. I have a call for room 501."

Poor Mr. Santos still didn't know my name.

"Lydia?" In Jon's usual roar. "It's Jon Sorensen, t'ank goodness I found you. My guys dug up a body in my cellar. They were pretty shook. A man. I can't get hold of your uncle. Tell him, please. And tell him I understand. And Lydia, I called Joe Mason. And the constables too."

"Jon, I'll tell him. Thankyou." I sat down like a popped balloon. A body in The Arms. Is that what Regan had seen? Kesey? Or his father? I thought I was going places, but now I wondered if I really wanted to be here at all. Yes, I did. Grand-Père said a ghost haunted The Arms and now a body had resurfaced, literally, in the cellar of that creepy old hotel. Constables? Joe? What about Uncle Michael?

Vancouver, Thurs Oct 8 1959: Lydia, Admissions

I grabbed my purse and key from the coffee table. The key wouldn't fit in the lock. It was Gerard's car key. No time. I rounded the corner into the main hall and *oh great*, Joe Mason came out of the elevator. I about faced and ran for the fire-stairs. Good thing I wore my sturdy pumps and not tricky stilettos.

The door slammed on Joe's shout, but I was already halfway down the flight to the fourth floor. I exited the fire stairs at the third floor and heard the fifth-floor door bang. I eased my door shut and dashed for the main stairs and hoofed to the top floor. I had to find my uncle and warn him. *And then what?* In the hall outside the dining room, I paused near a planter of aspidistras by the elevator and smoothed my hair. I walked the remainder of the hall gulping air and inhaling the scent of prime rib. The maître de smiled as I approached his podium, but Uncle Michael had seen me. He came forward, offering an arm, then his expression became intent.

"What's happened? Bad news?" I pulled his sleeve, looked over my shoulder, and headed toward the north fire stairs. Quick on the uptake, he held my elbow and kept up with my brisk steps.

"Joe Mason is chasing me."

"Chasing you! Why the bugger, I'll take his head off."

"No, not like that." I shut the door with a minimal plink. "Joe wants to ask me, and you, about that Kesey guy who disappeared years and years ago. And a body has just been dug up in The Arms. Jon called me because he couldn't get hold of you. He said he understands. And I think I've worked out why. But I want to hear it from you."

"You read the letter, didn't you?" My uncle aged ten years before my eyes. He leaned against the wall, and I thought he should mind getting chips of peeling paint on his fine suit.

The door banged open. Not Joe, Regan. Talk about aging ten years. A lock of hair hung in his face and his eyes blazed. He would look positively rakish on the silver screen. He was still pale and his hand on the door shook.

"Oh, it's you," he said, looking at my uncle. "The maître de said he saw a man go this way. I thought it was Birch. McCandless."

"Regan. McCandless is in the dining room with Gerard, Marcella, and Ellie. I'll talk to you, man to man, then we'll talk to Bertram together."

R. Rigsby

"We need to move." I had peeked through the strip of glass in the door. "Joe just came off the elevator. If the maître de is still in a helpful frame of mind, he'll send him this way. I've got Gerard's car key. I'm just not sure where he parked the car." I headed down the stairs. My uncle, helping Regan, followed.

"Joe who?" Regan's voice quavered but he kept up with our downward flight.

"Regan, Joe Mason is a private investigator looking into the disappearance of Calvin Kesey which is linked to the death of your father. Later, I will ask him to take me to his sergeant friend at the police station." He saw me look back over my shoulder. "Ellie told me about the man called Wilf." Regan groaned.

"I told Wilfred to go to Lydia's room and get the report. I told him Gerard was so doped he wouldn't be a problem."

"What did you give him?" We were out the side door, a door I had used more than I had the front entrance, and Gerard, bless his heart, had parked the Buick just down the street.

"Oh, something I take," Regan said. "I told him it was for my headaches. I do have those, but my other prescription isn't a good mix with alcohol. It would knock him out. You should have been asleep in the bedroom and Gerard zonked on the couch. Wilf said he could look at the register and lift a key. He wasn't supposed to bull his way into the wrong room and scare the bejesus out of poor Marielle." He opened the Buick's back door. "That crook at Empress sent Wilf to work with me. I'll need to speak to that sergeant too. Poor Wilf. He wasn't the brightest, but he shouldn't have died like that."

A few minutes later, following Regan's directions to a café on Denman, we sat at a table in the back staring into black coffees. Uncle Michael reached inside his jacket and pulled out a silver flask. Regan nodded, then after a micro-second, so did I. I hadn't had anything to eat in hours. The whiskey warmed my fingernails. Regan took a big swallow then looked at me.

"I remember you." Which I thought odd since I had head-butted him less than an hour ago. "No." He smiled and lost twenty years. No wonder Ellie was charmed. "I remember you from your christening party, and a, a friend's funeral."

Of all the things he could have said to me, that was the least expected. I stared with eyes that were probably losing focus. All I could do was smile in return.

"I'm sorry I was such a dick to you. Liz straightened me out on a lot of things." His expression of sadness and confusion would have melted a marble angel's heart.

"Which *I* should have done years ago." Uncle Michael said.

"A body has been dug up in The Arms cellar," I said. "Jon thinks it's Calvin Kesey." We may as well get all the chess pieces on the board.

"And who was Calvin Kesey?" Regan frowned.

Uncle Michael reached across the table and grasped Regan's hand. "Kesey worked for McCandless, but the body in The Arms is not Kesey. It's your father, Paddy Fitzroy."

Just as I thought. So Kesey is…? But Uncle Michael continued.

"It was an accident. A blow-up that shouldn't have happened. After, I should have gone for the constable, but I was a coward. Too afraid of losing my girl and my dream of being a big shot lawyer. Which is ironic because I'm a long way from being a big shot of any stripe. I thought the damage was done; nothing would bring back your father. I didn't know the memory of that night haunted you. I'm sorry."

Regan put his palms over his eyes. "All these years, I knew, I knew he wasn't in that graveyard. I never went there. My mother tried to take me, but I wouldn't go past the gate. She knew Dad drove booze for Birch, but she never knew about you."

Channelling Miss Primnase, I reached over and patted his back. The waitress lifted her eyebrow as she poured another round of coffee, matched with another round from the flask.

"Because I left to get my degree and didn't come back for over five years. I was a rumrunner though, make no mistake, even if I only minded the money. I saw your dad drive up that night and park in front of The Prairie Arms. When you followed, I went after you. Your Dad and Birch were fighting. I pushed you out of the way at the door."

"Birch killed my dad. I remember. I saw my dad fall. He died then didn't he?"

"He did. His bad leg gave out when he took a punch and he fell against the table. But Regan, Birch didn't swing that last punch. I did. I killed your father."

I stared at my uncle. Ice water flowed through my veins. He hadn't just covered up for Birch. I held my mug with both hands, which wanted to tremble.

Regan paled, and I thought he might again be on the verge of blacking out. He swallowed and gripped his own mug, not looking at us. "My dad wanted to quit. But Birch wouldn't let him."

"When we meet with McCandless, we will explain everything we did, and why."

Regan nodded and his breathing deepened. "Okay."

We all startled when the waitress poofed out of nowhere and stood beside our table.

"Closin' in five minutes."

R. Rigsby

I walked like a robot out the door, Regan behind me, while my uncle paid the bill. I wanted to keep walking, walking, all the way home to Regina, to the farm, and the drafty bedroom I once shared with Christine, but it was all I could do to walk to the car. I took Regan's arm. "I'm sorry about your father. You were a little kid; you shouldn't have been there. And Wilf. I know you feel it's your fault."

"It is my fault. A crazy plan."

"I saw Wilf in the lobby that afternoon. I think his heart failure was just a matter of time." If we talked about something else, I wouldn't think about the other thing. Why did my uncle hit Regan's father? "Wilf shouldn't have been able to get a key. Joe said the police found it in his pocket–"

"Did they find a gun?"

"Gun? Ellie didn't see a gun."

"It's mine. Wilf said it might speed things up if you gave him trouble. Maybe he thought better of that and didn't pick it up from where I stashed it."

My uncle came down the walk. Without looking at him, I handed over the car key and got in the back. Regan got in front. He turned toward my uncle.

"You were always so good to us, my mother and me. Always there when we needed something. You and, and, old Primnase. Why did you hit my father?"

"Birch fell over you, but your father laughed and didn't drop his fists. I just wanted it to stop."

Uncle Michael started the car and looked in the rear-view mirror. "I'm sorry Lydia."

Vancouver, Thurs Oct 8 1959: Lydia, Regan's Revenge

I let Uncle Michael guide me into the lobby, empty except for Mr. Santos who nodded at us and then left the desk to go into the back. I looked at the rack of keys and again thought of Wilf. Mr. Santos had to find another key for Ellie. What happened to the key I saw on the nightstand? I hoped the dining room was still open. I didn't want to eat, but my mind seized on anything to think about, other than, what, my uncle's betrayal? Ever since I read that letter, I assumed that Mr. McCandless, now revealed as 'Birch,' had been responsible for whatever had happened. Mr. Primnase thought so.

The elevator opened to Gerard, Marcella, Ellie, and a big man. In a grey suit. Mr. McCandless?

"Ah, Lydia, Michael, you missed dinner." Gerard stuck his foot out to stop the door closing, his briefcase in one hand and Marcella's hand in the other, "We gave up waiting for you. Regan, you look somewhat recovered. Good. Liz is running all over the hotel looking for you. I told her to wait in my room. You can excuse your truancy to her there and catch me up on everything tomorrow. I am taking," he put his arm around her shoulders, "Marcella home. She isn't feeling quite the thing."

They looked at each other with the goofiest of smiles. Marcella looked rosy to me. My eyes met Ellie's. Telepathy again.

A different intuition entirely crossed my mind when I saw Mr. McCandless. Birch. The man who got off the elevator when Lorraine blocked the hallway. It felt like ages ago but was only a few hours past. Mr. McCandless took over holding the elevator door with one hand, while the other held a large fat envelope. Another copy of the secrets. Gerard and Marcella walked away, and Mr. McCandless watched his daughter with the tenderest of smiles, sharply interrupted by Regan.

"Mr. McCandless. I'm Regan Fitzroy. May I have a word?"

"I know who you are son." McCandless' joviality was completely at odds with Regan's ominous tone. And completely at odds with the glitter in his eyes. I heard my father once say to Uncle Michael that he wouldn't trust, a name I didn't catch, as far as he could pitch his tractor. It wasn't an argument, but I sensed the tension. Neither of them noticed me on the hassock beside the bookcase. Brown on brown. Yet Birch had been Uncle Michael's friend for years, had saved his life in the war, and was apparently a doting father.

"Why don't we go up to the dining room to talk?" I slurred and swayed on rubber legs. Ellie stepped forward and linked her arm in mine.

"Yes," she said, "it's open for another hour." I dipped my head toward the restrooms. "Lydia and I will join you in a minute." The contained rumble of male voices, Regan and Birch, with Uncle Michael's even tones, were cut off by the swish of the elevator doors. We met Lachie in the hallway, jacket unbuttoned, and tie askew. He squinted at me and again I wondered if he needed glasses.

"It's him isn't it, with your boss's friend? I saw him earlier, going into the elevator, but couldn't find him, and he didn't show up down here."

"Who?" I said, not caring because the whiskey in my stomach had sent out a warning burp. *Uncle Michael?* Lachie had told him where he would find me. "Sure," I answered. Ellie closed the restroom door, and I made it to a stall in time.

"You shouldn't drink on an empty stomach." Ellie ran water into a glass.

"Since I got off the train, I've had trouble getting one decent meal a day."

"Then let's get you something." We waited at the elevator and then waited again while several people exited, all chattering about their terrific meal.

"Oh dear," Ellie said, "I think the dining room is closed after all." For once, my stomach didn't notice the mention of food. Instead, I doubled up. Ellie missed catching the elevator door, being engaged in holding me upright, "What did Uncle Michael tell Regan?"

"His father's body has been dug up in The Arms. They want to talk to Joe." Forming words had become work. I wanted to get horizontal. I could tell her the rest later.

"Joe's in the lounge. He didn't see me take the glass."

Did you hear that?" I had heard a muffled pop, then another. Then nothing. Ellie frowned and looked up. She'd heard something.

A few seconds later the elevator door opened. On a nightmare. Regan sprawled in the corner, eyes closed. Uncle Michael lay against him, eyes open, and blood gushing from a hole in his chest.

"Uncle Mike!" I screamed, but his eyes fixed on McCandless, crouched in front of him. I pushed into the elevator, the doors closing around my midriff as I dropped to my knees.

McCandless too had blood spurting from under the fingers he held to his neck. The other hand gripped a gun. He dropped it and slipped an arm around Uncle Michael's shoulders.

"Mike, Mike, look at me," McCandless panted, while I jabbered incoherently and pressed my hands over the bleeding hole.

"Birch, old buddy, this's it," my uncle wheezed, "Lydia, dear niece, don't blame…" He closed his eyes. Suddenly, strong arms lifted me and shoved me into Ellie.

"Come away, Lydia," she sobbed, "Let Joe help." She dragged me to the far side of the lobby to the armchairs under the window. Chaos. People rushed in from all directions: Mr. Santos, the maître de from the dining room, who must have come down the stairs, and the other barman from the lounge. Miss Primnase whirled around the corner from the stairs, then on taking in the scene, flew shrieking at the elevator. Then police and ambulance attendants, and stretchers going out the door. Sirens' wails faded as Joe appeared in front of us, blood on the knees of his pants and on his jacket and hands. Then we were in the lounge.

"He's dead, isn't he?" I hiccupped into one of the towels Joe had snatched from the bar. Blood on my dress, blood on my hands, blood on my towel. Ellie had her arm around my shoulders and held a bloody towel too. Joe took our hands, bloody towels and all.

"Your uncle, yes, I'm very sorry. So is the big guy, McCandless? He took one in the neck."

"Regan?" Ellie said.

"He's not dead. Not shot either, from what I saw. They took him in the ambulance. That crazy woman went with him."

R. Rigsby

Vancouver, Sun Oct 13 2019: Lydia, No Happy Ending

Gordon pulls his car up in front of The Sylvia. Mick eases his door open, maybe not wanting to disturb the ghosts. He needn't be so careful. No ghosts haunt The Sylvia. Ghosts haunt people, not hotels. I am trailed by the ghosts of everybody who was once in my life. That's some cavalcade of fantômes. Grand-Père would have laughed.

Janey stirs as if awakened, but her occasional hand squeezes told me she was there for the whole ride. Rennie, hunkered down on my other side, hugs her backpack. She hasn't said a word.

When I gasped out the last of the story, or where I ended it, she leaned forward, eyes huge behind her glasses.

"What about my grandfather?"

"I never saw him again. Mr. Santos told the police Mr. Jones had finished at seven and gone home. I didn't tell the police I saw him just before it happened. He was probably checking for his mother's ghost again. It didn't matter and he didn't need any more trouble with Santos."

Rennie waited. Had she thought Errol had confessed about Brenda Jones, and I'd kept it from her? What had Lachie written? I should have asked to read the letter. I tried again to make it clear that that was the end of my friendship with her grandfather.

"A few months later, I called the hotel and asked for Lachlan. I spoke to Mr. Santos who was again his usual smarmy self. He told me that young Jones had quit the day after the incident, as he put it, and he was glad to see the back of him. And Mr. Flynn had died in Vancouver on October 14. On my birthday."

That was when Kelsey came downstairs.

"That's more than enough for tonight," she said. "You girls will have a lot more time to ask Auntie questions," she turned to me, "if you would do us the honour of living here with us?" The uplift on the end of that sentence matched her uplifted eyebrow, an image of her mother. Mick, sitting in his armchair, smiled. The big secret agenda revealed.

I said it had been a wonderful Thanksgiving and birthday celebration, but I was tired.

I'm glad I told Janey about Uncle Michael. She will no doubt pester the daylights out of me for more family history. Despite my curmudgeonly acknowledgement of birthday wishes, I'm happy to celebrate sixty full years of adulthood. Not that some scrapes exhibited great examples of adult decisions.

Tomorrow, my real birthday, is also the anniversary of the deaths of Paddy Fitzroy, Calvin Kesey, and Errol Flynn. I can never observe a birthday without remembering Mr. Flynn's kind assurances that choosing 'work' (they didn't call it career then) over 'wife' was not a selfish thing. That poor troubled man, who Lachie was convinced was his father.

Janey opens the door and steps out, holding out a hand to me. Rennie leans forward across the seat, face eager.

"Did my grandfather call or write to tell you anything else?" I catch Janey's annoyed glance at her friend, but I pat her arm.

"I'm sorry Rennie, that's all I know." Rennie subsides into the seat, her backpack held to her chest. Mick and I assure them we can manage from here.

"Nightcap?" he says.

"Well yes, why not? I'm not likely to sleep." The lights are low in the lounge, and our preferred table is free. Mick, not waiting for the server, goes to the bar. I ease into a chair and look through my reflection to the bay. The clouds that moved in earlier have departed, probably to dump a load of rain on Coquitlam before sailing eastwards. Tomorrow, we will sail eastwards ourselves.

I examine the short glass of amber liquid Mick sets in front of me. Whiskey? I do my own version of eyebrow lifting, which probably makes me look like a puppy hoping for a biscuit. A Shar-pei.

"In memory of our uncle." Mick lifts his glass and sips. "You didn't tell the girls what happened next or how everything turned out. Was that on purpose?"

"Yes. Rennie had lost interest, and Janey, well, she knows there's more. And she will hear it."

"Refresh me."

Vancouver, Thurs Oct 8 1959: Lydia, Aftershock

I woke, or regained consciousness, stretched out on a couch, with my head on a lumpy pillow and a damp cloth over my forehead. I heard ragged sobbing and at first thought it was me. I opened my eyes. It wasn't me. Ellie, whose lap supported my head, smothered sobs in a handkerchief. We were in Gerard's suite. I sat up and took Ellie's hand.

Joe's voice boomed from the bedroom where, if he wasn't talking to himself, he was on the phone. He emerged, pinching the bridge of his nose.

"An investigator is coming up to talk to you."

"Do they know what happened, Joe? Ellie said."

I knew the answer. Regan. Regan, not two hours ago, had said he owned a gun.

"They won't confirm anything until after the gun is fingerprinted and such," Joe said. "Santos had me call Mr. Bakker, Gerard. He's shocked, but he won't leave his wife and her mother right now. Gerard believes Regan tried to get that report from McCandless. I mentioned the body in The Arms cellar, but Gerard doesn't believe his father-in-law or Michael Kerr had anything to do with that."

Glasses of water appeared on the table in front of us and I drank mine in one gulp. My head throbbed, but my stomach had settled. Uncle Michael. I stifled a sob. Did I want to reveal his part in a thirty-two-year-old crime? Was I that angry? I opened my mouth, but the only sound was a knock on the door.

The detectives were polite, considerate, and cool as they took statements. I told them my uncle and I went with an old friend to a café. We came back and met everybody coming out of the elevator. My boss took his wife home. The three men went up to the dining room and Ellie and I went into the restroom. When we came out, the elevator opened to the three men. Ellie's statement was even more brief, and Joe's merely said he had been in the lounge.

The detectives knew there was more. I could tell by their flint-eyed glances at each other and at Joe. I cried again when I thought of the bleeding men. Ellie sat beside me and shook, so they said that they would come back in the morning. Joe saw them to the door and stepped outside. Male voices resonated through the crack in the door.

I wiped my face and blew my nose. I should write down everything I wanted to say. The next interview wouldn't be as accommodating. The detectives would ask me the same question five different ways. I slid my holdall from the coffee table onto my lap. Only my steno book inside. And the umbrella. No notebook. I hiccupped. Uncle Michael. I looked under the table then got down and looked under the couch.

"Lydia, what are you doing?"

I went to the desk and looked behind the typewriter and on the chair. "My notebook. The one—Uncle Michael gave me. I left it here, when, when, I left to go find him and warn him about—Joe." No point hiding that detail now. Joe had come in the door and leaned against it, hands in his pockets. At my mention of his name, he looked up and a sad smile lingered on his face. I stifled another sob and knew every thought fanned across my face like a series of cards we used to flip when we were kids.

"Lydia, they think Regan fired at McCandless, who then got hold of the gun and tried to fire back at Regan. They think your uncle, either on purpose or by accident, got in the way."

I looked at my stocking feet. Where were my shoes? Why did Regan lie to me about the revolver? Was he that shaken and confused? Could it have been stuck in the back of his pants all along? Or in his pocket? You'd think you would notice a thing like that. Unless he picked it up outside the dining room. In the aspidistras? Where he had stashed it for Wilf?

"I should have taken my uncle to you."

"Lydia, it's not your fault. None of it."

My culpability hadn't surfaced in my mind, but at Joe's words, it erupted like the bloated carcass of a lost cow which bubbled to the top of the slough practically under our feet. My sisters and I had been wading and catching frogs. We screamed, but Marguerite, the most sensible of my sisters, grabbed a pink hoof and pulled it closer to shore. That thing had to come out of there. She tied it to a willow using her hair ribbon, a bright pretty tether for the stinking mass that my father and brothers later dragged out and buried. I would have liked to bury the memory of my last sight of Uncle Michael along with the bloated mass of my own guilt. The tether pinning it to the surface of my mind was neither pretty nor bright. I should have told my uncle about Regan's gun. It was my fault.

Somebody tapped on the door and opened it. A strong long-fingered hand on the door followed by a worried face.

"Richard," I shrieked and charged like the Roughriders right tackle. He lifted me off my feet and pulled me against his chest where I fell apart in gibbering sobs. At the same time thinking that I'd never seen him in a suit he looked wonderful the blue pin stripe was a smart choice and he even smelled good.

Over my head, he said, "The desk clerk, Santos?, gave me the awful news." At my renewed sobs, he held me tighter and patted my hair. I felt the pieces of myself coming back. I wasn't okay. I would never be okay again. Nor would Georgie and Aunt Lou and Ellie. Nor my mother or father. But we might gather up enough of ourselves to go on.

R. Rigsby

Vancouver, Wed Oct 14 1959: Lydia, Birthday Wishes

I sat on what had become my favourite bench overlooking English Bay. *Happy Birthday, Lydia, you have completed your first year of adulthood.* A sharp breeze pushed grey waves onto the shore and blew around my shins. My nose ran and eyes bleared. The seagulls screeched like neglected screen doors, but none of them wanted to pat me on the back and bring me a cup of tea. Which was why I had spent hours on the bench since last Thursday, when, I learned to say it, sometimes out loud, Uncle Michael died.

Mother and Dad, and Aunt Lou and Georgie, had flown in and taken charge of everything. Or rather Dad and Mother did. My heart broke at the tears in my mother's eyes. I don't think I had looked closely at her for a long time. Silver threaded her auburn curls and faint crinkles surrounded her eyes. She seemed smaller too.

"Maman," I squeezed her in a hug, "I'm okay."

She was shocked about Regan but adamant that he hadn't shot her brother. "He was such a sweet little boy. It wasn't his fault that his unhappiness and illness twisted his perception of his father's death."

Joe had learned that the body in the cellar of The Prairie Arms couldn't be Calvin Kesey. He was in the Great War, but unlike Paddy Fitzroy, he came home with two whole legs. And they found a wedding band. Joe said they would exhume Paddy Fitzroy's grave, and the police surmised that body was Kesey's.

I hadn't told Joe, or any detectives, about Uncle Michael's confession to Regan and me. Nor about Mr. Primnase's letter. I suspected that Miss Primnase would take care of the letter. Dad had given her Uncle Michael's keys and asked her to check for mail, and make sure there was no milk going sour in the kitchen, which even I recognized as code for taking care of anything incriminating. He had asked Aunt Lou if this was alright and she'd twisted her soaked hankie and said, "Yes, yes, André, whatever you think best." Georgie was a mess too. I wanted to offer my notebook, but it hadn't turned up.

I felt desolate without it. I mourned its loss as if the soul of the uncle I once knew resided within its beautiful covers. I was suspicious of Lorraine,

R. Rigsby

who I thought still blamed Ellie, and by association, me, for her nasty shock when she fell on top of Wilf. She won't clean the fifth floor anymore.

Gerard didn't give the closing speech at the conference, and Ellie helped him with other arrangements. He didn't need me to wash his socks, but he gave me a fat cheque, and I was on the payroll until again employed. Being his usual kind self, Gerard said he had a small task for me before I accepted anything. As if the lobby held a queue of prospective employers in need of a steno who wreaked havoc wherever she went.

The wind picked up and a spattering of rain splashed the rain already on my cheeks, then suddenly I was in the lee of a mountain. The mountain held an umbrella. My umbrella, or rather Georgie's.

"Georgie thought you should have this. I've been invited to your birthday lunch on the condition that I fetch you in." Instead of fetching, Joe sat beside me, holding the umbrella. "I didn't see your boyfriend with everybody in the dining room."

"He's not my boyfriend. But we have an understanding." Richard. I couldn't believe how glad I was to see him. A lifeboat in a churning eddy when I was going down.

"He seems like a good sort. Down to earth. Calm under fire. Working hard on his farm."

"He is." As well as kind and patient. And willing to give me more time. I was supposed to marry him. He had loaned me the money for my course with the promise that if I didn't get a job before my birthday, I would marry him right away. If I did get a job, I would pay him back, but with the implication that we would marry eventually, when I was ready. He went home on Monday, and before he left, we had a long talk on my bench.

He had said that the money didn't matter; he would wait for me for years if that's what I needed. He had held me close, and I leaned into his shoulder, my head under his chin. How wonderful it would be to be taken care of forever. To just say yes, let's announce an engagement right this minute. I opened my eyes and saw a sailboat scudding along on the bay. A man with blowing russet hair held the tiller.

"Should we go now?" Joe said. We stood up. "By the way…"

My birthday party wasn't as dismal an affair as I had anticipated. Despite his looming funeral, I felt Uncle Michael was with us in spirit. This was helped along with the spirits in a bottle of whiskey, Dad, of all people, procured and kept under the table. Mother, of course, abstained, and so did Marcella. However, I nearly fell off my chair when Mother ordered a glass of sherry and joined in the toasts to my good health and long life.

Marcella raised her glass of water. She was still devastated by her father's death, but I overheard her telling my mother that due to the circumstances, she was delighted that her mother would live with her and Gerard. Then Gerard made an announcement that explained some of those circumstances. In mid-March, he and Marcella would finally become parents.

We stood in a ragged ovation joined by Miss Primnase who soared into the room with coattails billowing and a radiant smile.

"Oh, Gerard, Marcella! Congratulations my dear!" She kept her arm around Marcella who, to my amazement, dabbed moisture from her eyes.

"How is Regan?" Marcella asked, which I thought might dampen a party whose celebratory spirit was an uncertain glow. We were still waiting on the police to make an arrest. When Regan woke up in the hospital, he couldn't remember a thing. Not just what had happened in the elevator, he couldn't remember most of that entire week. Then he had another episode, a bad one. They ran tests. That bullet in his head had to come out.

All eyes turned to Miss Primnase.

Miss P beamed her joy, oblivious that sympathy for Regan might be mixed. "The doctors said the operation went well. He woke up and knew who he was and recognized me."

Gerard put his arm around Liz, then everybody took seats as the head waiter bore a cake to my table with twenty-two candles ablaze. I blew without setting my hair on fire and laughed as I cut pieces for all.

Gerard turned to me, "Lydia, about that little task." I hoped he didn't want an answer because I had my mouth full of angel food. Ellie looked smug.

Before I could swallow, Joe said, "She already has a job," and laughed. I suspected he'd had my mother's and Marcella's share of the whiskey.

"Lydia," Gerard continued, "would you, with Ellie and Georgie, drive the Buick to Regina? After Mr. McCandless' funeral?" Ellie smiled and Georgie looked more alive than since she sobbed her way into The Sylvia five nights before. "Marcella and I will fly to Regina…then we will ship the car home." Then his mouth quirked, "After Michael's funeral."

R. Rigsby

Vancouver, Sun Oct 13 2019: Lydia, Whiskey Recap

Mick examines the whiskey in his glass. "Regan Fitzroy. When Noreen and I moved back to Regina, I met him, but he had no idea who I was."

"He didn't know me either when I went to see him a year or two later. He was glad to talk to me though, and we had coffee at The Cecil. I think I gave him my name three times. When I said I had to go, he thanked me for the coffee, but he had again forgotten my name. After his operation, Regan had no recollection of the conference, or getting on an airplane, or why he was in the elevator. The police had a hard time working out who shot who."

"It was eons ago, but they had pretty good forensics then."

I sip. I had no idea Mick is a connoisseur of fine whiskey. "Regan's prints were on the gun, but he said he last saw it in a drawer in his apartment. There was gunshot residue all over the elevator, but only McCandless had it on his hand."

"Gerard knew that Regan blamed McCandless for his father's death."

"Yes, but Gerard told the police he believed Regan was fixated on the secrets, and in his unhinged state, thought he could still take them to the competition."

"Did he know about McCandless's whiskey running?"

"If he did, he didn't disclose it for Marcella's sake, or his children's. Pinnace would never have survived without McCandless' money. Or Uncle Michael's. The Toronto plant cost more than expected. Pinnace might have gone under if our uncle hadn't invested. Gerard told Ellie when she became a director."

"And the bodies dug up in Regina–Paddy and Kesey?"

"Because of the still which burned up in the garage, they concluded that Paddy, Kesey, and Primnase had been rumrunners. A falling out resulted in Paddy's death and The Arms cellar was a convenient burial site. They knew McCandless was the primary owner but the few people who knew him from those days, including a Mr. Mutch, were emphatic that he was nothing more than a respected hotelier."

"And Miss Primnase?"

"She wasn't happy when the police linked her father to the deaths of Paddy and Kesey. But she couldn't tell the police about the letter without giving the police another motive for Regan shooting McCandless. She believed our uncle saved Regan when McCandless tried to kill him."

"With Regan's gun?"

"She claimed Regan had the gun for his own protection and McCandless got hold of it. I saw McCandless get off the elevator just before Lorraine went to Ellie's room. He had the report. I think he planned to leave it in Gerard's room. When Lorraine screamed out of the room, he could have gone in, and found the gun on Wilf. Anyway, Miss P never believed Regan did it. It caused a rift in her friendship with Gerard and Marcella."

"But you don't believe McCandless did it."

"No. Regan did it. When they got off the elevator, the maître de turned them away because the dining room had closed. Regan might have stashed the gun in the planter or somewhere nearby. He shot our uncle. McCandless grabbed the gun, but Regan shot again. Then he collapsed."

"But you didn't tell the police that. Offered Regan's revenge as another motive for their case? In fact, nobody mentioned anything about Regan's vendetta against 'Birch,' and our uncle's participation in the whiskey running. And you never told me that Uncle Michael caused Paddy's death."

"I thought Dad told you."

"No."

I look at my reflection, then at Mick. "How would that have changed anything? Other than ruin Uncle Michael's reputation? What he told Regan and me wasn't evidence. Jon Sorensen had nothing but Uncle Michael's drunken ramblings, which he kept to himself. He accompanied Kesey's body to Vancouver for reinterment. He had long ago promised to go to Vancouver with Jig and was glad to keep his promise."

"So, you making that choice wasn't the same as Uncle Michael making his?"

"I didn't say anything then, but now I have told Janey. Rennie only paid attention when I spoke about her grandfather. Even if I had told the police about Regan's real motives, it might not have been enough for a conviction. The man was so damaged. At the trial, his lawyer maintained he wasn't mentally responsible due to the bullet, and the prosecution couldn't prove he had fired the gun. Afterwards, Miss Primnase took him home to Regina, where they lived happily ever after." Mick snorts. "Well, they lived together after. Regan needed care and Miss Primnase needed to care for him. He lost his memories of what happened to his father and never mentioned him again."

"What did they live on? Was her school that profitable?"

"It lasted through the sixties, but Regan still leased out the farm, and she had her Pinnace shares. She willed them to Ellie and me."

"Ah. The indomitable Marielle. Uncle Michael's will was a surprise. Who knew he had so much to leave and so many people to leave it to? My inheritance funded my schooling and probably saved me from becoming a vagrant."

It's my turn to snort. Mick would have eventually set his sights on something.

About that will. The bulk of our uncle's funds and shares and property went to Auntie Lou and Georgie, but many other people inherited. He left his Pinnace shares to Ellie and me along with instructions. We receive dividends from stocks bought with rumrunning money and Kesey's stash. Pinnace thrives despite being forced to contract out to other countries. I get reports but have long let Ellie vote for me. She has a better head for it. The faux pas of Gerard's speech was her last mistake. Her sixth sense on financial matters rivals that of Birch.

How many other people still reap benefits from money made on prohibition? Of all my heirs, only Janey will inherit my Pinnace stocks. And now that I've told her about her Great Uncle Michael, she will inherit the ghosts too. But not too soon, I hope.

Mick twirls his glass on the table. It clunk-clunks in a circle, like his mind.

"Before you start listing pros and cons, we should move to that marvelous suite, if you aren't worried about offending Jasper and Desirée."

Mick stops twiddling his glass. He's probably considering another. But neither of us have lived so long without making some good decisions. He pushes it to the center of the table and sits back.

"I called Jasper. He's relieved because Charlie and his wife want to move home. With their kids. So there go our two rooms."

"Your grandson hasn't had the best luck. What happened?"

"He lost his job; she hates the city. They think the farm is the answer."

No more farm for us. We can watch sunsets from our deck or almost any room from the whole bottom of the house. It's immense. Kelsey intends to install her mother in the third bedroom. Des' brusque management of our welfare irks me, but am I ready to be kept like a hothouse plant behind that wall of glass?

This isn't how Mick or I envisioned our so-called golden years. Each of us should be with the one we loved best–his dear Noreen and my, well, it could have worked out that way.

Mick helps me out of my chair, and without hesitation, I head for the elevator.

R. Rigsby

Vancouver, Mon Oct 14 2019: Lydia, Finding Home

We stand in light rain outside The Sylvia. Michael, no, Mick checked this morning, and we will land in brilliant sunshine. Positively perverse. But that's the trade-off between Regina versus Vancouver. More sun, but colder. I've never bought the nonsense about 'a dry cold,' no, it's just freezing. Mick's laugh when I groused about that this morning gave me goosebumps. He looks and sounds like Uncle Michael. I have caught myself more than once calling him that.

Gordon drives up, and Janey bounces out of the car. Kelsey holds the door. And more than once I have called Kelsey, Ellie. Her hair is a shade lighter than Ellie's, when it was black, but she is as tall and willowy. And as generous and faithful. I really must call Ellie. She should retire. She and Mick get on so well, especially when lauding their mutual grandchildren: Janey and her brother, Royce, who didn't make it home for Thanksgiving but will try for Christmas.

The ride to the airport is uneventful, and I look forward to a few hours in which I won't be required to talk. Mick will fall asleep before the plane clears the tarmac.

"I can go through security with you," Janey says when Gordon stops at departures. We all kiss, hug, wave, and Janey helps us check in.

At our gate Mick wanders off to the kiosks. Janey thumps her backpack at her feet in front of our seats. "Auntie. I know why you told me about Uncle Michael. You're going to leave me your shares in Pinnace."

"I am."

"It's like a trust, isn't it? You trust me to do what's best with them? Like continuing to support 'Finding Home?'"

"I do." She smiles and there's no reason to explain further.

"Speaking of trust…" Janey rifles through her backpack and pulls something out. I stop breathing.

"Rennie didn't know until she heard the story how special this was to you." She strokes the worn leather surface now bearing scratches which only add to the patina. My notebook. "When her grandfather died, Rennie and her dad found this. Rennie wanted to keep it but changed her mind."

R. Rigsby

I take my notebook in both hands. Where my initials were once tooled, there is a bad scrape across the leather and only the LJ is readable. They must have thought it was for Lachlan Jones.

"Oh, Janey," I breathe, for once at a loss for words, "I can't believe it."

"Here's the letter. Rennie wants you to have it."

It's on a grocery memo. There's a cartoon image of an overflowing grocery cart on the top, and a brown ring stains the bottom. The writing is regular but spidery.

Dear Rennie,

You need to know about me and my father, Errol Flynn, but I won't be able tell you. You must find Lydia Jane Perrault. She is alive and knows about the ghost. Ask her about all that happened in October 1959 at The Sylvia Hotel. When you find her, you must return her notebook. She will understand. Love you, Gramps.

"Rennie thought of me right away when she read your name, but of course she Googled you and was amazed at what came up."

Amazed? That's one word for it.

Time has ticked on. Mick appears when the attendant calls for people with children, and all croakers to get first dibs boarding the plane. They don't word it like that, but that's what it means.

"Janey, my lovely." Words have returned. "We didn't talk about your studies, and why you aren't sure what you want to do." I'm an idiot. Janey laughs. I clutch the notebook in my arms. Mick drags me to the desk and yammers in my ear about getting out my passport.

"Don't worry Auntie! I totally know what I'm going to do!" She blows a kiss.

Within the hour, I'm in my window seat with a view of nothing. The pilot assures us we will soon fly under sunny skies for our viewing pleasure. Like a flight to Acapulco and not a two-hour commuter ride. I hold my notebook on my lap. When I showed Mick, he too rubbed the leather but smiled and handed it back to me. He's now snoring and may lay his head on the shoulder of the lady next to him. She stares at her screen.

I take a breath and open the notebook. A few yellowish ruled pages remain on the pad and disintegrating crumbs fall from the glued top. I lift the front pocket. No diploma. He must have thrown it away. I run my finger down the center and lift the tab to reveal the hidden pocket. Where Uncle Michael tucked that five-dollar bill. I pull out a folded page with my name in Lachie's spidery writing. It's wrapped around another sheet of paper.

Vancouver, Wed Oct 14 1963: Lydia, Every Wish

I get up to look for an envelope for the freshly typed invoice and snag a nylon on my desk's crooked and splintered drawer.

"Damn, the second time this week!" I say, without even thinking about Mother. After all, she's in Saskatchewan.

Joe comes to his office door. He looks at his watch but stands there with a mug of coffee. And a dopey grin on his own mug. Which alerts me that something is up. I've worked for Joe almost four years, enough to know that dopey grins aren't his usual expression. When there is one, I take note. I wait for him to tell me he has a new client–one he hasn't told me about.

Somebody pounds on the door, which Joe reaches in three strides.

"Happy Birthday, Lydia," Joe says, opening the door for two delivery guys who wrestle a handcart through the door. Strapped on the cart is a desk of gleaming dark wood. I waste no time in clearing my files, telephone, notepad, and pens, and the picture of my parents, from the old beast. They load it up to take away. For kindling I hope.

In the nick of time because I was about to bill Joe for another pair of ruined stockings. He did say that if my skirts weren't so short, my stockings would last longer. I told him his fashion sense peaked in 1950.

Joe retreats to his office and returns with a pot of chrysanthemums which he sets on my desk before going out the door.

"I'm going to see an old friend–the Maguire case. Back in an hour." Which means he's seeing a sleezy informant in an even sleezier locale. Probably one of the hotels on East Hastings. A place to which he won't take me, even in my capacity as useful observer.

Often, on such excursions, I sip a beer, cross my legs under my short skirt, and look as vacant as a ventriloquist's dummy. But one with working ears. Sometimes this distracts Joe's informant enough to trip him, or her, into saying something they probably shouldn't.

I rub my hands over my new desk, enjoying its shiny surface, its rounded edges, and its smooth-running drawers. My lovely plant, telephone, notepad, and pens are in place. I should make some calls–the Maguire case is just one of three which Joe and I have on the go, but it *is* my birthday.

I lean back in my steno chair and gaze out the window to the peek-a-boo view of The Sylvia. So much has happened since that week that changed everything. I did not marry Richard. When I started work for Joe, I told Richard that I needed a year on my own, but within six months I told him that I wouldn't marry. Not just him. Anybody.

I love my freedom. I have my own apartment. I walk everywhere: to work, shopping on Granville, to Stanley Park, to the beach in the summer. I have friends and for the first two summers, Ellie and Georgie spent a week with me. We hiked up Grouse Mountain, swam at every beach, and danced at The Cellar. When Georgie got married in the spring of 1962, Ellie and I stood as bridesmaids at her wedding. People kept asking us when it would be our turn, as if you could pick a date and Prince Charming would show up with enough lead time for a respectable courtship and engagement.

Ellie came to stay with me again this summer. Joe loaned me his car and we took a ferry to Vancouver Island, and then drove to a tiny village on the west coast. The Pacific's rollers pounding the beach lulled us to sleep in our rental cabin, but we were too nervous to do more than wade in the waves.

When I'm not dining and dancing, going to shows at the Orpheum, or exploring the city with friends, I enjoy my cozy living room, which is also my cozy bedroom. In my stuffed chair by the window, I people-watch, read, or write letters to my family.

Everybody is doing as well as can be expected after losing Uncle Michael. Mother and Dad appear to be back to normal, but I know from what Mother doesn't say that she still suffers. Dad calls me every two weeks, and of course I speak to Mother too. The family grows. I think I have eleven nephews and nieces, courtesy of Henri and my sisters. Mick isn't married, but in his last letter, he hinted that his latest flame might be more special than all the others put together. I'm going to Toronto next summer, so if the mystery lady is still a thing, I will meet her.

Ellie sees Mick often. They are as much like brother and sister as Mick and me. She's moving up with Pinnace; she manages the entire clerical department and joins board meetings. They have to let her in because of the shares we own, courtesy of our uncle. Gerard is her mentor, and she has become good friends with Marcella, who had twin girls, a happy surprise. Georgie and her husband now have a son they named Michael. No surprise.

I started working for Joe in January of 1960. When I drove Ellie and Georgie home for Uncle Michael's funeral, I had planned on returning immediately to Vancouver. But Ellie and I stayed with Georgie and Auntie Lou and helped them sort out Uncle Michael's things. We three mutineers, as my mother once called us, hadn't had so much time together in years. We talked about everything, including Uncle Michael's endless stack of filing.

Because Uncle M just lumped any of Miss P's business in the old folder he had for her father, Georgie had read that letter. She kept her mouth shut when she found it, not like me. Georgie knew long before me that our cherished uncle and father was once a rumrunner. When I showed my surprise, Georgie just rolled her eyes. From stories her grandfather, the banker, told her, she grew up knowing that illicit whiskey stills had been prevalent, if not rampant. Ellie too, learned this from Georgie, but Ellie hadn't found the letter and knew nothing of Regan. Where the heck was I? Stuck on the farm without a clue. Neither of them felt an inclination to share what they knew with the police, because really, why?

When Ellie flew home to her parents in Halifax, I too went to mine. Mother thought I was home for good, but Dad knew better. I stayed until after Christmas. Mick had come home for the funeral, and then again for Christmas, for our mother, but he and Dad found some common ground. I think Dad finally saw that Mick wasn't in danger of becoming a shiftless bum.

Mick had to go back to Toronto after New Year's, so I called Joe. Dad drove us to the airport, and we got lucky–both of our flights left on schedule with no weather delays. I cried all the way to Vancouver, but my heart lifted at the first sight of the mountains. And seeing Joe. He knew what I needed more than I did, because we came straight here to this office. And my scabby old desk where on some days, my phone didn't stop ringing.

Robert Kesey credited Joe for finding out what happened to Calvin. Joe has become good friends with John Kesey, Robert's son. When Ellie was here, John took her out. She's fond of him, but she's not ready for anything serious. Robert started a charity to help alcoholics–he calls it 'The Finding Home Foundation,' I think that. Joe helps. I had no idea that Joe was once much more than a social drinker.

Joe doesn't need me to take dictation, but I spend hours in libraries and city archives searching directories and such. I can usually find what he needs. And when a call comes in, I can sense a good case–good being one that will be relatively easy to solve and will pay well. Some days the phone rings more often than others, but we are doing okay financially. I have a new desk to prove it.

I look at my desk and at my phone, which, and I think this is a gift of mine, often rings when I look at it. It does.

"Hello, Mason Investigation, how may I help you?"

I hear a cough, and I wait for the person, a man I think, to regain his voice. Then a click, and nothing.

R. Rigsby

In the Air, Oct 14, 2019: Lydia, Heart and Home

I open Lachie's letter…

Dear Lydia,

I tried to kill him Lydia, but your uncle stepped in front and caught the bullet meant for my father, Errol Flynn. Then the big man reached out and grabbed the gun. It went off and I dropped it as the elevator door closed.

I'd taken the gun from Ellie-not-a-bimbo's room. I'd worked late that night and before going home I made my usual sweep of the fifth floor. That fat guy came out of the elevator, I heard the commotion, then saw the girl run down the hall. Gave me a fright because I thought she was my mother's ghost. I peeked around the corner in time to see you go into the room, and then come out. I had to see, but when I opened the door, the elevator dinged. Santos would be livid since I went off-shift an hour beforehand. I saw the key, so I took it, locked the door, and hung the 'Do Not Disturb' card.

Lachie had locked the door. I suddenly see myself in Joe's car, about to ask Ellie, but then I saw Gerard.

In case it was Santos, or his crabby assistant, I grabbed the tray and dishes. Just me doing my usual excellent job! Then I went home. The next morning nobody said anything about a disturbance in 502, so I went up. I still had the key. I found the fat guy on the other side of the bed and saw the gun on the floor. It must have fallen out of a pocket. I had it under my jacket when you ran into me in the hall.

So, Lachie, it never occurred to you to call for help? I suppose I knew Lachie was unbalanced. A good thing we never fell in love.

Later, when I stopped you on the stairs, I thought you had made notes and wouldn't tell me. I went up later to see you. When you left in such a rush you didn't see me at the other end of the hall. Neither did Mason. You looked beautiful. That shade of green suited you. Probably still does. You didn't take that ridiculous bag you lugged around. I was sure you wrote about my father, so I took your notebook from your bag. I hope you now lock doors. That evening, when I saw the man who I thought was Errol come in with you and the other man, I asked you if it was 'him' and you said yes.

My stomach knots. It was my fault. My uncle's death really was my fault. Despite Joe's assurances all those years ago, it really was my fault.
You thought I meant your uncle who I'd met earlier in the lobby.

If I had known Lachie meant Regan, who could have doubled for Mr. Flynn, I would have put him straight. If I hadn't been so drunk and sick.
But by then I was so angry. How dare Errol call my mother one of hundreds and not confess to using her. There was a reason I found that gun. He had to die. And then he did, five days later. By then I had learned of my mistake.

We hit some bumpy air and the 'fasten seatbelt' cue dings. I lift Lachie's letter to show the attendant. The other piece of paper slips from underneath. I unfold it. My diploma. Tears fill my eyes. Miss Primnase. Gone these twenty-five years. But then they are all gone. My parents, Henri, my sisters, and David–who remains in memory as a laughing young man with red curls–left one by one.
Mick and I, and Ellie, who keeps board meetings on track by thumping her cane, are the only ones left. Georgie, who lived with me for the last decade, died last spring. When she got sick, Ellie came out and we nursed her through her last weeks. We sat on her bed and the three mutineers relived our ancient days. Which did not include that week at The Sylvia, and I never told either of them about Lachie. I return to his letter.
I'm sorry I killed your uncle, it was an accident, I'm sure you see that. I wish you and I could have seen each other after. I called you at Mason's once but lost my nerve and hung up. I was afraid I would confess.

Ah, Joe. He never once asked me about what I believed took place in that elevator, or why.
I won't tell you all that I've done. I married, for a while. My son did better. Rennie is the only reason I hang on now because she deserves to know her roots. I trust you to tell her about my father and everything that happened at The Sylvia. I'm dying–days if I'm lucky. When I found somebody who could read your shorthand notes, I realized they had nothing to do with Errol. I should have told Rennie the story long ago, but one always thinks there's more time, so please

And there it ended. Lachie and Regan. Two aggrieved people who nursed their misbeliefs for years. As have I? Regan died believing he had killed Mr. McCandless and my uncle, and for sixty years, I have blamed him, and myself, for Uncle Michael's death. Well, I was half right. I will carry that guilt to my grave, like I carry my guilt for David's death.

But what's the use of that? Guilt and blame. Each feeds the other. Have I allowed my grief and guilt, and yes, anger, override the good memories of my uncle and of David? Did I let those haunting emotions, like unsettled ghosts, sustain my blame of Regan and Richard?

A few days ago, I thought of my legacy. Who would remember me? But I remember my family, Miss Primase, Gerard, Marcella, and Joe. I remember them for their best qualities, for the good times we had together. And Uncle Michael for his unfailing kindness, humour, and generosity. And his last words, "…don't blame…" He meant Regan, but not for the reason I thought. And if Regan had killed my uncle, it would be well past time to forgive. Forgiveness, the antidote to guilt and blame. My stomach no longer twists, my breathing slows and deepens.

I lean my forehead on the window. Far below: the prairie and home. I've often wondered how we recognize those pivotal moments when one choice or decision sets the course for the rest of our lives. I thought Rennie's request was a timely convenience for me to tell Janey about her great uncle. And be a respite from the farm to which I would return and await my end in the ennui of old age. But no. The fates have delivered other possibilities via my notebook and Lachie's letter.

It's too late to tell Regan he didn't kill anybody, to absolve his guilt and regrets, to tell him I don't blame him for the loss of somebody I adored, but it isn't too late for me to tell somebody else. How will Mick, and Janey, take the news that I won't move to Vancouver? Mick will have to entice Ellie to join him for that sailboat ride.

They belong with their family, but I belong, God help me, in Richard's kitchen. At least he can cook. Instead of waves on English Bay, I'll watch waves of prairie wheat from that big warm armchair. Where I will dictate my memoirs. Or write them in my notebook.

I dig in my purse and slide my new fountain pen into the tab. I fold the letter and tuck it into the pocket. Did Rennie read it? Would she believe her grandfather murdered my uncle? I clutch my notebook to my chest, and something small and metallic clinks on my seatbelt. There in my lap is a key. For room 502.

R. Rigsby

Acknowledgements

When my husband, Grant, first took me to the Sylvia Hotel for a weekend getaway, I was charmed from the beginning. As many are. Since then, we have stayed often. On none of our visits, did I catch a glimpse of the resident ghost that supposedly haunts a room on the sixth floor. Yet, I understand why the spirits of past visitors might choose to return to their favourite rooms.

We might have been in one of our favourite rooms when the tendrils of this story felt their way into my mind, but they refused to be ignored, growing, branching, and weaving like the shoots of the lovely creeper that clings to The Sylvia. Like those vines, this story needed time to achieve full growth, and I was encouraged by many, including the members, past and present, of my writing group, Pen & Inklings. My family too, as always, has been in turns audience, cheering squad, and a source of useful critiques.

I owe much gratitude to friends and in-laws, past and present, in the lovely province of Saskatchewan. My feelings of connectivity to that province are in no doubt influenced by my only elementary school teacher and her family, past and present. And perhaps genetic memory inherited from my ancestors explains my joy in seas of wheat and the sound of a soft wind ruffling the sloughs.

Lynne, my trusty editor, I thank for her forthright evaluations, suggestions, and attention to detail. She highlighted events and situations that were questionable or just plain wrong for the times. Who knew that in 1927 not all men carried wallets?

While I struggled to unite the plot, define characters, and refine all the little nuances that bring a story together, usually alone at my desk, Grant never once asked why it was taking so long. For your patience, and for all the wonderful times we've had at The Sylvia, thankyou.

R. Rigsby

Manufactured by Amazon.ca
Bolton, ON

35558139R00149

10/23